Wasteland Girls

and other stories

ALSO BY ANNA BAILEY

Tall Bones

Our Last Wild Days

Wasteland Girls
and other stories

ANNA BAILEY

doubleday

TRANSWORLD PUBLISHERS

UK | USA | Canada | Ireland | Australia
India | New Zealand | South Africa

Transworld is part of the Penguin Random House group of companies
whose addresses can be found at global.penguinrandomhouse.com

Penguin Random House UK, One Embassy Gardens,
8 Viaduct Gardens, London SW11 7BW

penguin.co.uk

Penguin Random House UK

First published in Great Britain in 2026 by Doubleday
an imprint of Transworld Publishers

001

Typeset in 11.1/15.2 pt Calluna by Falcon Oast Graphic Art Ltd
Printed and bound in Great Britain by Clays Ltd, Elcograf S.p.A.

The authorized representative in the EEA is Penguin Random House Ireland, Morrison Chambers, 32 Nassau Street, Dublin D02 YH68

A CIP catalogue record for this book is available from the British Library.

ISBN 9781529962048

FSC www.fsc.org MIX Paper FSC® C018179

For Aude, Lucy, Tamari and Matthew

Can you understand being alone so long
you would go out in the middle of the night
and put a bucket into the well
so you could feel something down there
tug at the other end of the rope?

Jack Gilbert, *The Abandoned Valley*

Contents

Wasteland Girls

Women in my family have always been magpies. Natural hoarders, attracted to bright, curious objects. Mama Ruth was the worst of us. My half-sisters and I were limited to picking up stray bones and pieces of coloured glass in the desert, but she'd had a whole lifetime to gather her totems, and as far out as El Paso our ranch was called the Junkyard, strewn with rusted car parts and peeling statues of saints, dream-catchers idling in the windows. When the wind came hustling over the dunes, our valley rang with the clamour of a hundred windchimes competing for dominion inside the collapsing porch with Halloween decorations that Mama Ruth had never taken down.

She wasn't really our mama. That's just what we called her, me and Bitty and Moth. Our fathers were dotted around from Dallas to Deadhorse, and our real mother worked in a chewing gum factory up north. Mama Ruth was her mother, our grandma, and she had a mouth like a papercut with a soul to match. She carried a cane with a glass handle, and petrified inside was a tiny dark figure, whom some folks claimed was the Devil himself, trapped by Mama Ruth during a séance in San Francisco in the sixties. You didn't cross our grandmother, is what I'm saying. Even the sheriff's men knew that, though their fear of her did not extend to the rest of us.

One afternoon, Moth and Bitty and I were down at Sometimes Lake. We called it that because it only appeared when the heavy winter rains came, and though the salt-crusted basin made the water bad for drinking, we liked to lay our coats out on the shore and pass a bottle of Wild Turkey back and forth, letting the sun heat us up like lizards.

'You think you'll stay here for ever?' Bitty asked, holding the bourbon up so that it cast golden shadows over her dark skin. At seventeen, she was the oldest of us. Her daddy had been a nature photographer from Louisiana, and she'd inherited his wanderer's spirit. 'I want to know what different cities smell like.'

'Exhaust fumes and garbage, probably,' I said, picking dirt out from under my thumbnail. 'You know what Mama Ruth says, San Fran was bad for her. The cards told her to get out.'

'Oh sure, the cards.' Moth smiled. She was the daughter of a Kentucky miner, and pale enough that you could believe she'd crawled out of some deep, sunless cavern.

I sat up and looked at her. She was beautiful to me; both my sisters were. At fifteen, I was the baby, just slat and bone. 'You don't believe Mama Ruth?'

'I believe she believes it,' Moth said. 'The Tarot readings and magic circles.'

'Prophetic dreams and astral projection,' Bitty added with a laugh. 'Come on, you don't still think all that's true, do you?'

I wrapped my arms around my chest and hugged myself. 'Lots of people believed her, back in the day.'

'Yeah, lots of other doped-up hippies,' Moth replied. 'No offence, but when I'm seventy-three, I don't want to still be living in the Junkyard dropping acid so that I can talk to the moon.'

I thought the shadow of the mountains grew longer then, reaching out to us over the lake, and a cactus wren took flight from the nearby scrub, sounding the alarm. That was when he appeared.

'Bunch of little witches,' young Deputy Amos said. His boots were worn down to the sole, like everything out here, but the gun on his hip flashed in the sunlight. 'Not old enough to be drinking this.'

He picked up the bourbon bottle from where it had fallen, took a swig, and then flung it hard on to the stony shore, making us tense as the glass shattered everywhere.

'I guess you girls think you're pretty grown-up?' Amos was looking Bitty up and down in a way that made my skin crawl. 'Guess you don't meet a lot of guys your age, am I right?'

I bolted towards her, wanting to put myself between them, but the deputy's fingers snapped to his pistol, and I knew well enough to stop where I was. When Amos leaned in closer, my sister spat at him, and he raised his hand, but before he could bring it down on her, the sun vanished behind a thick bank of cloud, and Mama Ruth erupted from the cottonwoods, swinging her Devil's cane.

'Get away my granddaughters!' Her voice was like a shout in a cave, her white hair flying, as the shadows drew closer and the surface of the lake trembled. She frightened him, you could see it in the sudden hunch of his shoulders. Deep down, she frightened me too, because I could not explain how she did it – how she could make a grown man with a gun back away, although not before he'd returned Bitty's spit, right in her tearful face.

Mama Ruth used to be a preacher's wife, someplace back east. I know this because I found a picture of her standing with a little girl – my mother – and a man who I guess must have been my grandfather, who wore a rattlesnake around his neck. None of them was smiling. When I asked why she didn't live with Grandad any more, Mama Ruth told me not to call him that.

'I wouldn't raise my daughter in a house where beating on your wife was only frowned upon but questioning your husband was a mortal sin.'

'How did you get away?'

Mama Ruth tapped the side of her crooked nose. 'I used my magic.'

I thought about Deputy Amos's pistol gleaming in the sun. 'I wish I knew magic,' I said. 'I don't feel anything when we do the Tarot readings. Burning incense just makes my eyes water.'

'That's set dressing. Real magic is something you feel, same as when you lose yourself in a song or you get real mad. It's when you get those big, loud feelings that you're at your most powerful.'

I asked her again how she'd done it. How she had gotten away from her husband.

My grandmother stroked her cane and said, 'I made him disappear.'

*

I loved the winter best. With summer came the promise of dust storms and ruin, but in winter the desert seemed to me like a lovely old face, her crevices and creases revealed by longer, darker shadows, and cooler hours in which to explore.

Vultures were hanging overhead as my sisters and I hiked down the old trail, clockface cacti and horse-crippler clinging to the slope by exposed roots, salt flowers blooming in shades of ochre and pink, fed by meltwater from the mountains that flanked our valley. Barb-wire fences battered by the wind gave way to towering walls of plutonic rock, which funnelled sand into a box canyon, and that was where we found it.

The crown.

At least, that's what I called it. Bitty and Moth just told me to leave it alone.

'But don't you think Mama Ruth would like it?' I said. The sheep skull looked clean to me, bare and white and grinning at us out of the earth in which it had been partially buried.

Bitty wrinkled her nose. 'Mama's got enough old bones.'

I knelt down by the skull and ran my finger along the ridged horns. Someone had wound thread through the eye sockets and tied flowers into the empty holes, so the departed animal seemed to see in bursts of desert colour.

'Those flowers are fresh,' Moth pointed out. 'Someone did this recently. You shouldn't touch it.'

But like I said, I have always been a magpie, and so the crown came home with us.

Mama Ruth had driven upcountry to visit our mother, and so she wasn't there to advise me either for or against putting the skull in my room. I set it on my bedside table, next to my other treasures. A fragment of eagle's egg I'd found on a mountain trail. An old coin that smelled like blood. A photograph of my father in his furry hat and snow goggles, waving with a gloved hand at the camera, while a towering crane laid some massive section of an Alaskan oil pipeline behind him. The oil company paid him decent. I know that because I heard him yelling it at Mama Ruth one night, years ago, saying he wanted to take his little girl back. But it wasn't the angry kind of yelling – it had sounded like a sob being squeezed out of him.

Mama Ruth had said, 'She doesn't want to go with you, she wants to stay here with her sisters.'

I remember thinking that both things could be true.

'You don't want to leave me, do you?' she'd said, and my answer was enough to turn my father away without the use of any magic. I don't think my grandmother was necessarily always a kind person, but then, she had learned at the feet of an unkind man.

That night I had two dreams.

I was squinting at the dark little figure frozen in the glass handle of Mama Ruth's cane. At first it looked kind of like the effect inside a marble, some sort of twisted coloured glass. But as I looked closer, I saw that the figure was moving, twitching from side to side like an insect trying to squirm its way out. And I was certain, in that way you can be certain only in dreams, that this was my grandfather.

The sheep skull watched me roll over in my sleep, and in another dream, I saw my grandmother, clear as a burning house at night, her face bruised and swollen as she raised that cane and cracked it over her sleeping husband's head.

I was woken by an engine snarling out in the yard, the yellow glare of headlights distorting as they moved across the wall, making it look as though my room were underwater. A fierce wind had picked up while I slept, and now it screamed around the Junkyard, in between the clapboards and back again, but not loud enough to drown out Deputy Amos calling.

'Come out, come out, little witches!'

The porch timbers creaked. Hollowness beat through me.

Mama Ruth had warded the house with coal dust and horseshoes, but what good were her spells without her here to believe in them? Amos kicked in the door like it was nothing but cobwebs, and I could hear his voice ringing through our home.

'Not so tough without that old hag around, are you?'

My hands shook, but it wasn't fear this time. There was something in me – something big and loud that made me rise up off the bed and take the crown by the horns. I wanted to put it on, but it was so heavy it felt as though it still had the whole sheep attached, so I tucked it against my hip and climbed out of the window into the night.

The sky was buckshot with stars as I crept across the yard. I could hear the door banging on its broken hinges, my sisters calling out in alarm. On the porch, Amos turned and spotted me, and his mouth slouched off to the side in something like a smile.

I thought of the spit on Bitty's face. I thought of my grandmother tapping her crooked nose. I lifted the heavy skull in my arms, saw the deputy's eyes go wide, and before he could reach for his gun, I brought the skull down on his head, like magic.

Long Way to Come for a Sip of Water

He has dreaded this. Dreaded who would call and who he would be obliged to speak to. But it's only Thomas's nurse whose voice bustles down the line, all the way from West Texas, giving Ready the impression of a large, matronly woman with little patience for the excuses of men. This turns out to be true, at least the latter part.

'Come or don't come,' she says. 'Everyone here says you won't, and your brother says that's the reason you will.'

Ready scoffs. He hears the nurse take a drag on a cigarette, and it makes him feel mildly revolted, looking at his own nicotine-stained fingers, imagining someone changing his underwear and sponging him down with yellow hands like that.

Well, that's what you get, he thinks, and he directs this privately at his brother. Thomas could have stayed in the hospital.

Ready had always expected to get the call after the fact. A

last-minute invite to the funeral, perhaps, or someone diligently doing the rounds of Thomas's address book, letting people know he'd passed, without realizing that so much had gone between the brothers in the last few decades, the death of one would hardly seem like a milestone to the other. So he can't for the life of him figure out what Thomas is doing, getting in touch now. Unless he's prepared to hand it over at last. Well, goddamn.

'He signed a DNR,' the nurse goes on, even though Ready had not asked. 'Do not resuscitate. You understand?'

'Uh huh.' He is slouched on the back porch, watching dusk fall over the pasture, the shadows of the horses grown long and distended, insects like pinches of dust in the blue bug-zapper light.

'He reckoned you'd say that,' the nurse replies, and Ready hangs up on her. Doesn't care for the judgement. It was the same with his first wife, Helen. She thought that just because she'd married him, she'd married into the whole sorry business too and that earned her a stake in it. Well, it didn't. Nobody but him and Thomas get to scrap over that one. Whose business is it but his if he's about to come up trumps at last?

And yet his little brother had been right about one thing – the best way to get Ready chomping at the bit for anything was to tell him he wouldn't do it.

Like a badge of honour, Ready McGowen wears the same pair of steel-toed boots one of his mother's boyfriends had used to kick the shit out of him when he was fourteen. He was long-limbed and ropey then, a collection of shaving cuts, torn denim and bloody teeth, and while he hides his childhood scars with thick stubble now, there is still something a little lanky about him, like he hasn't grown into himself yet, even at the age of forty-four.

These days he only scrubs up for funerals and weddings, two of which have been his own. Mothers of the bride have sighed and said he could have been James Dean in a past life, if the rebel without a cause had lived long enough to snort his weight in methadone and get his eyes blacked at every bar brawl between Texline and Amarillo, which is to say he is handsome, but the kind of good looks that got run into the ground.

Hundreds of raw, red miles out there, and still he had always felt like the wrong shape for that place. Got out and headed east quick as if he had the Devil on his heels, and maybe by then he did. It was '95 when things turned rotten, or so his brother said, but Ready still remembers the boyfriend with the boots and thinks that the problem with rot is that it always goes deeper than you realize, right down to the foundations.

'It's been a bad time,' Midge says now. Midge-from-next-door, Addie calls her, because Addie grew up in Dallas, where people have next-door and upstairs and downstairs neighbours, although Midge lives about two miles out from the McGowen property. It bothers Ready that his wife keeps saying this, like she hasn't adjusted to living out here, between the suburbs and the prairie. Like she does not especially intend to.

'It's been a bad time for a long time now,' Addie agrees, pouring three glasses of nameless red wine out of the box on the kitchen counter. She hands one to Ready without looking at him on her way back to the couch. 'We got war and pestilence checked off, and famine is on its way, you bet, judging by the price of eggs.' She jabs a finger at Midge with a kind of manic glee. 'And you know what comes next.'

Ready rolls his eyes. He finds this kind of talk exhausting – leave it to the preppers on Route 380, that's what he thinks, buying up their clean water filters and .44 calibres. 'What, if the end times come around, you gonna eat bullets?' he'd made the mistake of saying once, and he'd gotten a hole through his windshield for his troubles.

'Might be going away for a time,' he announces, and Addie looks up sharply. The sun is setting through the west window, making her mousy hair look briefly burnished. The living room is all slices of orange light. The cross above the TV drips its shadow down the wall.

'First I'm hearing of it,' Addie says.

'Because it's the first I'm telling it.'

'Where you headed?' Midge asks, always eager to defuse tension, to play Addie's gallant protector. Took one look at Ready the day they moved in and got a notion in her head that his wife needed protecting.

'Haring,' he says. 'Two or three days maybe, there and back.'

Addie raises her drawn-on eyebrows. 'Your brother's out that way. How long's it been since you last seen him?'

Later, Ready rolls over in bed and does not speak to her.

He sets out early, night still caught between the truckstops and the car dealerships like dregs in the bottom of a wine glass. Daylight is marked by how faint the neon grows as the interstate carries him further from the metroplex, goodbye to Braum's and Dairy Queen. Past Decatur it's just miles and billboards: *DIRT 4 SALE. GOD LOVES YOU!!!! A HEART BEATS AT FOUR WEEKS*. And still East Texas has always felt jammed up to him, even at this time of day when it's only Ready and the truckers on the road.

He grew up out west. Not Haring, but near enough, close to the border with New Mexico. Prehistoric landscape, all arrowheads and hot wind. A man had space to breathe out there.

He swerves to overtake a church bus with Alaskan licence plates – you can get just about anything on these roads – and thinks of the old house. Built back in the days when men might have robbed stagecoaches in those parts, it was a great wooden pile, far enough from the highway that you didn't have to listen to the howl of traffic all the time. He and Thomas would go digging for fossils in the dried-up creek bed on the other side of the chain-link fence. He can still feel the pressure of that rust-coloured dirt compacted under his fingernails. Mama kept a jar of ammonites that Thomas added to loyally over the years, although when Ready brought her the skull of a bird of prey he'd found one afternoon in the scrubland, she'd smiled stiffly, and later he discovered it tossed away with the rest of the trash. It was like that. There was much between Ready and his mother, including all the space his father had left behind.

'You're the man of the house now,' she would say, and she would send Ready to buy cigarettes from the gas station three miles down the road, even when he was too young to drive. Bright pink lipstick, that's what he remembers, and the acrid taste of hairspray gumming his tongue to the roof of his mouth, Mama humming Willie Nelson and glancing at Ready's reflection behind her in the bathroom mirror as she prepared to go out dancing. She looked like what she was: a woman coming up on middle age with too much dust in her eyes to see it.

'You want me to do your eyeshadow?' she laughed. She was always laughing at him, until things weren't so funny any more.

*

He drives into a storm, rain like the report of assault rifles, the world beyond the windshield reduced to finger smudges. Traffic slows around Wichita Falls, the wind putting its muscle against the cars. The air coming through the vents smells waxy and cold, and the sky turns an unhealthy colour, just as Ready's phone lights up with a tornado warning for a neighbouring county. He barely glances at it. That's what you get, he thinks, close enough to Oklahoma that he could hit it with his spit if he rolled down the window, which he is not inclined to do.

'You really showed up to my deathbed looking like a drowned cat,' he can imagine Thomas saying, a smug smile on his little rosebud mouth. How Mama used to fuss over that mouth – *cherubic*, she called it, but Thomas was no angel.

A jeep looms large in his rear-view, coughing up black fumes, couple of mini Confederate flags on the roof snapping in the wind. Ready thinks maybe it's easier for certain folks to stay mad about things from before, wearing a comfortable groove in old arguments, rather than having to face the state of the world in goddamn 2021. More dying every month from some variant or other than were killed in the whole of 9/11. He can sense in his country a great sadness, the way grief comes on only after you've buried the body, although he is not sure which body it is they have buried. He can tell that he is part of a generation to which this world is no longer especially interested in catering – neither old enough to demand respect, nor young enough to preen over not getting any. Ready McGowen simply is, and even that feels like a stretch these days.

*

When did his rope run out of give? Oh, he knows. When he and Thomas fell out. When Javier dos Santos stopped coming around, flashing his quick, dark eyes at them.

'You got blood on your hands ain't never gonna wash off!' Mama hurled at him that day, slamming the door.

Well, that's what you get.

The rain stops as quickly as it came on, steam rising from cars and blacktop alike as the heat boils the water back to heaven. Ready catches sight of the tornado on the far horizon, suspended from the clouds, and it lingers there in his wing mirror for an hour or so, but he doesn't pay it too much attention. Always been good at turning his back on things, that's what Mama would say.

He's hitting West Texas now, where the little towns are bone quiet, most of the businesses boarded up or whited out. Around noon, he stops to gas up and grab a pack of cigarettes, while the strip lighting hums overhead and the cashier watches him listlessly. His stomach groans for food, but he'd just as well eat one of the flattened armadillos baking on the edge of the highway than put a truckstop taquito into his body. Stopping was a bad idea. He can feel the exhaustion of an early start and too many hours behind the wheel catching up to him all at once, so he buys a Red Bull, even though the cashier warns him that the cooler packed in last week and they're still waiting on someone to fix it.

'Whatever,' Ready says. He needs the caffeine. The cashier shrugs. When she wishes him a good day, he can see she is missing some of her teeth.

'You're too picky with women,' his first wife, Helen, said once, although this was after the divorce had come through.

She still liked to call sometimes, just to check that she was doing better than he was.

'Well, you're too picky with men,' was the best he could come up with in response.

'Ain't picky not to want a guy who only ever goes on about how hard he's had it. You wouldn't know a hard time if it flashed its titties at you. The veterans I work with at the shelter, some of them ain't even got arms and legs—'

Ready always hung up when she got around to talking about her work. Someone had to look after folks like that, he figured, and it was good that Helen did it, but another sad sack getting dealt a shitty hand didn't make his set of cards any more fun to play with.

It wasn't like he had nothing to offer a woman. Indeed, his second wife had seen the value of a man who knew how to cook and wash stains out and do any manner of repairs she needed. That was how they'd first met, in fact, him working with a plastering company at the time and being sent over to Addie's apartment to fix a wall finished poorly by his predecessor.

'Your dad teach you how to do all this?' she'd asked once, when she was watching Ready from the bottom of a ladder, two glasses of sweet tea perspiring in her hands. When he shook his head, she said, 'Your mom then? Wow. I'd like to have met her.'

'No,' Ready replied, meaning that as an answer to both statements. Everything he knew, he had taught himself, mostly by trial and error, and he had lost half his thumb trying to put in a new window at the old house one summer, when the latest of Mama's boyfriends had thrown his shoe through the original. Ready had bled and sweated over that house so much, there'd be enough of his DNA mixed up in the paint and the grouting for him to consider the place a blood relative.

That house belongs to him.

Doesn't matter what Mama wrote in her will, doesn't matter that it's Thomas's name on the deed. He is owed that house. How does the saying go? He'll get what's owed him, even if he has to prise it out of his brother's dead hands.

Ready stands in the meagre shade of a gas pump and takes a few swigs of the Red Bull, before the sugary warmth of the drink makes him gag and he tosses it away.

He blows a tyre somewhere before Childress, bald rubber spanking the tarmac and then flying clean off with a bang, throwing him into the hard shoulder. An eighteen-wheeler thunders past, blaring its horn and churning up red grit that sticks to Ready's face as he scrambles out of his truck to curse at the driver. The highway is otherwise empty, which would be a good thing if he were anywhere else in the world – less risk of being flattened, anyway – but out here the nothingness is uncanny. Dream-like, in its way. Just fields of pale stalks all the way to the horizon, still swaying from the passing hauler. It's like looking out at the ocean. He can see too far, and it makes him dizzy.

He calls AAA. When they ask for his location, he tries to bring a map up on his phone, but the battery dies. He swears loud enough that a flock of dark birds takes off from the nearby field, and he remembers suddenly a time when he'd startled the crows in the back yard, and Mama had told him, 'That's the Devil taking flight. Even he don't want to stick around you too long.'

Ready rubs a hand over his face, pushing back sweat-slick

hair. It's mid-afternoon, and the rain from this morning may as well have happened in another country, it's so far behind him now. The sun here is punishing. If he stays outside, he could get heatstroke, but if he just sits in his truck and waits to be rescued, he could end up being cooked alive. He scuffs his boots in the dirt and weighs up his options, while a vulture buzzard makes a wide arc overhead.

He could run the engine a little while, enough to charge up his phone and keep the AC going. He wouldn't need much battery to call AAA back, could always tell them he's somewhere outside of Childress and see if they can track him down that way. But like as not they won't, and then he'll have drained the truck's battery in the process, stranding him here until someone either charitable or wrong in the head offers to pick him up.

No, thank you. Spent too much time out west to trust a stranger on these roads. He still has half a tank of gas and three working tyres, enough to limp on to Childress, by his reckoning.

It's slow going, like working a splinter out of a wound, but eventually he gets himself clear of those strange pale fields, and the town welcome sign drifts into view. A Lone Star flag ripples on one side, while on the other, the speed limit has been graffitied over in red lettering. *UN-VAXXED! UN-POISONED!* it reads, bold as brass, and who's going to scrub it off around here? Downtown's brick streets make the truck shudder. It gives Ready a headache.

This could all be some prank on Thomas's part, couldn't it? *I'm dying, come and see me.* What if he gets there and his brother jumps up from his sickbed and laughs in his face? What a good joke, making Ready drive all those lonesome miles out of his way, luring him in with the promise of the house that should be Ready's by right. But he's come this far.

He eats a drive-thru special that tastes vaguely yellow while he waits for the mechanics to fit him a new tyre, and he imagines fitting his hands around Thomas's throat.

Wouldn't be the first time.

When he reaches Amarillo, he can barely sit upright at the wheel. The city appears out of nowhere on the horizon, distant windows blazing with the sunset. What a place, like a child came up with it: sticking a giant cowboy statue here, an oversized fibreglass milkshake there. Ready gets himself a motel room out of pure spite for the road, and collapses into bed without taking his boots off, feeling from head to toe like some long, withered root.

Better to sleep before this next leg of the journey anyhow. It's not only Thomas's company he's thinking of, but what will come before that – the highway slipping through ancient desert country, narrowing to just one lane either side at certain points, like it's trying to make itself small, trying to go unseen by the coyotes and the scorpions and all the things that know men and their engines do not belong out there. It would be a bad place to come off the road. Only a fool would drive it in the dark with sleep fraying him at the edges, and Ready, despite the testimony of two wives, does not consider himself a fool.

But what fool does? – his brother's voice this time. The sonofabitch always has to have the last word.

Ready dreams of split knuckles, of a throat yelled raw.

You can't smell anything in dreams – he doesn't remember

where he heard that, although it sounds like something Addie would have said back in their early days, lying in the hammock he'd put up for her in the pasture, while she read his palms for him. He didn't buy into all that, but he liked having his hands touched with something other than violence. You can't smell anything in dreams, and yet when he wakes in that cinder-block room, the vinyl drapes only half shutting out the sun that makes his eyes sting, he swears he still catches a trace of copper in the air. The ghost of old blood.

He downs a packet of instant coffee mixed with greasy motel faucet water, and then he's off again, peeling out into a landscape that shrinks his car to the size of a flea. He has always liked that about this part of the country, how you can look in any direction you want without seeing a hint of mankind. Addie is the churchgoer, not him, but even so, he could believe that God lives out here, creeping over the earth, watching from between the mesas. After an hour, he passes the burnt-out skeleton of a car a little ways off in the scrub-land. Another hour after that, blood drying brown all over the blacktop. Maybe it's not God out here, but something older, more feral, with a long memory and plenty of its own scores to settle.

Haring is about twenty miles north of where they grew up, him and Thomas. If pressed, he would say the town into which the old house had been incorporated went by the name Ever Rest, although he and his brother never called it that. It was just The Town, because it was the only one. Same as the road was The Road and the house was The House, because they were young and dumb and their lives were so small they couldn't imagine being anywhere else.

Ever Rest was the kind of place that made you think about the difference between living and surviving. Ready had decided there was a difference, after he moved away from their mother. But Haring is not much better. Thomas's apartment sits in a block of adobe lodged between a boarded-up building that may once have been a bank and a motel that looks like it hasn't been refurbished since the 1950s, despite the sign outside that promises: TV, WIFI, JESUS. Why Thomas picked such a dump to settle in when he's had the old house at his fingertips all this time, Ready will never understand. Except that perhaps his little brother, too, grew weary of mere survival.

The apartment is surprisingly cheery on the inside, however. Walls painted cream to catch the best of the light, mason jars of dried flowers dotted here and there, a bowl of oranges on the coffee table that nearly takes Ready aback after his long, colourless drive.

'He said you'd come. We had a pool going; you cost me fifteen bucks.'

Ready had been expecting the matronly nurse, but instead he is shown indoors by a long-limbed young man with a mop of white-blond hair that reminds him uneasily of the field where he'd broken down the day before.

When Ready asks where the nurse is, the young man says, 'I'm looking after him now. You can call me Pearl.'

'Pearl? What sort of name is that for a guy?'

He looks like a doll. Like his whole face has been painted on to porcelain, and if you tapped him too hard, he might splinter into slender shards.

'What sort of a name is Ready?'

'I'm gonna use the bathroom,' Ready says, because he wants to be away from delicate Pearl with his weird name. To Ready's horror, however, the bathroom door does not lock, and so he pisses with one sweaty fist closed tight around the handle. He has the awful sense that Pearl is watching him somehow. Trust Thomas to keep that kind of company.

But when he emerges, Pearl is at the kitchen counter, trying to prise open a whole pineapple with his bare hands. 'I saw this video online,' he explains. 'You're supposed to be able to get into it without using a knife.'

'Why would you want to do that?'

'For the fruit-on-fruit violence of it all, I guess.' Pearl laughs to himself. Then, without looking up, he adds, 'You can go see your brother if you want. He's in his room.' As if Ready is just supposed to know where that is.

Thomas was often sick, growing up. He had a hole in his heart, which Ready pictured as a gaping flap into which he could poke his finger. It was usually his job to drive his brother over to the specialist in Amarillo, where the doctors were constantly re-estimating how many years the poor kid had left. One time Thomas collapsed from the heat, and they seemed almost pleased about that. Perhaps they'd had a pool going too.

He'd needed surgery that they couldn't afford. Thomas had been twelve and Ready sixteen, and on the weary drive home through the desert, he'd played Metallica as loud as he could on the fuzzy car stereo, and told Thomas to have a good long scream if he wanted. Thomas had just asked him to turn the music down, in the same tone their mother would have used.

'You've gotten old,' his brother says now, shuffling in his sickbed until he's sitting upright, resting on a couple of sweat-stained pillows.

'You've gotten uglier,' Ready replies.

'I'm dying. What's your excuse?'

Ready doesn't know where to put himself. Despite the buoyancy of a vase full of sunflowers on the desk, the room feels clammy and has a sour smell to it. The nurse had told him on the phone that although his brother had recovered from COVID, the virus had drastically exacerbated Thomas's cardiovascular issues. 'You understand what all those words mean?' she'd said, and Ready had told her to mind her own business. During the drive, he'd envisioned a bed surrounded by beeping machines that dragged Thomas's life out another day at a time, but the room is surprisingly empty, save for a fan shifting the stale air around and a pile of books on the nightstand.

'You read all those?' he asks.

'Not even started. Pearl keeps bringing them to me. Look at this.' He holds up a thick paperback with some French title that Ready doesn't understand. 'He says it's required queer reading.'

'Guess he would know.'

'Now, now. He's very good to me.'

'He looks about half your age.'

'How old is Addie, again?'

Ready flips him off, and Thomas says, 'Sit down. It's making me edgy looking at you standing around.'

The only place Ready can see to sit is on the bed, and he does not want to sit there. It feels like some ill piece of Thomas might get stuck to him, so he settles for a compromise, leaning against the wall. Thomas says, 'Well.'

'Well. You know why I'm here?'

His brother smiles sadly. 'I'd like to think it's because you wanted to see me one last time, but sure. I know why you're here.'

'That house is mine.'

'Yup,' Thomas says, drawing the word out slow. 'I've kept it up, Mama's old place. Not as well as you used to, but it's in decent shape. I want you to do something for me first, though.'

'I already drove four hundred miles for you.'

'Don't kid yourself, that wasn't for me.' Thomas cocks his head. The hollows around his eyes are plum-coloured and tender-looking. 'I'll give you Mama's house if you tell me why you did it. Why did you beat me up that day?'

Ready huffs out a laugh. 'That's it? You know why. Mama loved on you too much. Someone had to toughen you up.'

'So it had nothing to do with me kissing Javier dos Santos.'

'Who?'

'That boy in your class. We used to do 4-H together after school.'

When Ready doesn't reply, Thomas sighs. 'I think Pearl put a fresh jug of tea in the fridge. Go have something to drink. Take a shower. You smell like roadkill.'

The water pressure is good, unlike the motel, where it had felt as if someone was pissing on him gently. This is the scalding kind of spray that really hoses you down, although Ready is too distracted to enjoy it, poring over whatever answer his brother had been seeking.

'I suppose you'll be wanting a towel too,' Pearl had said, standing in the doorway with his arms folded.

'No, I'm gonna shake myself out like a dog. 'Course I want a towel.'

'Don't clog up the drain with all that hair.'

Thankfully there is no sign of Pearl when Ready steps out of the shower. He feels a little less like spoiled meat, but he could do with something to eat. Dripping past his brother's room on the way to the kitchen, he hears the shush of quiet voices, and through the crack between the door and the frame he can see Pearl sitting beside Thomas on top of the covers, brushing his hair slowly. He has a faraway look in his eyes. Thomas is saying, 'He's never known how to ask for the things he wants, so he fixates on what he can't have. And he punishes everybody for it.'

The journey has worn him out, and yet, come evening, Ready feels oddly keyed up. Alert from too much coffee, or from the subtle wariness that comes with staying in a stranger's house.

Thomas won't let him in his room again. He claims he is too tired and is going to sleep for a hundred years, and so, at a loss for what else to do, Ready heads across the street to the bar. A band is playing on a makeshift stage – some white trash bluegrass cover of a pop song he'd heard on the radio the other day, although what the musicians lack in swagger, they make up for in banjo picking. He takes a seat at the bar with his back to them and orders a beer. A voice to his left says, 'Oh, it's you.'

Pearl is sitting next to him, one bar stool between them, nursing a Coke with more than a little Jack in it, judging by the smell.

'Who's watching my brother?'

'Himself,' Pearl says. 'He says he doesn't like me hovering over him all the time.'

'Can't say I blame him.'

'Does it ever get tiring, this whole mean-son-of-a-gun thing you work so hard on?'

'You sound like my ex-wife.' Ready takes a sip of his beer and wishes he hadn't said that.

The truth is he feels nervous about Pearl being here. The other patrons seem normal enough – a couple in leather jackets who are not bikers in the classic sense but probably enjoy folks thinking otherwise; muscular middle-aged ranch wives with red hair right out of a bottle; men with their baseball caps pulled low to cover balding heads, their faces moist and pink from too much summer – but their normalness is where the problem lies. Pearl, with his dainty doll features, is so clearly something else, and you can never tell who's going to decide to make that their problem.

The band finishes their song to a limp round of applause, followed by an interlude of tuning strings, the frontman clearing his throat and drawling out some joke that only gets a few laughs. There's nothing personal in people's lacklustre response, Ready thinks. It's just been a long summer. A long decade, really, and they're only two years into it.

But when the first few chords leap out of the banjo, Pearl sits up straight, grinning as he declares, 'This is my song!'

Ready cocks his ear and listens, abruptly jolted back to a muggy school gym where boys and girls kicked chalky balloons around the edges of the dancefloor instead of holding one another by the waist, although even in this there was a sense of togetherness. Ready had been sixteen or so, a flask of bourbon stashed in his blazer pocket to pre-empt the hollow knowledge that no one would ask him to dance, at least not the person he'd wanted. This song had played on the speakers, he's almost certain. Something about a rose and a grey tower. The bluegrass boys are doing a decent cover, better than the last one anyway, and more upbeat than the original, even if it does sound a little crooked with a country twang. Ready wrinkles his nose all the same.

'What're you doing? Don't make a fool of yourself,' he says, as the chorus hits and Pearl tosses his head back to join in.

The bartender turns, some unreadable look in his heavy-lidded eyes. The others at the bar all stare in Pearl's direction, and Ready leans away, as if to say, *I'm not with him*. But then one of the ranchwives laughs – a belting, honest laugh – and joins in, and she catches Pearl's eye, and he points at her, beaming his way through the lyrics. As if they'd been waiting for permission, her friends join in too, and not just the women, but their men as well, smacking each other on the arm, one of them cawing, 'Sharona, you couldn't hit that note if it was two feet in front of you!' The singer on the stage whips his hat off with renewed energy and everyone raises their voices to the strains of the fiddle as they come to the final chorus, and the banjo player strums his fingers red finishing it off, the last few notes lost beneath a roar of laughter and applause.

Ready sits there feeling much as he had at junior prom all those years ago, which is to say, on the outside of things.

'That was a dumb thing to do,' he tells Pearl, as the kid takes a long swallow of Jack and Coke, still buzzing like a plucked string. 'You shouldn't draw attention to yourself, not in this kind of place.'

'You're too negative about people.'

'I'm realistic. On a different night, any one of them might have knocked your teeth out.'

'Okay.' Pearl shrugs. 'But they didn't. They just wanted to sing.' The lights above the bar make his hair gleam gold, and Ready feels like a thief in noticing this. 'I think everyone's tired of being unhappy. Aren't you?'

*

Their mother's funeral was the last time Ready had seen his brother, before he drove all the way out to Haring. It was the weekend after Fourth of July, fourteen years ago, and Ever Rest's Main Street was strewn with tattered confetti crushed into the nooks and crannies of the sidewalk. In some parts of town, you could still smell the fireworks in the air. The heat was so bad all the flowers had wilted before the service was over, which seemed appropriate, considering how the day ended: Ready, marinated in whiskey, driving his truck into the side of the little brick church.

'Mama would have been ashamed,' Thomas told him. Mama, who had drowned in the municipal pond – not an easy thing to do by any account, but, as she would have said herself, she'd never done anything because it was easy.

'Surprised they let someone like you set foot in here, in God's house,' Ready had slurred back him. What he didn't say was that he had been ashamed of their mother too.

When they were still small, they used to listen to her getting into fights. She was a real one for bloodletting, used to beat her boyfriends as bad as they beat her sometimes. And it was during those fights that Ready would lead his brother up to the attic at the top of the old house, where he would tip over the hurricane lantern and cast a parade of shadow creatures on the blank wall with only his hands.

'You guess what this one is? Dog, yeah, that's right. Smart kid. What noise does a dog make? No, don't listen to them down there, you just tell me what noise a dog makes.'

In his brother's apartment now, he lies on the fold-out couch, night pressing at the windows, thick as molasses. And above the clunk of ice cubes calving in the freezer and the hum of the AC box jammed into the window, he hears Thomas cry out. Pearl hurries from his own room and rattles the door handle a couple of times, his voice growing high-pitched and frantic, but Thomas does not get up to answer. Ready thinks about kicking the door in. He thinks about shaking Thomas, and then propping a lamp on its side to reawaken the old menagerie for him. But he doesn't, and come morning, as if to spite him, his brother is dead.

Pearl is sitting in a mustard velvet armchair in the corner of the living room, his legs drawn up, his chin resting on his knees.

Ready does not look him in the eye. 'Where is it?'

The boy only wipes his cheek with the heel of his hand and shakes his head.

'I said where is it, kid? I ain't hanging around. Where's the goddamn deed?'

'Is that all you care about?'

'Condolences and all, but it's a long drive and I got a wife to get back to.'

There's something slightly wild about the stare Pearl fixes on him then. A kind of savage delight, and Ready should have seen this coming – the way you can see everything coming in the desert, the view going on for ever – but it still feels like knuckles to the gut, Pearl saying, 'You know he already sold the house, right? Last year. He sold it to a charity in Potter County for queer youths.'

'You're lying,' Ready says, because he feels compelled to, like he's reading off a script. 'There's no charity for queers out here.'

'You've been gone a long time.'

'Not so long that folks have changed their minds about that, I can tell you.'

Pearl looks at him with something like pity. 'Well, some people decided to do something about it, your brother being one of them. He sold the house. It was never gonna be yours.'

Ready feels like he's burning up under his clothes. Only two times he's ever felt like this before, the first being the day he beat his brother bloody, the second being when he drove his car into the church, and it seems like those are the only two paths he can see before him now. As if sensing this, Pearl goes very still, staring at him with big, glassy eyes, and Ready's right hand twitches at his side. He can hear Pearl breathing fast. He clenches his fist until his nails dig into his palm, and then he pivots on his boot heel and storms out into the midday sun, crickets and katydids seething in the weeds as he slams the truck door.

He drives. The emptiness on the horizon feels like a wall he can drive right into, grit pinging off his hubcaps, the engine whining the way his brother had in the dead of night. Hefty columns of cloud tower over him, heralding storms that will probably blow themselves out long before they reach this county, but it makes him think of his teens, how he would race the rain up and down these roads because he had nothing better to do.

He grips the steering wheel so tight he can see his joints straining at the skin, and he doesn't think about it, the way he heads south, towards Ever Rest, towards the old house. He doesn't think about anything, except that maybe he still has a chance, if he can only get to the house and stake his claim, just like the old ranchers who built that place, displacing native peoples in a tide of blood. Hasn't it always been a matter of blood out here? He bled for that house, and for his mother, who couldn't make up her mind what he was to her, and when he couldn't replace his father, she seemed to have no use for him at all.

He lets his anger run him through, too focused on the electric feel of his own fury to notice the dead thing in the middle of the road. A deer, perhaps? At the last minute, as he swerves and the car flips over, he thinks he sees an antler sticking up out of the pulpy mess. But bent at that angle, it looks more like Thomas's arm had looked when Ready was finished with him, back in '95.

'How was that your song?' Last night, he'd leaned up outside the bar with a cigarette propped at the corner of his mouth, while Pearl finished the dregs of his Jack and Coke. 'You can't have even been born when that came out.'

Pearl smiled. 'How young do you think I am?'

'Younger than loverboy up there,' Ready said, and jerked his thumb towards the apartment block across the street. No lights were on in Thomas's place, and it made that side of the building look like a Halloween mask, blank space where the eyes should be.

'He's not my lover,' Pearl said. 'He's a friend. You know gay people can just know each other, right? Same as you're not hooking up with every woman you meet.'

'How'd you know?' Ready winked at him, and Pearl snorted.

'I'd like to think they had better taste than that.'

Ready was surprised at his own relief. He had not liked the thought of anyone touching his brother's body, worn ragged as it was, and this revelation made him feel more companionable. 'So what is it you're doing here then?'

'You weren't wrong before, I guess. This isn't the friendliest part of the world. You know how many fundraisers there are online for kids trying to get out of towns like this?' Pearl shook his head, and Ready thought he saw a heaviness overtake that doll face, something that made Pearl sink deeper into his narrow shoulders. 'I guess what I'm saying is, Tom's been my friend, and I've been his. We look out for each other.'

Ready watched the boy raise the glass to his mouth. There was a thick blue vein on the back of his hand, and for a moment that he could not get a handle on, Ready pictured being a rattlesnake and biting down on it. 'I know what it's like,' he said, before he could stop himself. 'Wanting to get out of a place. Feeling like you've gotten too big for it. I know.'

'Oh yeah? Then how come you want your mom's house back so bad?'

'Because I made it what it was.'

'A big stack of splinters? I've seen it.'

This caught Ready off guard. He'd sort of imagined that Thomas kept his distance from the house, considering he wasn't living in it. It was odd to think of him still moving between those rooms, not quite a ghost, but getting close enough.

Maybe it was being startled like this that made him say, 'I could never get anything out of her. I couldn't scrape the love out of Mama if I tried. Least I can get is her house. She owes me that much.'

Pearl had looked at him then. Really looked at him, as if previously he had only been glancing, the way one might glance at a cross at the side of the highway before driving swiftly on. 'You want some?' he said, offering the glass.

Ready wet his lips with his tongue, his mother's funeral still on his mind. 'I think I'll get some water.'

'Long way to come for a sip of water.'

Pearl moved closer. His body was soft and soundless against the pebbled wall, his mouth rosy and glinting from the liquor. When he was only inches away, Ready didn't even think about it. He leaned in and kissed him. Pearl's lips were warm and tasted of whiskey, and Ready thought he felt him breathe out shakily, like there was some relief in it.

'I ain't like this.' The words came out mechanically, as if Pearl's breath in his mouth was a coin slotted into him to make him go. But the next thing he knew, the boy was jerking away, his pretty face scrunched up.

'You're such a—'

'Don't,' Ready said, without knowing what the end of that sentence might be. His voice was hoarse as it had been when his mother saw what he'd done to Thomas, the way they'd screamed at each other like Ready was one of her boyfriends.

But Pearl didn't scream at him. Didn't say anything. Only swallowed and turned and walked away towards the shadowy apartment, leaving Ready alone.

When he finally comes to, the sun has already set, leaving an orange stain along the seam of the world. Ready's tongue tastes musty, probably from the airbag, which has left his face feeling tender. Everywhere else he is numb. He can see the broken glass in his hands, but it only bothers him in a faraway sense.

The truck is a wreck, crushed on to its side with all the windows smashed to pieces. He will have to climb out over the gear stick and the passenger seat, seeking places to put his hands without risking getting more glass in them, but then what? Not a single car has driven by in all the hours he's been lying here. With a shudder, he recalls the burnt-out vehicle he'd seen on the edge of Amarillo, and he thinks a whole convoy could have driven past and not looked twice. People aren't meant to live with this much distance between them.

Now the sun is gone, it is cold in the wreckage. The wind that hurtles across the desert and plunges through the broken windows is no summer breeze, but the scouring kind that turns the earth on its axis. Ready shakes like a starving man. He never believed it, people saying your life passes before your eyes when death gets its grip on you, but as the truck turned over, he had thought of certain things in the freefall. Not of his mother, or of Thomas, or even of the old house. But he had conjured the boy with the soft mouth and the ways that seemed strange to Ready, perhaps because Pearl found no shame in them.

Above the sound of his chattering teeth, he can hear another noise now, and his ruined hands grapple blindly inside his jacket, feeling for his phone. Maybe it's Addie wondering when he'll be back, or Helen wanting to gloat. He doesn't dare hope it might be anyone else.

Splintered glass glints in the fading light as his fingers close around a familiar shape. He can't believe it survived the crash. He'd call it a miracle if he thought God held any sway out in the desert, but as it is, there are only the stars, spilled from one end of the sky to the other, and his phone ringing on and on. Clear as someone singing in the dark.

The Girl in the Ground

The cassette whirs. Clicks. The rewind complete, the interviewer's voice – a man's – comes through clearly. 'Can you tell us where you've been, Elizabeth?'

'Eliza.' A female voice, faintly southern, a little muffled, as though she is speaking from another room, or perhaps from somewhere further still. Missing girls never really come back all the way. 'Nobody calls me Elizabeth.'

A pause. Then, 'All right, Eliza. Can you tell us what happened to the others?'

'What others?'

'Your friends. Your friends who went into the cave with you that day.'

'There was nobody else.'

'Bobby Henshaw, Adam Tremethyk, Paul Cannery. August 10th, 1976, the four of you went into the Saint's Jaw cave system together. Do you remember this?'

'Oh, right,' Eliza says, very calmly. Almost bored. 'I don't know.'

'You don't know if you remember, or you don't know what happened to them?'

'I imagine they're dead.'

Silence, interrupted only by the interviewer scraping his chair across the floor. When he speaks again, a trained ear can tell he has put a little distance between himself and his subject. 'Do you know what today's date is, Elizabeth?'

'I told you, nobody calls me Elizabeth.'

'Your parents do. They've been very worried about you.'

'I don't think so.'

'Now why would you think that? I can assure you they have been.'

'That's not possible. They're definitely dead.'

Static picks at the audio, making it crackle.

The interviewer clears his throat. 'Your parents are not dead, Elizabeth, they have been waiting for you to come home for a long time. Do you know what date it is? It's June 30th, 1995. Do you understand that you've been reported missing for nearly two decades?'

The tape whirs and whirs.

'Why did you come back to the cave?'

'I didn't come back.'

'Come on now, Elizabeth, there's no point lying. You were found outside the cave. You don't expect us to believe you've spent the last nineteen years down there? Can you tell us where you've been?'

A long sigh. The sound of fingernails tapping on the tabletop.

'I've been right here.'

*

Claw rewinds the tape and listens to it again. Sitting in his sweltering car, window cracked to let in some air, he turns up the volume as loud as he dares in order to hear it over the lazy bustle of the drive-thru parking lot. He recognizes the interviewer's voice from their recent phone calls. Craig Hollis, a deputy with the county sheriff's department. He talks like the two of you are running side by side and you're failing to keep up, but, in the recording, what stands out the most is the way Hollis addresses Elizabeth Dunn as if she were a child. Perhaps because, in so many people's minds, she still is.

She was only thirteen years old when she disappeared at the height of summer, when Claw was a scab-knuckled teen himself, hotboxing his big sister's El Camino, David Bowie on the radio telling him these were his golden years. He'd heard nothing about the case at the time. A bunch of kids getting lost in a cave – it was only a local news piece, happening on the other side of the state. May as well have been on another planet.

The first time he remembered really hearing about it was during college, when he was staying over at a girlfriend's place and couldn't sleep. Ended up surfing the dregs of late-night television, and there, between a phone-in psychic and a middle-aged man trying to sell vacuum cleaners, he'd stumbled upon some hokey unsolved mysteries show. That was when he first saw the faces of those four missing children. At the time, the case was already half a decade old.

Bobby Henshaw loved the outdoors, the narrator said. A grainy photograph showed an African-American boy on the cusp of growing into his long limbs. One hand was caught mid-wave at the camera. The other hand was holding a large frog. Bobby was going to be a biologist, or a geologist, or anything he wanted, said a tearful Mrs Henshaw in an old newsreel, but by then the only thing her son had become was a question mark.

Adam Tremethyk looked like a little rockstar, all long, wavy hair and torn denim. He'd lived on his uncle's cattle ranch just outside Saint's Jaw, the no-stoplight town that lent its name to the nearby cave system, or perhaps the name-lending went the other way around and people had simply come to think of the town as more important. The Tremethyk cattle were all afflicted with a kind of mange and gave bad milk. People said the family had never had much luck. It sounded to Claw as if they had never had much of anything.

Paul Cannery, in contrast, was a prince. Son of a farmer who'd struck oil back in the early sixties. The photo of Paul that flashed up on the TV screen showed a boy who looked much closer to manhood than the other two, a stern confidence in those deep blue eyes, hard, tawny muscles on display under his basketball vest.

An unlikely group of friends, perhaps, given their different backgrounds, but none so unlikely as Elizabeth Dunn. A new girl in town, she'd been incorporated into the group within only a week or two of her family's arrival in Saint's Jaw. She was a trailer park kid. Her father worked at a slaughterhouse and her mother read people's fortunes. The narrator relayed this like you were supposed to glean some additional meaning from it. A kind of conspiratorial nod of the head. 'You know, one of *those* kinds of families.'

There were only two photographs of Elizabeth on record. One of her as a very small child sitting atop a plastic brontosaurus, and the other a school picture, a black-haired girl with a wide, flat face like that of a barn owl. She was scowling at the camera. Looking life right in its bloodshot eye.

One afternoon in 1976, the four young teens had cycled out to what was known as a sky island – an isolated clutch of mountains where the terrain leapt suddenly from parched scrubland to dense forest, yuccas and shin daggers giving way to junipers and piñon pines. The kids often played up here, the documentary narrator said, where the trees offered some respite from the heat that collected down in the valleys. Apparently, Adam Tremethyk's uncle had expressed a wish that Adam not go up to the sky island any more. He said it was dangerous, the mountains riddled with caves that sank way down below for God knows how many miles. But Claw wondered if Mr Tremethyk had ever actually said such a thing, or if he only wished he had.

The facts themselves were few and tantalizing.

This group of friends had gone into the mountains. Officials knew where, because one of Bobby Henshaw's sneakers had been found at the mouth of the cave, his name written on the sole in faded marker pen.

The kids had gone inside the cave too. Further in, crime scene investigators had discovered one of Elizabeth Dunn's black hairs caught on a rock, but there the trail went cold.

Nineteen years ago, these four young people had walked into that cave, and none of them had ever walked back out.

Until now.

Claw is just what his colleagues at social services call him. Claudio Galardini is a mouthful and a little old-fashioned. A man still clinging to his mid-thirties, Claw holds himself like a pack of cigarettes that's been clenched in one fist. He and his sister were raised primarily by grandparents, after a brief stint in a foster home, where he remembers being spoken to with sympathy but little more than that. A sense of being skirted around still dominates those early years of his life, as if he were a feral animal rather than a child. At that point, maybe he and his sister were a little of both.

He and Angie had been found in their parents' empty bungalow, eating food out of the dog bowl, the windows black with flies. People said afterwards, 'Their father fought in Korea,' as if that explained things. No excuses were made for their mother. Neither she nor their father were ever heard from again, and the police had written Mr and Mrs Galardini off as another pair of useless beatniks, before dumping little Claudio and Angie into the system.

A girlfriend once asked Claw if that's why he'd become a counsellor. Because of what his parents did.

'I have no idea what my parents did,' he said, because that was the truth.

In the drive-thru parking lot, Claw rubs a hand over his face, recoiling a little at the sweat pasting his hair to his forehead. Crazy to think this whole part of the country was a seabed a billion years back. Feels like there's never been anything here but heat.

'Tusk' comes on the radio as he peels out on to the highway, conjuring up an image of his mother dancing in her long tie-dye skirt, her bangles clinking as she spun around the kitchen. *I could have been Stevie Nicks*. Claw has a feeling she never actually said this; he just added it later, trying to flesh out a woman he barely knew. You don't remember someone *maybe* saying something, he thinks. You either remember the way they said it and know it to be true, or you're just guessing. But he does know this: that, once, while dancing to Fleetwood Mac, his mother had scooped him up and held him against her chest so that he could dance with her. Sometimes he feels the absence of her in the cup of his palms.

Claw turns off the radio. The landscape beyond the window blurs into shades of brown and burnished gold interrupted by the occasional rocky outcrop, or the rusted skeleton of a windmill. Plenty of real skeletons here as well, no doubt. Mule deer and pronghorn and the odd steer that's strayed from its enclosure. Belowground, too, are the imprints of ancient bones pressed into the rock an unthinkable number of millennia ago. Exactly the sort of place where a group of kids could get swallowed up by the earth and no one would be any the wiser.

But from what Claw has gleaned from those late-night unsolved mystery shows, and from trawling old newspaper stories, it wasn't just the kids' disappearance that put Saint's Jaw on the map. Something else had happened at that cave.

According to hearsay, printed in defunct magazines for the UFO/Bigfoot crowd, and the few police reports he'd managed to get hold of by calling in favours, another incident had taken place shortly after Elizabeth Dunn and her friends vanished. An incident which, despite long nights spent hunched over on his couch, staring at the pages spread out on the coffee table until the words stopped making sense, Claw still struggles to believe.

The local police had looked after the case to begin with, this he does know. The chief back then was one Burn Rowler, a blocky, white-haired man with a face like someone hit him sideways with a shovel. He'd been old enough to escape the draft, though there were few who'd call him lucky, not after this case.

His people had done a surprisingly reasonable job for a three-man police department in the seventies. They had found Paul Cannery's shoe and Elizabeth Dunn's hair, had ascertained that there were footprints in the dust leading into the cave but none coming out. They'd handled the local press too, the pressure cooker of frantic parents and neighbours demanding instant answers. By all accounts, they'd kept on top of things. But then, about a week after the disappearance, Chief Rowler had gone up to the Saint's Jaw cave, and all of a sudden, according to one of his officers, he just ran inside.

Said he heard a voice, somewhere back there in the dark, the officer's statement read. They had all been questioned by the state police afterwards, the two officers and the chief himself, or what was left of him.

QUESTION: Did you hear this voice, deputy?
ANSWER: No, sir. I guess I did not.
Q: What happened then?
A: I had to shine my flashlight in to see him. Even on a bright day, not much light gets inside, but I could see him there in the shadows.
Q: And what did you see? Deputy . . . what did you see?

A dust-coloured town, caught between a desolate stretch of pumpjacks at one end and a peeling Marlboro billboard at the other. With a sense of running aground, Claw pulls up outside the Saint's Jaw local police department, which hasn't been the department of any local police for about fifteen years. Not long after the 'incident' with Rowler, the county sheriff had absorbed the town into his jurisdiction and then promptly forgotten about it. Bobby Henshaw, Adam Tremethyk, Paul Cannery and Elizabeth Dunn were given up for dead. It's just not possible, the sheriff at the time had said. Not possible that four kids could still be alive down there in that cave. Well, it was the seventies, Claw figures. The sheriff was probably busy misplacing vital serial killer evidence, or writing off a rape case as 'just one of those things'.

The current sheriff is using the former police department as a 'debriefing space'. She meets Claw in the lobby and offers him a brisk handshake, calling him Galardini. She is older than him, somewhere in her forties, with high cheekbones and a dark, solemn face. Her uniform is smart, top button done up, her hair pulled back into a tight knot, but for all her attempts at formality – because this is what it is, Claw thinks; this is a person who wants very much to be taken seriously – she too is falling prey to the climate, her shirt sweat-wrinkled, her hair wilting at the edges.

'You can call me Claw,' he says, because everyone does.

The sheriff looks him over, and he finds himself straightening up, as much as anyone can after being jammed into a car for a two-day drive. He must look a mess, not to mention he's had a headache blooming ever since he stepped off the street. The abrupt shift into the shade and air conditioning of the cinderblock police station makes him feel slightly nauseous.

'You can call me Marquez,' the sheriff replies. 'Or ma'am.'

So, it's going to be like that.

'Have you done this kind of work before?' she asks, as she leads him down a dingy corridor.

'I've counselled trauma survivors before, yes.'

'Is that what the Staties told you you'd be doing here?'

She is walking ahead of him, the corridor too narrow for them to manoeuvre comfortably side by side. He wonders if he's only imagining the sharp edge of a smile in her voice.

The police station looks much as Claw imagines it must have the day that Chief Rowler and his two officers packed up their things. They pass a dusty water cooler with something green growing on the inside. What looks like a bullet hole in one of the windows has been patched over with cardboard. Marquez shows him to a break room, where a corkboard on the opposite wall hangs heavy with yellowed posters and flyers – a forgotten history of lost dogs, petty criminals, and a town Founders' Day advertised in retro bubble font. Claw wonders how much sense of community remains in Saint's Jaw, holding out against its tragic past, or if the disappearance of those four kids back in '76 gutted this town.

'How come you brought her here?' Claw asks. 'Elizabeth Dunn, I mean. How come you didn't take her back to County?'

Marquez breathes deeply through her nose, buying herself a few brief seconds to weigh up her options, he thinks. 'We thought Miss Dunn would feel more comfortable in familiar surroundings.'

Claw nods, deciding not to push it for now. Let Marquez come to him in her own time. He would prefer to get along with her, if possible. Would prefer only to have the one headache out here.

'Have her parents come by to see her yet?' he asks.

'Sure, they've come. Miss Dunn didn't want to see them, though.'

'Did she say why?'

'These people aren't her real parents. That's what she said. Said her real parents are dead.'

She had sounded very sure of that on the recording too. 'Have you had her examined for head trauma?'

'Of course.' Marquez crosses her arms. 'Mr Ortiz – the man who found her, he's a rancher, summers his cattle up near the sky island – he brought her straight to the clinic here in town. That was four days ago. Doc knew who she was, of course, called us right away, but he examined her on site. Said she had some minor cuts and scrapes, a little dehydration, but nothing serious. Nineteen years, and she gets away with "nothing serious".'

'Gets away with?'

The sheriff raises her eyebrows. 'Mr Galardini, your work with the state police has been predominantly on criminal cases, no? Did you really think you were here just to provide trauma counselling to a girl who got stuck in a cave?'

'So you think she's done something criminal?'

'Did something. Knows something.' Marquez shrugs. 'The fact is, we've still got three missing persons, and the only individual who can shine a light on any of it is being deliberately vague. Your superiors gave you the tape, I assume you've listened to it. There's a complete lack of concern there.'

I imagine they're dead.

'The boys could have been killed accidentally,' Claw says. 'Caves can be dangerous places. They might have fallen down a shaft or drowned in one of the underground pools.'

'We've got a lot of caves out here, Mr Galardini. I'm aware of the hazards.'

'Right. Sorry. I just mean, there's nothing explicit to suggest she killed them.'

'So her friends all met grisly, albeit accidental ends, and she just lit out, is that what you're saying? Never bothered to mention it to anyone, not even when she heard the story on the news? I don't think so. She's hiding something.'

Claw sighs. 'Even if that were true, even if she chooses to reveal something to me, I wouldn't be at liberty to tell you. It's a matter of confidentiality.'

'You don't have to tell us anything, Mr Galardini. You just have to convince Miss Dunn it's in her best interest to talk, which it is, provided she doesn't want to end up facing criminal charges.'

'You understand I'm not a lawyer, right? Does she have legal representation?'

'She didn't want any.'

Claw stares at the sheriff. 'You've been holding her for four days without a lawyer? Is that even legal?'

'Feel free to ask her if she's changed her mind, though I doubt she has. She doesn't seem to like visitors very much.' Claw can see the muscles tensing in Marquez's jaw. 'You know my deputy you heard talking to her on the tape? Later that same day, he went to interview Miss Dunn again, and she went for him like a dog. Took a bite right out of his cheek.'

Marquez decides that Claw will interview Elizabeth the next day. Not today, she says, you've had a long drive, though her concern seems distant.

'It's fine,' Claw tells her. 'I'm eager to get started.'

'This station runs off a generator, and we're low on fuel. Past seven tonight, the only room with any lights still on will be my office with one of my deputies sitting in it. Take it from me, Galardini, you don't want to be locked in a cell with Miss Dunn in the dark.'

Claw wonders why she didn't just say that before. Marquez

is already holding the door open for him, keys in hand, keen to get out of here. Saint's Jaw is far from the county seat, and she probably has a long journey ahead of her. Maybe she's hoping, too, that a night in darkness will make Elizabeth feel a little more talkative in the morning.

He and Marquez part ways with a stilted goodbye, and he crosses the disused freighter tracks to what is purportedly the livelier side of town, which is to say it has a bar. It's not much of a place, brick and linoleum, steel bars on the only window up front, but it's a decent spot to people-watch. Claw sees a young man with a skateboard perched upside down on his lap, tweaking a set of wheels. A cluster of older women are gathered around the pool table, shooting bourbon and trying to pretend it isn't playing havoc with their throats. A guy with smeared prison tattoos stares blankly out the window. Claw takes a seat at the bar and orders two fingers of Jack, which he drains in two gulps.

'One of those days?' the bartender says. She's a small, stocky woman in her fifties.

'Long drive,' Claw says.

'Didn't think you looked like a local. Where you headed?'

'This is the end of the road for me. At least for now.'

The bartender nods like she's considering this. 'Figured you were only passing through. Most people are.'

Fleetwood Mac is playing on the overhead speakers. Claw could do with someone to talk to, instead of Stevie Nicks telling him about snow-covered hills, making him think about his mother again. The bartender eyes Claw's empty glass, and he nudges it towards her. 'Have one with me?'

That makes her laugh. He can see the black fillings in her back teeth. 'Go on then. Been a while since a young man bought me a drink.'

'Not true, Rosa,' the kid with the skateboard pipes up. 'I got you a tequila shot last week.'

'Yeah, and you know I hate tequila.' Rosa shoots Claw a look like they're somehow in on this together. 'Tequila is for narcos and college kids, of which I am neither, though I was married to one once. I'll let you make up your mind which.'

She pours Claw another Jack Daniel's and one for herself, knocking their glasses together before she throws her head back and downs it in one. 'All right,' she says, 'you got my attention, stranger. What bad business are you on?'

Claw can't see any reason not to tell her. If this Rosa is a local, she'd have been in her thirties when it all went down.

'You heard about the Dunn girl?' he says, and immediately Rosa stiffens.

'You a cop?'

'I'm a kind of social worker. I'm here to speak to Elizabeth, try to figure out what happened.'

'You tell that girl her mom's worried sick,' someone says, and Claw looks around to see two of the women from the pool table returning empty glasses. They're dressed the same, men's shirts tied above their sagging midriffs, cut-off jeans that expose tanned, ropey legs, and dyed hair tied up in messy ponytails.

'Sadie Dunn's a friend of my sister,' one of them says. She has a dreamcatcher tattoo fading on her forearm. 'Or she was, before she and her husband moved to New Mexico. Must be hell for them having to come back here, only to hear their daughter doesn't want to speak to them.'

'Any idea what that's about?' Claw asks.

The women look at each other, and Dreamcatcher shrugs. 'Always something off about that girl. My Nancy was in her grade at school, invited her to a birthday party once when they were very small, and Elizabeth spent the whole day saying she could see the cracks at the edge of the sky. Freaked the other kids out.'

The other woman nods sympathetically. 'You ask me, I wouldn't be surprised if she's been down there this whole time.'

'In the cave?' Claw says. 'For nineteen years?'

He hears Rosa make a clucking sound with her tongue like she disapproves.

'What?' Dreamcatcher says. 'That cave ain't natural, ask anyone.'

Rosa refills their glasses and waits for them to return to their game, then shakes her head. 'Ignore them. They talk a lot of shit when they've been drinking.'

'You're not convinced by their theory?' Claw asks.

'Honestly? Those kids were thirteen, fourteen, hormones flying all over the place.' Rosa leans across the bar, lowering her voice. 'I've always thought those boys took Elizabeth up that mountain to have their way with her. And if she finished them off, then good for her.'

Claw stays long enough to have another whiskey, and from Rosa he learns that most of the families of the missing children moved away in the late seventies or early eighties, when it became clear that law enforcement was letting the case fall by the wayside. Bobby Henshaw's parents went north to Colorado Springs. Paul Cannery's family moved up to the Panhandle. Mr and Mrs Dunn lived in New Mexico, but were currently staying at a motel out by the highway and wouldn't set foot in town unless they were expressly sent for by their daughter. Only Adam Tremethyk's uncle, who Claw still remembers so vividly from that old documentary, has remained in Saint's Jaw. Not like he could afford to go anywhere else, Rosa says. He let the ranch go after Adam disappeared, like all the fight just went out of him. Works at an oil refinery now, about forty miles out.

It sounds to Claw as if the four kids weren't the only thing that cave took out of this community. He swills his whiskey and ruminates on fate's strange sense of humour, that he should end up here, entangled with a case like this, when as a child he was terrified of caves.

The idea of a mountain being able to hide whole rivers and lakes inside it used to make Claw wonder what else they might be keeping from him. His grandmother once told him how the priest in her childhood church said that caves were haunted. Being Calabrese by extraction, she'd grown up running through tunnels full of ammunition abandoned during World War One, around old men who buried their money in holes in the ground, wild boar spit-roasted in the village square, tarantella and blood oaths.

'When you get close to a cave mouth and feel the cold air blowing out,' she said, 'that's the Devil's breath.'

But Claw's grandfather would have none of this. He had left Calabria behind, seeking work in America, as many of his countrymen had, and he did not hold with what he called 'old country superstitions'. Claudio, he said, was not to pay attention to that kind of talk.

Claw tries to bear that in mind now, thinking of what the women at the pool table had said. When he has finished his drink, he makes his excuses and heads out, glad to get some air. It was stuffy in the bar, and he stands out front inhaling deeply and listening to the insects in the sagebrush. Even in the dark, the stars light the desert flats all the way to the horizon, and the massiveness of the world, which usually brings him a kind of peace in his blessed irrelevance, this time leaves him feeling exposed and totally unprepared.

Elizabeth – or Eliza, as she insists on being called – reminds Claw of a piece of trivia he once heard about the last shot of *Carrie*. They'd filmed Sissy Spacek walking backwards into her house and then played the footage forward so that it had a slightly off-kilter quality. The way Eliza moves feels a little like that.

Sheriff Marquez has had her cuffed to the table, on account of the biting incident with Deputy Hollis. Now Eliza sits picking dirt out from under her fingernails, occasionally twisting her head to one side and then the other, like she's trying to stretch her neck. The strip light overhead drastically deepens the shadows in the sockets of her eyes and hollows of her cheeks. Someone has combed her hair – the doctor, perhaps – and dressed her in a big plaid shirt and jeans that don't look quite the right size. Marquez says the clothes she was found in were filthy and torn to shreds, though what little was left has been sent away for analysis.

'My name's Claudio.' The light fritzes overhead as Claw sits down opposite. The station generator has been refuelled, but it doesn't exactly feel high tech in here.

'I just want to go home.'

Claw looks up. Eliza's stare is cool, distracted.

'Well, okay,' he says. 'That's what everybody wants. For you to go home. That's why I'm here, actually, to ask you a few questions, and then hopefully we can get you back to your parents.'

'Not that shit again.' Eliza grunts, leaning back in her chair as far as her handcuffs will allow. 'How many times do I have to tell you people? I don't know who y'all have gotten me mixed up with, but I don't have any parents. Cops got grapefruits for brains, I swear.'

'I'm not a cop.'

'Oh yeah? What are you then, a shrink? They haven't tried with a shrink yet.'

'I'm a little like a shrink, sure.' Claw lays his hands palm-down on the table. 'I heard an interesting story last night.'

'Tell someone who gives a shit.'

'It was about you. And the others who disappeared at the same time you did. Eliza, did you ever have any problems with those boys?'

She just blinks her big black eyes at him. Her mouth is one unmoving line.

'Did they ever hurt you?'

Eliza's fingernails have been roughly cut and left unfiled. For some reason, Claw also pictures the doctor doing this. Her desert-brown hands feel very out of place in this metal and concrete room. There is a wrongness to her being here, Claw thinks, though he cannot quite articulate why. The longer he watches her, the more he can sense his headache returning.

'Bobby Henshaw,' he says, clearing his throat. 'Paul Cannery, Adam—'

'Adam was my boyfriend.'

Claw is tempted to turn around and look back at the two-way mirror, behind which he knows Marquez is standing, but he doesn't want to disrupt the flow of things with Eliza. As far as he's aware, this is completely new information.

'Adam Tremethyk was your boyfriend?'

'What I said, wasn't it.' Eliza tries to roll her shoulders, but her movement is limited while being cuffed to the table. 'He was my boyfriend for five months and eighteen days. I don't know those other guys.'

'How'd you mean?'

'I mean what I said, shrink.'

'They weren't friends with you and Adam?'

The gears in Claw's head are turning fast. Is it possible, he wonders, that Eliza and Adam were somehow in on it together? Maybe the police and those documentary filmmakers preferred the story of a gang of friends going missing, instead of daring to probe any further. Maybe Eliza, living in a trailer, and Adam, growing up on his uncle's dirt ranch, had privately despised the wealthy Paul Cannery, had been jealous of Bobby Henshaw's loving home. Maybe they'd taken those two boys up to the cave to get their pound of flesh. Childhood has as dark an underbelly as anything else, Claw knows that much.

But Eliza taps a jagged fingernail on the table and looks at him like he's slow. 'They weren't friends with us because I *don't know them*. What are you not getting? What kind of a psychologist are you?'

'I'm not a psychologist, I'm a social worker. My name's Claudio Galardini, and I was sent—'

'Wait, *what?*' Eliza laughs, a scraping, brittle sound. 'Man, I get it now. You're here to fuck with me.'

Claw gives her a questioning look, and she says, 'Come on – Claudio Galardini? Did that bitch Marquez tell you to say that, or did you come up with it on your own?'

'What are you talking about? That's my name.'

'Sure. And I'm John Wilkes Booth.'

Claw doesn't know what to say. He presses the flat of his hand to the back of his neck, trying to ease the burgeoning ache from the base of his skull, but the pain in his head seems to shift, and he pictures it like wax in a lava lamp, stretching and floating as it relocates to a space right behind his eyes. He winces, and clearly this isn't the reaction Eliza was expecting, because she suddenly seems less sure of herself.

'The Galardini case?' she says, but her voice has less shit-kicker swagger than before. 'Do you even know what that is, or did Marquez tell you to give me a fake name to screw with my head, and you just went along with it like some chump?'

'Nobody's screwing with you, Eliza.'

Maybe she's paranoid. They should have gotten someone local in to do a psyche eval before he arrived, and Claw almost can't believe that Marquez didn't send for a proper psychiatric specialist, especially after the biting incident. But then again, they're a hundred miles from anything and anyone out here. She could have called the feds for all Claw knows, and they still wouldn't get here until dark.

Claw breathes in through his nose and tries again. 'No one's messing with you. Not Sheriff Marquez, not me, not anyone in this police station. All we want to do is figure out what happened to you and those boys, and then get you home.'

The suspicion Eliza had regarded him with a moment ago has bled into something warier, and she narrows her eyes. 'Who are you?'

'I'm Claudio Galardini.'

'Fuck.' She breathes this out, rather than saying it.

Claw grits his teeth around the pulsing pain beneath his eye sockets. 'What is it about my name that's bothering you, Eliza?'

'Well, man,' she laughs. 'It's just that you're dead.'

'Excuse me?'

'You were tied to a chair and beaten to death.'

Claw does turn around then, glancing at the two-way mirror for some indication of what the hell he's supposed to say to that. But if Marquez is there, she is standing silently, passively, watching it unfold. Am I only here so that she didn't have to subject any more of her own people to this? he thinks. He turns back to Eliza, and she looks almost sorry for him now.

'The Galardini kids?' she says. 'You seriously don't know? It was like, one of the state's biggest child murder cases back in the seventies. Some sicko broke into their house and killed the kids while Mom and Dad were at work.'

'What are you talking about?'

'How can you not know? Everybody knows.'

'That's not . . .' Claw swallows. The pain is immense now, his vision darkening faintly at the edges, as if he's looking up at Eliza from a hole in the ground. 'What you're saying – that's not possible. That didn't happen. I'm Claudio Galardini.'

Eliza shakes her head, though this, like every other movement, somehow manages to look out of sync. 'Nah, don't screw with me,' she says. 'I saw it on TV. I still remember the mom crying on her knees when they brought the bodies out in those tiny black bags. The look on her face, man. I won't ever forget that.'

Having stayed in a lot of motels in his life does not mean Claw especially likes them. It's the furniture, he thinks, that's what puts him off – the cracks in the bathroom tiles, the sweaty prints of hands on the wall when the light hits it just so, the odd stray hair in the plughole. All these things amount to a place that has existed before he got here and will continue existing after he's left. They are supposed to be temporary spaces, but more often than not, they just make him feel temporary instead.

In his room, he swallows a couple of Tylenol, sloughs off his jacket, and lets the conditioned air waft over him. It's the middle of the day, and he can hear room service hoovering next door, the growl of a motorcycle somewhere outside. Claw wipes uselessly at his perspiring face and picks up the phone to call across the state.

It's Wednesday. Angie doesn't work on Wednesdays, so Claw knows she'll be in, and after a couple of rings, his sister answers with her typical demanding, 'Hello? Angelina Galardini-Peterson. What do you want?' She took her wife's last name after the civil ceremony because she liked having something longer to yell at strangers on the phone. 'Makes me seem more official,' she'd told Claw, drunk at her own wedding.

'Hey, Ange.'

'Oh, it's you. Look, is this about the money? Because you know, Claw, I can't give you anything else until my cheque comes in.'

'I'm not asking for money. I just wanted to talk to you.'

'Huh.' Angie sounds like she's chewing gum. 'Okay.'

He doesn't hold her wariness against her. They're the kind of siblings who have been through hell together, and as such, are afraid to get too close again, in case they can still smell the traces of a bad time on the other's skin. Angie had paid for his driving lessons with money she'd saved working at an abattoir. He'd twisted a boy's arm behind his back in high school because the kid had called Angie a dyke. Years later, Claw had donated his sperm so that she and her wife could have a baby. They had done these things for each other, and done them with no small amount of love, but such acts were easier, because they were wordless.

There is something almost obscene, Claw realizes, about barging into his sister's day without warning. He is a reminder of a darker part of her life, and it feels unkind to unearth it for her, but he doesn't know who else to turn to.

'Ange, what do you remember about Mom and Dad?'

'Don't call them that,' she says. 'They don't deserve it.'

'I had a weird conversation today.'

'With one of your junkies or something?'

'Don't call *them* that. And no, not exactly. I mean, I don't think she's using any drugs.'

'But you talked to some nutso about our parents?'

'Come on, Ange. My patients aren't "nutso".'

But Claw rubs the back of his neck; now that he's faced with the prospect of explaining the conversation with Eliza, it does sound ridiculous. He and his sister clearly weren't murdered in the seventies. Their parents abandoned them, and maybe it made a few local headlines in Austin, but it certainly wasn't a state-wide news story. Back then, Texas was busy covering those guys who'd dissolved kids with lime outside Houston, or Tex Watson finding God while doing jailtime for killing Sharon Tate along with the rest of the Manson Family. This state has always been bloody ground. Too much space, with people too cut off from one another. You can lose sense of how a person's supposed to live. You can get up to plenty far away from prying eyes.

Claw has always held that his parents were products of

their generation. Sixties teens turned seventies adults who liked the *idea* of doing things more than the act itself, and who, when faced with the prospect of raising two children on welfare, decided to hitchhike on to greener pastures. He has never once pictured his mother crying for him. Never, until Eliza said it. Now he feels as if he's been given a glimpse of something powerful, as if he's seen his mother through a door that was then abruptly slammed shut, and he doesn't know how to open it again.

But his sister says, 'Look, Claw, I've got to go. I'm supposed to pick Sammie up from daycare.'

'Hey, Ange? Do you think there's any chance . . . maybe they were murdered? Mom and Dad?'

She's right – the epithets do feel strange in his mouth.

'You know,' Angie sighs, 'to be honest, I don't think about them at all. I've got Monica and Sammie, and Nonna and Nonno, and you. I don't think about the family I don't have.'

'Sure,' Claw agrees. And then, perhaps a little uncharitably, he adds, 'But you've got a lot more family than I do.'

He regrets it as soon as he's said it. He knows Angie doesn't deserve his jealousy, but it doesn't matter. She'd already hung up before he spoke. The hoover next door suddenly switches off, and the silence in the room seems to expand, the weight of his words settling on him heavy as the midday heat.

The following morning, there is a storm on the horizon. Ranchers out early stand in their fields and raise a hand to their brows, shielding their eyes for a better look at the black stain building on the edge of the world. This will be a violent one, recompense for the temperature. Don't ever say God is no fair dealer. Already the Lone Star flag outside Claw's motel is beating against its pole, the bunchgrass bending back as the gust front rolls in ahead of the storm.

Claw drives through a moonscape of blasted rock and dead plant life, the footprint of nearby oil extraction. Towering pumpjacks peck at the earth, and beyond that, Callaghan Drilling Co. sits like a steel city on the horizon, a mass of pipes and shafts and steaming vents, belching white smog into the sky. There is something smothering and artificial about the air here, something that leaves a metallic taste in the back of the mouth, as if Claw's throat is bleeding.

He is grateful he doesn't have to drive all the way up to the refinery. Most of the men who work there are housed in an array of low-slung buildings that form a sort of shanty town nearby, all corrugated roofs and dirty walls, trucks scattered outside in the sand. He finds Adam Tremethyk's uncle here.

A burly man in his forties, Jago wears a stained boiler suit rolled down and tied at the waist, revealing bare arms mottled with dark patches, like fruit that has been dropped too many times. At first he doesn't want to speak to Claw. Claw can't exactly blame him, but ever since that conversation with Eliza yesterday, everything has taken on an absurd urgency, as if Claw's afraid he'll burst into flames should he take his mind off the case. He follows Jago across the makeshift parking lot to Jago's truck and offers him a cigarette, but Jago looks at Claw with some alarm, and then retches out a laugh.

'Kid, I'm three parts petroleum these days. You spark that up for me, there'll be nothing left but our shadows.'

Claw lowers his eyes, feeling a little dumb, but to his

surprise, his embarrassment seems to thaw Jago a little. When Claw asks about Adam Tremethyk, the man he remembers from a fuzzy late-night TV spot all those years ago heaves a deep sigh.

'Adam's dead.' Jago looks away towards the steaming towers of the refinery. 'Sometimes you just know.'

'Certain people in Saint's Jaw seem to think Miss Dunn might have been trying to hurt those boys,' Claw says. 'Or vice versa.'

Jago scoffs. 'People in that town got nothing better to do but run their mouths. Those kids were this close,' he says, holding up two thick fingers, crossed as if for luck.

'Adam got along okay with the other boys? I understand Paul Cannery especially could be kind of . . .'

He doesn't know how to phrase it for someone who must have actually known the Cannerys, but Jago beats him to it: 'Bratty?'

'I was going to say spoilt.'

'Well, he sure was that. Parents handed him the world on a silver platter. But kids like each other differently to adults, at least that's how it seems to me. Those kids didn't care what their parents thought – those boys and little Elizabeth – they were all crazy about each other. Adam wouldn't have hurt a single one of them, understand? Not one.'

Claw nods again to show he does understand, or at least that he wants to. 'I mentioned I've been speaking with Miss Dunn. She said something about Adam being her boyfriend at one point, is that right?'

'She said that?'

Jago glances over his shoulder at the other men getting ready for the day, washing brown necks in cracked bowls, hacking at stubble with razors, using tiny shards of mirror propped up by stacks of porn rags and loose bricks.

'Tell you something,' Jago says, turning back to Claw. His voice is lower now. 'I never heard nothing about that from Adam.'

'It's kind of personal though, a girlfriend. Is that the kind of thing he would have shared with you?'

'Didn't need to.' Jago's eyes dart back to the other men again. 'I just know Adam didn't have no girlfriend. You can take that to the bank. Him and Elizabeth . . . well, she used to dress him up in her mom's blouses.'

'Oh. Right.'

Claw pictures Adam Tremethyk as he is in the case file – slouchy and sullen with that mass of rockstar curls. He had a face that seemed to say *so what?* Maybe he really hadn't been interested in girls, though it doesn't rule out him and Eliza as a couple, Claw figures. They were only thirteen, it's possible neither of them was aware the attraction only went one way. Adam could have kept close to Eliza to ensure the other boys didn't get suspicious. Claw remembers his sister doing something similar with a guy in her English class. Eliza could have been telling the truth, but that doesn't mean she and Adam had nothing to do with Paul and Bobby's disappearances, and it doesn't explain what happened to Adam himself. Or where Eliza has been all these years.

What they really need, Claw thinks, is someone else who was there. Someone else who was part of that little group, who understood its dynamics. Everyone he's spoken to, every interview he's read, every file he's pored over has claimed that the four kids were thick as thieves, so why is the only surviving member insisting she never knew the other two?

No, Eliza knows something. Claw is certain of this. And if she's refusing to talk, it seems to point to her having had a hand in what happened at the cave.

The Callaghan refinery glints eerily against the murky sky. Even with the encroaching storm, the workers are beginning to migrate towards their various transports, and Jago hefts himself up into his rust-scabbed Ford, just as Claw says, 'You wouldn't come talk to her, sir? Miss Dunn might feel more comfortable around a familiar face.'

Jago wrinkles his nose. 'No. I've got no interest in that.'

'But she might be able to tell us what happened to your nephew.'

'My nephew died. Knowing how it happened won't make that untrue.' He slams the truck door shut so heavily that Claw feels the sound right up through his legs. 'I stay away from any and all to do with that cave. Nothing right about it. You heard what it did to Chief Rowler?'

The skin prickles on the back of Claw's neck. He recalls the transcribed interviews with one of the former police chief's deputies, back when they were still handling the case.

Said he heard a voice, somewhere back there in the dark.

'Decent guy.' Jago turns the key in the ignition and the Ford snarls to life. 'In his coffin before his time.'

What did you see? Deputy . . . what did you see?

'You know what actually happened up there?' Claw shivers in his shirtsleeves. The truck rumbles, as impatient to get going as its driver.

'Rowler was up looking for the kids, when he saw a hand come out of the cave. Just reaching, right out of the dark. But it wasn't no child's hand. It was a grown man's.' Jago lowers the sun visor, not looking at Claw any more. 'It was wearing Rowler's own wedding ring.'

The former sheriff's station is more awake than Claw has seen it since he arrived. The couple of deputies Marquez had brought with her from County are bent double against the wind, scarves pulled up around their mouths and noses, as they nail boards to the windows and fit tarp over the AC boxes. Their muscular police jeep is already covered with a thin layer of dirt tossed up from the parking lot, and Claw spots Marquez loading an eight-pack of plastic water bottles into the trunk.

'You headed somewhere?' he calls, rolling down his window. The sheriff's movements look awkward, and as he pulls up alongside the jeep, he can see that she's wearing two of her fingers in a splint. 'Jesus, what happened?'

Marquez is grim-faced, fighting to keep her hair out of her eyes as the wind whips it about. 'You want to tell me where you've been?'

The way she says it tells him she already knows.

'I think we're about done here, Mr Galardini.'

'Excuse me?' Claw gets out of the car, and the dust in the air makes his eyeballs itch.

'You've grossly overstepped your position,' Marquez says, adjusting the bandana over the lower half of her face.

'I thought I was here to help find out what happened to those missing kids. I don't see how I've done anything that contradicts that.'

'Questioning family members is police work. We had a call from Jago Tremethyk's supervisor. Complained about some scrawny guy hassling one of his workers.'

'I assure you I wasn't hassling Tremethyk, I was just talking to him.'

'About an ongoing case.'

'His nephew vanished!'

'And yet you sought him out to pick at old scabs unnecessarily.' The sheriff raises her eyebrows. 'Listen, Galardini, we appreciate you coming all the way out here, but it sounds to me like you've gotten a little too close to this case. Nobody's blaming you. It happens sometimes. But I think it's best for all parties if you return to Austin.'

Try as he might, Claw can't get the calm of her voice to match up with the words coming out of her mouth. She is sending me away, he thinks. She is sending me away because I've gotten too close – *to what?* Surely that was the point, to get close, to zero in on the truth?

'I'd like to talk to Miss Dunn again,' he says, 'if that's possible.'

'I'm afraid it isn't. I'm having her transferred to County.'

'With a sandstorm bearing down?'

'I'm driving her myself. We'll keep ahead of it. Frankly, I'm done with mollycoddling her here. She's refused every opportunity to cooperate with us, and this morning she almost broke my finger.' Marquez holds up her splinted hand. 'I want her contained in a proper facility with the necessary staff, and that includes psychological analysts, so like I said, Mr Galardini, your assistance will no longer be necessary.'

'Sheriff, please, I've established a connection with her. You heard what she said about Adam Tremethyk being her boyfriend, she'd never mentioned that to anyone else.'

'And if that piece of information turns out to assist us in our investigation, we'll be grateful to you,' Marquez says, slamming the trunk of the jeep shut and nodding to one of the deputies. 'We're good to go, you can bring her out now.'

'I think you're making a mistake. Something else happened up at that cave. Even Chief Rowler—'

'If this is about old Rowler's hand, I've heard the *X-File* story. I'm here to deal with facts, Galardini.' Marquez pulls the bandana down from around her mouth like she wants to make sure Claw damn well hears what she's going to say, but she doesn't get the chance.

The sound of a man screaming makes them both turn, in time to see Eliza standing at the station side door, her arms straining around a deputy's neck, the chain of her handcuffs digging into the wheezing man's throat as he clutches uselessly at the air.

Claw sees Marquez go for her gun, shouts, 'No, don't shoot!' at the same time as he hears the crack of another firearm. Bullets ping off the metal station door. It feels like a swarm of insects has descended upon Saint's Jaw, a constant mass of motion as the storm pours in. Claw loses sight of Eliza in the dust, but the guns keep going off. A figure looms out of the writhing haze, and Claw lunges towards it, crying, 'Stop! Stop shooting!' but then a voice that sounds like Marquez yells, 'Get down!' and an elbow connects hard with his windpipe, knocking the air out of him. Claw staggers back, stumbling over something that feels horribly like somebody's leg. He feels his head collide with the side of the jeep. Then all the lights go out.

He wakes with a start, suddenly thrust back into the world. Cool air that smells of stale vents is ghosting over his face, and his throat feels like it's been stuffed with cotton wool. At first he thinks he must be dreaming. A clock set in the jeep's dashboard reads 10:46 a.m., which should be full daylight, and yet the inside of the jeep is dim. He cannot hear the wind, but he feels it in the tremor of the vehicle, the way it wants to go one way, pushed by the harrowing gusts, but the woman at the wheel keeps them on course.

'No use pretending to go back to sleep, murder boy. Your breathing's changed. I know you're awake.'

Rubbing his eyes, Claw can see that the windows are covered in sand – desert dust packed up on the glass. Eliza, hunched in the driver's seat, is navigating by a tiny patch in the windshield kept open by one working wiper blade. The landscape beyond is all the same colour, and Claw recognizes nothing.

'Where are we?'

'I don't know.'

'Is this the sheriff's jeep . . .?' Claw breathes in sharply as he turns his head, the pain starting little fires under his temple where he'd fallen against the car. 'Is she okay? What happened, what am I doing here?'

Eliza sighs, raking her greasy bangs out of her face. Her handcuffs dangle from one reddened wrist, while the thumb on her free hand lies swollen and disjointed against the wheel. 'You were unconscious. Figured I might need you at some point.' She must see the way he's looking at her, because she laughs – a bleak, deflated sound – and adds, 'As a navigator, not a hostage. You already died once.'

'Quit saying that.' Claw feels a shiver across the back of his shoulders. 'Where are you trying to get to?'

He half wonders if she's hoping to flee across the border to Mexico. Technically she's on the run from the police, and that's not even taking into account the missing persons enquiry.

But Eliza shrugs. 'The cave. Where else? Except I can't tell where I'm going, everything's the wrong way round.'

'I don't know what good you think I'm going to be. I'm not even from here.'

She's wearing the same expression she'd had during their interview, when she told him to quit screwing with her, and Claw is expecting her to lay into him again, but then Eliza just turns back to the windshield and the scrap of road beyond.

They drive slow, headlamps nosing a faint path. Sweat sticks Claw's shirt to the small of his back, the wind battering the doors and windows like mortar shells. A nervous energy fills the car between them, as if they both know they are on the brink of something, even if he cannot say what.

Claw tries to remember the maps he'd seen on the late nights he'd spent examining the details of the case. The kids had cycled from Saint's Jaw to the sky island, before hiking up to the cave, so it can't be too great a distance. Even a pro cyclist would struggle to cross too many miles of open desert in the heat of the day. Eliza tells him they've been driving for about twenty minutes. Claw tells her to head south next time she sees a turn-off, which is easier said than done in the murk of the sandstorm. He grips his head, trying to get around the pain that builds like some solid thing behind his eyeballs. Before long, he can hear Eliza muttering, 'This is weird, this is trippy as shit . . .' as a sign looms at them, warning of cattle crossing the road. More than once, Claw swears he sees a flash coming from behind them, but when he checks out of the back window, there is only the dirt piled up against the glass.

'What exactly are you hoping to achieve, going back to the cave?' he says. 'You can't hide in there. Marquez and the others will hunt you down, after what you've done.'

'What's it matter to you?'

'You dragged me into it.'

'I told you, you're not a hostage. Once we get to the sky island, you can keep the car, get out of here. I mean it. I think we both got in way over our heads, and I just want to go home.'

'You really mean that, don't you?'

Eliza smiles stiffly, sadly, still peering out of the gap in the windshield.

Claw sighs. His skin feels pulled tight over his bones from the heat and the grit. More than anything right now, he wants to go home too, but he doesn't really know where that is. Not his grandparents' place, for they were long ago displaced to a retirement facility. Not Angie's condo with wedding photos framed on the walls and her kid's toys strewn around the carpet – evidence of a life in which Claw plays little part. His apartment back in Austin is all blank light and bare boards, interrupted by a few desiccated house plants that seem to want to be there as much as he does.

By the time they come to a stop, the storm has faded to a dirty red mist that lingers in the air like the aftermath of a bonfire. At their backs, the desert looks altered beyond recognition, cacti torn out by the roots, barb wire from ranch fencing scattered around, and great mouthfuls of earth eaten away. Without the bellowing wind, a quietness has descended, so thick that Claw feels he could take a bite out of it. Ahead, the land rears steeply, scrub giving way to pale grasses, and then above that, the greenery of oak and pine, topped by towering cliffs. When Eliza sets off, Claw follows without a word. His eyeballs still itch, though the visibility has improved, and now he can see two police cars roaring through the immense flatness of the landscape behind him. He wonders if Eliza hasn't noticed, or if she simply doesn't care.

She moves fast, her dislocated thumb growing increasingly mauve and swollen, though if it bothers her, she doesn't let on. They climb through the stony scenery and the trunks of madrones trained by muscular winds into fantastic red coils. It is cooler up here, the smell of hot asphalt replaced by pine needles and damp air so unhampered by pollution it is almost difficult to breathe. The silence follows them. Claw hears no bird calls, no animals rustling in the undergrowth, but he doesn't hear the engines of the police cars either, and he can't tell if this is a good thing or not.

Perhaps Marquez and her remaining deputies have reached the foot of the sky island. Perhaps they are already on their trail. They could, at this very moment, be closing in behind them, but Claw doesn't look back. He watches Eliza's boots cutting footholds in the soil, and he follows her steps, reminds himself she knows where she's going. For better or worse, she has done this before.

The cave appears as a black slit in the rock. Lurking beneath the weather-beaten overhang, it has the sense of a lair. As he stands at the entrance, Claw is greeted with a blast of cold, wet air, and he thinks of his grandmother's old superstitions. Devil's house and Devil's breath.

'You don't have to come,' Eliza says.

But he has come this far, and in that moment, the sum total of what he has to go back to doesn't seem enough of a reason not to see this through to the end.

They have to scramble in one at a time. Eliza has brought a flashlight from the jeep, and as its white beam curves across scalloped walls, the tunnel echoes with the crunch of their boots and the steady drip of things eroding. Claw's eyes strain, and he glimpses various offshoots and passageways leading away into total darkness. Eventually the tunnel spills out into a wide cavern, so huge it seems like a shout would take a day to reach from one side to the other. Wavelike formations rise up the walls that glint electric blue when the flashlight beam hits them, and stalactites protruding from the ceiling have an eerie yellow glow.

'It's the bacteria in the water,' Eliza says, her voice magnified in the vastness of the cavern. 'When I first came here, I thought maybe it was something nuclear. They used to test bombs just across the state line. This place caught some of the fallout, I think.'

They shuffle along. Claw feels he should ask how deep she plans to go. How far under the earth. Does she mean to stay down here until she thinks the coast is clear? She can't hope to outlast the sheriff's department when she has no supplies, surely? But Claw does not mention any of these things. Eliza isn't stupid. And even now, as he ducks and scrabbles and crawls after her through impossible spaces, Claw holds on to the belief that he is going to understand, that Eliza is going to show him what happened to her. She is going to give him the answer at last.

At one point they find themselves wading through an icy stream, their heads scraping against low rock, until they heave themselves up on to a narrow beach of dry stone. Their muscles ache as they bunch themselves up, trying to leave the other enough room, but when Claw's jaw won't stop chattering, Eliza puts her arm around him and rubs his shoulders until he settles.

He thinks maybe he's slept. He can't be sure, though he can sense the tension in Eliza's body, can tell she has remained alert, even as he drifts down here in the dark. She tells him they should head on, but they can stop whenever he needs, that the air is thinner in this place. He asks if she means the oxygen. Eliza only slips her hand under his arms and helps hoist him to his feet.

Eventually, Claw thinks they have come in a circle, because he can see a shred of light quivering up ahead. They emerge into the same landscape, with its limber pines, its corroded cliffs pitted with holes and stained by centuries of buzzard faeces. Claw feels rubbed raw by the interior of the cave, and he shudders, even in the warmth of midsummer. Eliza wipes her palms on her filthy jeans. Her hair is thick with knots, her face lashed with little cuts and scrapes, but she grins at him, and it is a real smile. There is no sign of Marquez or her deputies. There is no sign of anyone at all.

There seems to be nothing else to do but follow once again, as Eliza begins her steady hike down to the scrubland. Claw's movements are unsteady, with the dragging slowness of someone walking in a dream. Sometimes Eliza stops and waits for him to catch up, but increasingly, as they near the foot of the slope, she forges ahead, and Claw finds himself having to jog the rest of the way down the track.

'I don't feel right . . .' He leans over with his hands on his knees, trying to catch his breath, and then he sees the car.

Claw squeezes his eyes shut. Takes a deep breath through sore lungs, then opens them again. 'I don't understand.'

The stolen jeep is gone. The vehicle in front of them is a Dodge pickup the colour of old denim. Eliza sets about clearing away the twigs and leaves that appear to have covered it, and then she reaches up under one of the front wheels and retrieves a set of keys, jingling them in Claw's direction.

'Give you a ride?' When he only stares at her, she shrugs. 'Don't worry, I'll look after you, murder boy. At least for a little while. Guess I owe you a good turn.'

She opens the passenger door for him, and he can't think what else to do but climb inside. The air smells stagnant, but when the engine kicks in and the AC comes on, Claw draws deep breaths, clenching his fingers between his knees to stop them shaking.

'Are you really Eliza Dunn?'

'What kind of a question is that? Of course I am.'

Beside him, Eliza pushes her hair out of her face and throws the truck into drive. Claw watches her, and the sudden fluidity of her movements – no longer that awkward jerkiness he'd witnessed in the sheriff's interrogation room – makes him say, 'But you're not the little girl who went into that cave, are you.'

She hums, reaching across him to recover a pair of sunglasses from the glovebox.

'Do you know where she is?' Claw asks. 'Where any of them are?'

'This is big, wild country. Plenty going on out here that folks don't have an explanation for. My guess is those kids went in too deep, got stuck or lost. Died down there.'

'Jesus Christ.'

'You take it personally, don't you?' she says, though her voice is not unkind. 'I wonder if some part of you knows you weren't so different. That you were a dead kid too, at least here.'

'What do you mean, "here"?'

'If I understood it any better than you, I'd have told you back at the police station, but you have to understand, you weren't making any sense to me. Bobby whatshisface and Paul somebody – maybe *your* Eliza knew them, but not me. And as for Adam, my Adam, I saw him at CVS two weeks ago, but none of you wanted to hear that.'

The car bounces over a pothole, the thermals making the desertscape shimmer around them. They pass the road sign again, warning them of cattle crossing in the area, but the silhouette of the animal is facing in the opposite direction.

Claw feels pent up and wrung out at the same time. After a little while, he says, 'My mother. Is she here?'

Eliza glances at him and smiles. Behind her enormous sunglasses, he cannot see her eyes, only his dim reflection, so distorted by the glass and the ordeal of the cave that he barely recognizes himself, but maybe, he thinks, this is no bad thing. They keep on driving. They follow the curve of the road until it joins the highway again, the sun hitting them head on and filling Claw with heat. The frigid waters of the cave are only a memory now. Like something that happened a long time ago, to somebody else.

Riddles

'The more there is, the less you see. What am I?'

'That's easy,' Ramona says. 'Darkness. Give me a cigarette, would you?'

Annie clicks her tongue, skirting around her wife's propped-up ankles with a pair of sweet teas in hand. 'You know what the doctor said.'

'That twelve-year-old was a doctor?'

'I think he was thirty.'

'How's having a Dunhill supposed to make my memory better or worse? That's all I want to know. If the clock's ticking, I'd like to enjoy the last few hours, thank you very much.'

Annie swats her wife's slippered feet, settling down beside Ramona in one of the patchwork deckchairs their daughter-in-law made them. She is a rawboned woman, Annie, with a face you'd call 'full of character' rather than handsome, and a tendency to hunch forwards like a mesquite tree being pulled by the desert wind.

'You've got a lot longer than hours left, dummy,' she says. 'Especially if you lay off the Dunhills. The clock's not ticking yet.'

'Clock starts ticking the day we're born.' Ramona's voice has been ground to grit by years of smoke. She's built like a tomcat, low to the ground and hefty, complete with nicks in her ears from all the earrings their son ripped out when he was small. She would say love leaves scars worse than violence sometimes. She would know best.

Currently she is staring away to the south, and Annie knows she is seeing further than the scrub and the horses enclosed by wire. Further even than the horizon, a white-hot lake of heat trembling at the foot of the mountains. Beyond that natural border lies another, man-made and punctuated with regrets. Ramona lets out a slow sigh. Then she takes a sip of sweet tea and demands, 'Another one, my girl. Ask me another one. Doctor also said I had to keep my mind busy.'

Annie chews her lip, as she often does when she's thinking hard. Harvesting the skin right off in translucent strips. Her mother once painted Annie's lips with goat's blood to get her to stop, but Annie pushes that memory down. Her mother is long dead. Her mother is just strips of old skin now too.

Eventually she says, 'Who can finish a book without finishing a sentence?'

Ramona taps one of her slippers against the porch rail, making the whole structure shudder and the windchime rattle overhead. Gazing out at the endless distance, she shoots Annie a sly smile. 'A prisoner.'

*

Annie did not grow up a prisoner, but sometimes she thinks the way her mother made her live was supposed to be some kind of criminal boot camp. Aiming low to prepare her for a down and dirty future.

Annie was an only child. Her mother had given birth young, back before the hillbilly heroin got at her face and aged her past the good will of any man. It was the end of the war in the South Pacific and men were coming home with ideas in their heads about meeting nice girls and starting families. Corporal Johnny Hewitt, US Marine Corps, managed the latter half of that, at any rate. But he'd been at the liberation of certain POW camps in Japan, and he once told Annie's mother about a British soldier he'd seen, barely out of his teens, with pressure ulcers so deep and rotten that Corporal Hewitt could see right down to the bone. He saw other things at those camps too. Things he wouldn't talk about, but they must have been bad, Annie figured, because her father got a tickle in the back of his throat that only a shotgun muzzle could scratch.

Her mother was the one who found him. It wasn't long after that she started on the pills. Used what was left of Corporal Hewitt's soldier pension, figured he owed her that at least, and when the funds ran out, she spent the rent money, until the bank account was as empty as Annie's stomach.

Annie remembers turning thirteen, sitting on the hood of her mother's car at a gas station south of Amarillo. Every time she blinked, she could see black spots out the corners of her eyes. When she asked her mother where they were headed with all their clothes jammed into one suitcase, her mother told her they were going into the desert like Jesus. When Annie asked if she could have a cigarette as a birthday present, her mother cuffed the back of her head and asked her did she want to set the whole damn place on fire?

Annie considered the question but said nothing.

It was 1968. No one at the gas station paid any attention to a teenage girl with ratty hair and no shoes on.

'What grows up while growing down?' Annie is making up the pull-out bed on the couch. Ramona's ankles have swollen, so she and Annie will sleep downstairs for a while, until it passes.

'Another easy one,' Ramona scoffs. 'A duck.'

Outside, the sky is the colour of apple skin, and one of the horses trots through the slatted shadows of the mesquites. Annie will have to go out and feed them soon, but for now she is happy to keep her wife company.

Ramona fidgets and huffs in her armchair. If she's in pain, she doesn't say so. The specialist in El Paso, their nearest city, told Annie that people with dementia can sometimes lose the ability to express discomfort, but that doesn't mean they aren't feeling it. So Annie asks her wife often, sometimes every hour, if anything is bothering her, to which Ramona will roll her eyes and say, 'You, my girl! You're nagging me like I'm a man who can't wipe his own ass.'

Annie doesn't mind that. She knows a day will come, even if she cannot quite picture it yet, when the disease will blunt Ramona's sharp edges. A day when Ramona won't remember Annie's name or who she is, so Annie will take all the insults, eye rolls and groans she can get for now, hoarding them like you might hoard tinned peaches to prepare for a nuclear winter.

Hector, their son, always liked tinned peaches. Used to

pretend they were big fat worms and that he was a mole tunnelling through the sand looking for his lunch. That used to make them all laugh. He was a funny kid with a big imagination. Annie does not think Hector's own kids are all that funny. Whenever she sees them, they seem to speak entirely in references to things she doesn't understand – things they don't want her to understand, it feels like. Ramona says it's because they spend too much time on their phones, which is probably true, but Annie thinks they do this because they're understimulated. They live in the city, where Hector and his wife are both lawyers. They spend their lives being ferried from school to basketball practice to math tutoring to microwaving dinner themselves because their parents get home late. They don't get time to watch the sun setting. They don't see how it sets the desert all on fire.

Ramona spends a lot of time on her phone too. She plays memory games and reads about conspiracy theories. Not because she believes them, but because she knows it makes Annie groan and laugh when Ramona tells her how some people believe the Egyptian Pyramids extend all the way down to a secret chamber at the centre of the earth, or how Texas's stone mesas are the stumps of giant trees, harvested by long-ago visitors to this planet and fossilized by time.

'What is it with people in this country?' Ramona says now. 'They can't just let life be. It's always aliens or Bigfoot or Jesus. There has to be some great cosmic reason for everything. Well, tell me this: why is God scraping my grey matter away like it's a block of Parmesan? What's the divine point in that? Nothing. It's nothing. Shit just happens.'

Annie straightens the sheets on the pull-out. 'It was the aliens,' she says. 'I didn't want to say anything, but they abducted you and probed your brain. That's why you're like this.'

Ramona snorts. 'Give me a riddle. A hard one this time, come on.'

Annie nudges the pack of Dunhills to the other side of the coffee table so that Ramona can't reach it. 'They can be harboured, but few hold water,' she says. 'You can nurse them, but only by holding them against someone else. You can carry them, but not with your arms. You can bury them, but not in the earth.'

Ramona frowns. For a moment, Annie thinks she has stumped her and finds she is almost disappointed by this. Not yet, she thinks. Please not yet.

But then her wife shuffles in her chair again and mutters, 'Grudges.'

When Ramona Martínez Amador was twelve, her father tattooed prayers on her fingers to match his own. She grew up with God like a shard of glass stuck in her foot that nobody ever took out, and she swears on her grandmother's bones that it hobbled her.

Hers was a childhood of votive candles and limpias, shrines along the roadside to murdered children, new saints birthed from hit and runs, the Virgin of Guadalupe in her blazing shawl. The sacrament tastes different in the desert than it does up north, Ramona once told Annie. You can really taste the flesh and blood. Not that Ramona has set foot in a church in many years, and it would have been many years more, Annie knows, if Ramona had had her way. As it was, Diego Amador decided what was best for his daughter.

Annie never met him, but by Ramona's accounts, he was

a hard man. Not in the sense that he was unkind, no, but life had covered him in callouses, even before the family came to Texas. He was a field worker, intent on following the harvest north. He had two children to feed and a wife with another baby on the way, and although he was afraid, Diego had discussed it through many hours of prayer, and what he believed was that God wanted him to cross the Rio Grande. God wanted Diego's children and his pregnant wife to cross the river too.

Ramona remembers the towering sides of a gorge. She remembers how she felt like she'd been shrunk down so that she was smaller than her own fingernail. Vultures drifted in the sky overhead. Catclaw and algerita sprung up through the cracks in the rock, tight little buds closed around yellow flowers, and she remembers the secondhand dinghy that took hours to inflate. Her little brother Juan whined and moaned and told Ramona he was boiling to death and he was going to peel his skin off to cool down. She thought he was disgusting. Sometime later, she caught him throwing rocks at a lizard. It was hurt but still alive, and Juan kept hitting it and hitting it, like some biblical punishment. Ramona had picked up a rock of her own and slammed it against her brother's ear.

Juan fell down then and lay very still. She thought she had killed him, and she almost burst into tears. But then Juan started moaning, and Ramona helped him sit up and gave him some murky river water to drink, which he spat back in her face, so she said fine, be like that, and slouched off to help with the dinghy.

It was springtime. Meltwater streaming down from the mountains had swollen the river and given it legs. Ramona and Juan and their mother were going to sit in the dinghy while their father pulled them across. It would be all right, he told them, the water would only come up to his waist. He held his hands out to the side as he said this, palms turned upwards, as though awaiting some kind of blessing.

The dinghy smelled of hot rubber. Sometimes Ramona claims she can still smell it, though Annie thinks maybe she is making that up, because the more mundane details there are in a story, the more grounded in the real world it feels. What happened to Ramona that day was awful. Annie can understand how a twelve-year-old girl would want to make sense of it. Would want to ground it in terms she could understand.

Ramona and Juan and their mother sat in the little dinghy, and Ramona was glad because her brother had stopped complaining. He had stopped speaking at all, and when their mother told them to hold on tight, he just grunted, his eyelids drooping.

It could have been heatstroke, Annie said, the first time Ramona told her the story. He could have been suffering badly in the heat, he was only eight.

But Ramona shook her head and looked away to the mountains.

She had hit him. She had done something to his head when she hit him with that rock, and so when they reached the middle of the river where the water was running fast and churned up by ancient stones, when their father had to hold on to a buried tree branch to keep his balance, when the Rio Grande barrelled into their little float and almost tipped them out, Juan was too unconscious to realize what was happening. Ramona remembers. She remembers him going over the side in silence and the river holding him down.

*

'What walks on four feet in the morning, two in the afternoon, and three at night?'

They are lying side by side on the pull-out bed. Outside are the moon and the stars and the purple brush, and the darkness covers them over kindly. When Annie turns to look at her wife, she can imagine they are both young women again, like they were the night they met – at a bar where Annie sang Delta Dawn on the karaoke, and Ramona bought her a beer because she thought Annie 'had balls' to get up there in front of a crowd of dumbass cowboys.

'Mona,' she whispers. 'What walks on four—'

'I heard you, I heard you. I'm thinking.'

'Too hard for you?'

'I didn't say that. I said I'm thinking.'

There was no point at which Annie could say she realized she wanted a woman instead of a man. There was only the gradual growing into herself that happens to everyone at the beginning of their twenties. Suddenly you find yourself looking back on the last few years and you realize you're not the same person you were at eighteen, though you would be hard pressed to say why, or when exactly it happened.

Things became clearer to her when she left her mother passed out in their grimy apartment and walked away. Away from Amarillo, and the truckers her mother brought home to fund her junkie jitters, and the boys who made eyes at her – all the people who knew Annie to be this one thing that she was quietly certain no longer fit. She hitchhiked south, got a job in a mobile library, where she consumed books the way a man running from a fire might take gulps of air. She learned the expression 'the scales fell from my eyes', and she thought, yes, that was exactly what it felt like.

She talked about this with Ramona, that night after the karaoke. They switched it up from beer to sangria and poured their lives out to each other while George Strait strummed over the bar-room speakers, and Annie felt pumped up because she could not remember the last time she had talked to anyone like this. Pulling out what was inside her and showing it to someone, and Ramona saying, *Me, me too!*

There were times, Ramona said, when she felt cut off from her own sense of place in this world. The immigrant's dilemma of wanting to belong but not wanting to leave too much behind either. But year after year, as she shifted from student dorm to her own rented apartment, from degree studies to a job guiding tourists through the canyons on horseback, she learned to look at the landscape and relish that feeling of being part of something ancient. The cities, the roadkill, the borders – all of this was temporary. When human beings were long gone from the desert, only scars would remain. The fossils embedded in the sides of ravines, the river-carved valleys, the glacial moraines – these, like the tattoos on her fingers, were all proof that people and places could go through hell and come out shaped anew and glorious.

That second night was, for many years, the best night Annie could remember, the sex almost secondary to the conversation, and Annie still tells their friends that Ramona is both the match and the flame of her life.

'What was it?' Ramona says now, and lying close in the dark, Annie can feel her wife's breath against her cheek. 'Your riddle about the walking thing, what was it?'

Annie sighs. It was a stupid choice. 'A man,' she answers quietly. 'The times of day represent a lifetime. He crawls as a baby, walks as an adult, and walks with a cane at the end.'

'At the end,' Ramona grumbles. 'Well, I don't have a cane, so I guess it's not the end yet.'

Ramona's ankles improve, but almost in rhythm with this, she begins to complain of fatigue. Annie suspects this is because she has not been out of the house in a while. Sleeping in the living room becomes the norm. Sometimes Ramona will spend whole days on the couch, watching back-to-back episodes of *Ghost Adventures* and scoffing at the TV. If Annie goes out to buy groceries, she will come home to find the living room rank with smoke, and Ramona hastily stubbing out her cigarette with a look of both guilt and frustration. She does not like feeling guilty, she tells Annie. She does not like feeling like a little girl who has done something wrong.

'You've done nothing wrong,' Annie assures her. 'Not ever. Not to me. I just don't want you to smoke. Don't you get it? I want you for as long as possible.'

And Ramona will huff and ask, 'Tell me a riddle.' It has become her go-to response when she doesn't know what else to say.

Hector comes by and makes a fuss. He has very grown up ideas now, Annie thinks. She cannot imagine her little boy, who slurped tinned peaches as if they were worms, using terms like 'palliative care' and 'live-in nursing'. No, Annie says, no, she couldn't possibly do anything like that. Cannot even consider it, in case the idea starts to seem rational and she feels obliged to implement it.

Hector stands in the kitchen drinking sweet tea and glances through the living room door to where Ramona is slumped on the couch like a heat-struck horse. He is keeping his distance because she scared him when he first arrived.

She'd asked about his kids like she thought they were still at preschool, and Hector had done a solid impression of a jackrabbit in headlights and said, 'Mamma, Jackson and Gabbie are in high school now.'

He tells Annie he doesn't want the kids to see their grandmother like this. Annie thought Ramona was sleeping, but her voice cuts through the hum of the ceiling fan in the living room: 'What the hell do I care about someone else's kids?'

That night, after Hector has driven back to El Paso, and Annie has made up the couch bed again, she wakes in the dark with the distinct feeling that something is not right. The room is too quiet. There is a coldness beside her where her wife ought to be.

Annie calls out to her. She goes into the kitchen, but it does not feel like her kitchen all of a sudden. The dresser with their wedding crockery looms at her in the shadows. The tinny echo of the dripping faucet seems only to highlight the emptiness, the lack of Ramona. She does not find her in the bedroom or the bathroom either. Annie is standing on the landing in her pyjamas, hands pressed to her cheeks, when she sees through the window a fleck of white among the indigo swathe of the brush. She is already running on bare feet down the stairs and out into the dust when she hears the cry like a fox caught in a trap.

'What in God's name were you doing?' They are sitting on the porch steps, waiting for the ambulance to arrive. Annie wraps a blanket around Ramona's shoulders and scolds her, 'You could have stepped on a snake. Could have snapped your ankle in a prairie dog burrow.'

'My wrist hurts,' Ramona says, cradling her left hand in her right. 'I landed on it when I tripped.'

'Nothing less than you deserve.' Annie frowns, but she puts her own hand on her wife's knee and squeezes.

A blue light flashes on the horizon. On their flat stretch of earth, they watch the ambulance approach for nearly twenty minutes, huddled against one another, the vehicle's wheels sending up great plumes of dust.

The EMT is a local boy by his accent, and he helps Ramona shuffle to the ambulance with his big arms and his big smile, saying, 'Now, what were you ladies up to in the yard at this time of night? Witchcraft?'

Annie is standing close enough that she can hear Ramona mutter, 'My brother's waiting out there. He's waiting for me. I was going to go get him.'

At the hospital in El Paso, a nurse takes Ramona's blood pressure and asks her some basic questions – address, insurance company, standard things, but Annie can tell it's getting on Ramona's nerves.

'She thinks I'm nuts,' Ramona stage-whispers, when they are exiled back into the waiting room. Annie suspects they will be sitting here a while, until the harried on-call doctors find space between the Saturday night gunshot regulars and a drunken teenage car wreck out on the highway.

'Nobody thinks you're nuts,' Annie says.

'You did. When I fell, out in the yard. You thought I was crazy.'

Ramona lets her head fall back against the waiting room wall. There is something about the gesture, and about the way the muscles of her face begin to sag, that seems to say she has come to the end of something. Breathing out deeply, letting the body deflate, the way one would at the end of a long hike.

Annie touches her wife's knee again. 'I didn't think you were crazy. I was just scared for you.'

'It's okay. I think maybe I *was* crazy. Sometimes it's like I'm standing next to myself, watching myself say and do things, and the real me is thinking "Ramona, what on earth . . .?" but I can't do anything to stop it. Shit just happens, right? Life just happens. Or it has happened, and now I'm in the fine print.'

'Now you're being morbid. Tell you what,' Annie says, joints clicking as she pushes herself to her feet, 'I'm going to go find a phone and call Hector. Maybe we can stay at his place tonight, instead of trying to get home this late.'

Ramona shoots her a sad smile. 'He'll say no.'

''Course he won't. This is Hector. We raised him better than that.'

'You did, maybe. Maybe he'd say yes if it was just you.'

Annie sits back down. She doesn't know what to say to that, most of all because she has a horrible, guilty feeling that it is true.

For nine months, Ramona carried their son, but after he was born, she never let herself get so close to him again. She laughed at his jokes, his stories, she sang him songs and drove him to school and dates and dances, but she never put her arms around him, and a child notices the space you leave, Annie thinks. Annie, whose father put a shotgun in his mouth, whose mother flew away every night in a handful of Oxy. She knows. Just as she knows why Ramona couldn't take their son's hand in hers, any more than she could catch the hand of her little brother as the river took him away.

What a life. What a pair, the two of them. But it doesn't *just happen*, Annie thinks, we each of us fill in the gaps that the other lacks, like we were made to fit together.

'Go on then, my girl,' Ramona sighs. 'Give me a tough one.'

Annie looks at their hands, overlapping on her wife's broad knee. Like this, she can't tell exactly whose fingers are whose, it's just an entanglement of gnarled skin and knuckles, bitten nails and old scars. Annie would take some of Ramona's scars if she could. She would take them all.

'You know I love you, don't you?'

'That's not a riddle.' Ramona glances at her then, eyes widening in momentary alarm. 'Is it?'

Annie shakes her head. She squeezes her wife's hand, lets her rest her chin on her shoulder, and thinks, You remember that, if nothing else.

Yukon, 1940

He was dead. The ground was frozen, and she would not be able to bury him until spring.

Sea poured between the rocks and spilled over the sodden bladderwrack and patches of snow that would settle again just as fast in this fresh flurry. Already there was a greasy film on the water where the slush was forming, giving way to incisors of pack ice further out in the bay, the great white mouth of winter that every day swallowed a little more of her life. Would that it had swallowed him too.

Otta's husband sat slumped in his wooden chair – the one he had made himself, because he was very good at making things – looking down at the bowhead whale's pelvic bone they used as a coffee table. He had stripped the whale himself, because he was also very good at that. On the table was a mug of coffee, from which he had taken only one sip before he died, because Otta was not very good at making coffee, and he had been in the process of telling her this when his face suddenly went slack and he went out of the world like a snuffed candle.

Now Otta stood in their little cabin with the profound feeling that she was trapped between two futures, even though she was already living in one of them. Her husband was dead and somehow life would have to move on from here, only she didn't see how it could. The wind moaned between the clapboards, and she thought, Oh I wish he would have died outside.

The house was her only refuge on this scrap of land, cast out ruthlessly into the Beaufort Sea, blind-wrapped in fog and cold. A land of teeth and claws and harpoons. A land of long night and men creeping about under ice-scabbed cliffs with only thoughts of murder and money to warm them. How many had come here before? Native traders and fishermen; Scottish, French and Russians seeking fox and mink and wolf; missionaries with their crucified god in tow; English explorers hunting for a passage through the ice; Americans hungry for gold. How many, still, arrived with dreams of striking rich, but found only crumpled waves as far as the horizon. Otta's husband was one such man, having made the long crossing from Norway with his hakapik and his seal gun, trying to escape the Nazis. This land was his domain now – he had deemed it so. Only the house belonged to Otta, and he had gone and died in it.

His final insult, she thought. She had been permitted so little out here, but, even dead, he managed to take up so much space.

It was not unheard of for hunters to bring their wives along to overwinter in the north. When Otta was last on the mainland, she'd read an article in the local newssheet in which a Canadian woman jauntily recounted shooting her first polar bear as a 'Pure thrill!' The journalist had been quick to add, of course, that the lady in question had also served the bear up for supper. 'And what a fine cook she was too.' Steak and potatoes with seal stew. More column inches were given to the excellent spread the huntress prepared at mealtimes than her marksmanship. Even so, Otta had envied her.

Otta was a reedy, flat-faced girl of nineteen with a tight braid of colourless hair and a look in her eyes like she was outnumbered, even when she was alone. She was known in the town where she grew up for her neat handwriting and for an incident at a cousin's birthday party where she had sung very badly. Though she could draw the Norwegian coastline from memory, she had never left her own harbour until the day she was married, and then her life had felt like a spool of thread suddenly dropped, rolling away and never picked back up.

She could not load a rifle, though one hung by the door on a crooked nail.

She could not skin a seal, though they relied on the pelts for their livelihood.

She could just about handle the rowboat that lay upturned outside the cabin like some huge resting beetle, but with the sea now freezing and many weather-soaked miles ahead, Otta knew she'd be tipped over and drowned before she ever caught sight of the mainland.

The full horror of her situation hit her with all the force of one of the surly blasts of wind that filled her mouth with cold and froze the hair inside her nostrils. Winter had her by the throat. She was trapped here on the island until the thaw brought the spring fishermen, who might ferry her to Herschel or one of the larger islands, although even that wasn't a given. She lacked her husband's knack for English and easy confidence when talking to strangers. She doubted she could charm them, but she would have to try. With no seal skins to sell, she would have no money to pay for the passage. And if she could not hunt, she would have nothing to eat.

Otta went outside and stood shivering in the purple dusk that hung between the cliffs and the sea most of the day now, the sun no longer rising above the horizon. She took great lungfuls of dark air, heard the rasping cry of a cormorant, and spotted it down on the rocks, stretching out its great black wings to dry. A bad omen, her husband would have said. Cormorants were the souls of dead men trying to find their way home.

Otta glanced back at the cabin where her husband's body sat, and then picked up a stone from the pebbled shore and hurled it at the bird. She missed, heard the stone splash in the slushy water. The cormorant simply looked at her, and she wondered what it saw. A pitiful shred of a girl that could not feed herself or hit a target only a few yards in front of her? Some small, quiet thing that could not even cry, because her husband had taught her not to.

They had met at a dance, where she trod on his toes. In her hometown, not far from Tromsø, the post office doubled as a dance hall, the timbers imbued with the smooth, pungent smell of cod liver oil, corners piled high with bundles of rope, nets, buckets and buoys, fishermen's boots with wooden soles hanging from the ceiling. Otta had come from a long day cutting the tongues out of stockfish down on the wharf, and she was aware of the ripe stink of her own body as she moved through the hall's hot fug, squeezing between men in their best tweed and ladies in their good dresses, cotton shipped all the way from Oslo. Unable to see where she was going – but wanting to go, wanting to get to the other side of the room as fast as she could, where it was quieter and a half-open window provided some cool relief – Otta walked right over his foot. It was the first and only time in their lives he had ever been beneath her.

Back then, he'd been curious about her, this grim-faced girl with little dark eyes, who answered questions about herself with all the flair of a prisoner under interrogation. She could tell he'd decided to take this as a challenge, assuming that her reticence must be a veil for hidden depths he intended to sound. She wanted to tell him: 'No, this is all there is, this is all I am.' But her mother said, 'Don't scare him off, Otta, for heaven's sake. A sealer, now, he'll take you out, show you a bit of the world. And who else will have you? You don't even look men in the eye when they speak to you. You'll be an old maid before you know it.'

She was sixteen, at the time.

Winter pressed on, and Otta drew down into the cave of herself. Huddled in the cabin with the rest of her husband's things, she burned whale oil, chewed on dried cod, sketched icebergs in the margins of a Bible. She listened to the bay cracking and groaning as it froze, and she waited for a sunrise that would not come.

Removing his body had been a punishing task. While there were still a few scant hours of light in the day, she'd rolled her husband in a bedsheet, heaved him out of the cabin and dragged him as far away inland as she could before she collapsed in the snow, her lungs burning. She'd piled rocks on top of him so that bears and scavenging birds couldn't get at the remains, and then she'd crouched on her haunches beside the cairn and said quietly, 'Well, here we are. I don't think you were a very good husband, but you did not think me a very good wife, and I suppose we knew both these things to be true before we were married, so more fool us.'

But after the long trek home, she'd discovered that her sweat had frozen inside her thermal underwear, and she had to wait and thaw herself by the stove to avoid pulling her skin off along with her clothes. As she sat there, she'd stared at the chair where her husband had died, and heard him saying, as he so often had, 'Isn't there anything you can do right?'

She slept a lot, to conserve energy. The thin supply of salted fish and tinned soup was not intended to last the whole winter, but she would have to make it stretch. She thought of the Canadian woman who had learned how to shoot a polar bear, and Otta wondered why her own husband had never taught her to do the same. Surely it would have made her a more useful partner to overwinter with? But then again, he had not liked sharing things with her, and he treated all aspects of hunting and skinning as if they were arcane knowledge she could not possibly hope to grasp. Perhaps he had been afraid she might turn the rifle on him.

Because she slept often, she easily lost track of time. It could have been well into January for all she knew. Her only company was the pack ice grinding out in the bay, and sometimes she would simply lie there thinking about the immensity of it, how it stretched up to cover the top of the world. How, if she'd wanted to, if she'd possessed the energy and the know-how, she could have walked all the way to the North Pole, down to the Kola Peninsula, and across the tundra to her very own Norway.

Oh, but it frightened her. Not the ice itself, but what lay beneath. Miles and miles of black ocean, whales with jawbones the size of a man, sharks that could live for hundreds of years, swimming down, down into the shadowy depths where only the shipwrecks and the green bones of old sailors lay. Where her father and brothers lay.

They had all drowned, some five years back. Taken under by a vicious little squall on the way home from escorting a group of English scientists up to Spitsbergen, though it later transpired that the scientists had eaten their meteorologist that winter, which everyone could agree was probably worse than drowning. Plenty of men expected to die at sea, to go down as heroes in legendary storms. Graveyards in coastal towns were usually the domain of women, buried in the dirt and forgotten.

Otta woke to the sound of dogs barking. She scrambled to the door, opening it a crack, though the cold was so sharp it made her eyes water. The sky was a net, its mesh clogged with stars, but in the hazy bruised half-light, she could make out three figures crawling around the seracs in the frozen bay. Then one of them stood up, and gunshot tore out viciously into the dark. Dogs were barking again, but she could not see them. Then came another shot, and Otta knew the report of that rifle, for it was the same make as the one that hung in her cabin. Her whole body tensed at the sound; not dogs, she realized. It was seals barking. These men were hunters.

Had she been someone else, had she been her husband,

she might have gone out to them, might have tried to trade something for fresh food or lamp oil. But the figures shuffling around on the ice with their guns and skinning knives made her flesh creep. She wanted nothing to do with them, guessed they would make quick work of a woman alone in the dark. She buried her head under her pillow so that she wouldn't have to listen to the seals, wailing like men going down in a storm.

She managed a few hours' sleep, but hunger pulled her insides into one central point of pain. There were fawn-coloured bruises on the backs of her knees and under her arms, although she could not remember having bumped into anything. Her mouth was stiff with the salt from her dried cod, and so she forced herself to put on her boots and coat and venture out in search of clean snow to melt for drinking water.

Once outside, however, curiosity got a hold of her and steered her towards the bay. Solitude could press down on a person, demand that they make something happen, and the monotony of her widowhood had left her eager for anything different in her day-to-day. So, with her lantern in hand, she went and stepped out on to the frozen sea.

It felt solid enough, and yet as she walked, she was sure she could feel the space beneath, wondered if the animals down below could hear the muted echo of her footsteps. Certainly, she could hear nothing else. The world was silent. Even the ice had gone quiet, and in the dark, the stillness seemed an invitation to let down her guard. Ahead of her was nothing but empty miles. When she looked back, her little cabin was further away than she'd expected – a single lantern glowing in the window, throwing long shadows across the snowy ground.

That was when she heard it. A long, mournful cry from further out on the ice.

A shudder ran up the length of her spine, making her scalp shrink. When she lifted her lantern, she saw that the snow in front of her was smeared, and above the sweet-scented cold, a metallic reek hung in the air.

The sealers must have done their skinning here. Otta's husband had always preferred to haul his kills home and work outside the cabin, where the meat could be easily stored or handed over to Otta for cooking, and many times she had watched him at his task. Straight cut from jaw to tail, knife under the blubber layer, removing the pelt from the carcass, and then the fur had to be washed in the sea as soon as it was off, so as not to be stained by the iron-rich blood.

Otta was a fisherman's daughter, a sealer's wife – animals had to die for her to eat them, and she knew this the same way she knew that the whale pods followed the herring, or that a polar bear's heart was the same size as a human child's head. Some things were facts of life, and facts did not trouble her. What troubled her was the way her husband would kick the seal bones around after he was done, or how he had once hunted down a walrus for the tusks alone and let the body sink into the sea. She thought there was a difference between killing something to eat it and killing because you liked the colour of blood on snow.

The long cry came again. Otta took a step forward, holding her lantern out ahead of her. Whatever it was, it sounded as if it were in great pain.

'Hello? Is somebody there?'

In reply, she heard a snort. The sound of snow crunching under something heavy. She smelled it before she saw it, the briny scent rolling towards her like a stormfront, and in another few paces she found the seal lying on its side, panting frantically.

It was enormous. Seven feet long at least, with a copper-coloured face and immense drooping whiskers that curled like a gentleman's moustache. In the lamplight, she noted a large gash in the animal's flank, and she had encountered enough dead things up here to know a bullet graze when she saw one.

Her own small body strained with hunger. Her limbs were weighed down with exhaustion. The seal's mottled grey fur looked dry and fluffy, was specked with snow; evidently it had been out of the water for some time, and Otta suspected it was either too tired or too hurt to make its way back to its hole. It was the ideal prey. Already downed with nowhere to go. A seal this size, she could probably live off it for the rest of the winter. She should have been relieved, and yet when she looked down and saw the panic in the whites of its eyes, watched it thrash then give up with another painful moan, she could not help thinking that they were both trapped here. Two ragged survivors who just wanted to go home.

The better place to tend to it would have been indoors, but the seal was far too large to carry back to the cabin, and every time Otta got too close, it would bare its teeth and snap its thick jaw at her.

'Who raised you?' she said, brandishing her lantern. 'Where are your manners, miss?'

In fact, she had no idea if it was male or female. Bearded seals were all hefty and moustachioed regardless of sex. All she knew was that the animal had a foul temper, and eventually, though she was loath to do so, she had to part with a few pieces of dried cod in order to get it to stop biting her coat.

The seal chewed loudly. It had a jaded kind of watchfulness, the result of a long and bloody history.

'Don't make that face at me,' Otta said. 'You're lucky I'm not eating *you* right now.'

They sat there, side by side on the ice, her teeth chattering, while overhead an aurora wove itself between the gaps in the clouds.

There was a primitive first aid kit back at the cabin, though she couldn't very well wrap the seal in gauze and give it a lick of akvavit. The wound in its flank was deep and needed cleaning, but saltwater would work better as a disinfectant and would be less likely to upset the already ornery creature. The seal had to have a hole nearby, a gap in the ice where it had come up out of the sea and where it would have made its escape, if the hunter's bullet hadn't found it first. Otta hoped she could find water there. She would have to go back to the cabin for a bucket, but the scent of blood in the air worried her. If she could smell it, no doubt bears would pick it up as well.

After a clumsy scramble across the ice, she gathered a bucket, the last of the salted cod, and the only sealskin her husband had taken that winter. She also unhooked his rifle from the crooked nail on the wall and slung it across her back, fixing his knife to her belt too for good measure. Never killed anything in her life, but she was not going to forgo this seal as dinner just to let some other animal eat it.

So Otta made her little camp out on the ice. Ideally she would have built a fire, but she sensed her new acquaintance probably wouldn't care for that, and she didn't like the thought of signalling to the hunters either. Besides, the seal gave off its own kind of staggering warmth, half-heat, half-smell, and bundled in her thermals, jumper and coat, Otta found she was no colder than usual.

The coat had been a gift from her husband. Sea-green wool with a rabbit-fur trim. It was her treasure, not because he had bought it for her, but because no one had ever bought her anything before. All her clothes had been hand-me-downs from her brothers, or been stitched by her mother during the long days when the sun refused to set and sleep was elusive. At first, Otta had taken his purchase as a sign of affection, though after they were married, she came to see it for what it was. He was starting to see the plainness in her, to understand there were no hidden depths after all. Just a void of a girl that he was trying to patch over with pretty things.

In the end, she didn't have to go far to find the sea. Otta had imagined herself stumbling around on the pack for hours, if she didn't slip and break her neck first, but after clambering over a wind-whipped ridge, she saw the white of the ice give way abruptly to nothing. Not so much a hole as a lesion, and bigger than she'd expected, as wide as a man was tall.

The whole group of seals must have used this spot as a haul-out, the lucky ones disappearing the same way when the hunters came. Otta approached the edge almost in a crouch, smelled the salt and the cold and the deepness of it. The sound of the water lapping at the edges was like some distant conversation she had not been invited to join. She took what she needed, but she did not stay for long.

Through the long night, she sat with the seal. It honked and snuffed at her when she poured saltwater on to its injured flank, but it did not try to flee. She fed it more scraps of dried cod and said that it was doing a fine job, since she thought that must be a nice thing to hear.

Daylight came in a wash of murky blue. The snow-veined slopes rose until they vanished in a coronet of mist, and Otta watched with gritted teeth as the mist rolled down and out into the bay, bringing with it a brutal hail of snow. She burrowed under her sealskin, heard the wind roaring all around her, her bones aching with how hard she was shivering, while beside her, the seal bore it in silence. She should have gone back to the cabin, but she did not want to leave the creature, or they would both be alone.

The snow didn't last long. The sun would not come up from behind the mountains, but its watery light made the thin clouds jewel-toned – pink, green and purple, as though someone had blurred a rainbow with their fingertips. A polar cloud, her father used to call it. Rare as eagles' teeth. Otta huddled in her sealskin, tired and hungry, but watching the colours shifting with the thermal winds, she thought she'd never breathed such fresh air in her life. She thought, too, that her cabin looked even further away.

Twice a day, she dragged her body to the hole in the ice to collect saltwater. Every time, she wondered if the hole was a little larger. On the second day, in the milky light, she saw other seals under the surface.

'Hello!' she called, her voice cracking through lack of use. 'Hello, your friend's up here!'

The seals slid over one another in silence. Their flippers, which always looked so awkward on land, billowed and contracted in the water with grace, like the wings of a bird. To swim as fast as they could, she supposed, must feel like flying.

Otta sat down cross-legged and watched them. She still wasn't sure which ones were the males and which the females. Her seal, with its big, raffish moustache, looked so much like old Jørgensen who'd run the post office back home that she sometimes thought of it as male, and yet at the same time, its hardiness and curt huffs in response to everything she said reminded Otta of her mother.

Little bubbles of air floated to the surface as the seals began to dive. One by one, their sleek grey shapes slithered into the depths until they seemed to become part of the water themselves, and Otta thought things like that – like being husband or wife – probably didn't much matter down there. After all, none of those seals was expected to keep house, make coffee or learn how to shoot a gun. They were all born with the same sharp teeth.

Her own seal trilled at her when she returned, snorting as she washed its wound. She could feel her exhaustion like rocks tied to her ankles and eventually she sat down a few feet away, pummelling her legs to get the circulation going. Suddenly there was something hot and damp against her side, and Otta looked up to find the seal nosing at her coat, searching for more dried cod, no doubt.

'You moved!'

The seal blinked slowly, little fishy puffs of steam escaping from its nostrils. Then it headbutted her, knocking her sideways, and Otta cursed at it.

'You great spoiled thing. You've got all that fat to live off and you still eat twice as much as me. Have you been able to move this whole time? Why don't you get back in the water and catch your own fish?'

But the seal did not understand her, any more than it

understood why she had rewarded it with cod every other time but now. Otta thought of her husband, how he had bought her this coat and then never anything else. How his kindness towards her had waned along with his interest, though she hadn't done anything different, had not somehow become more boring, just as she supposed the seal had not become more spoiled. It only expected food because she had started feeding it. Really, she thought, her husband had been starving her for a long time.

She gave the seal two pieces of cod and ate one herself. They watched each other while they ate, and she mimicked the way it chewed with its mouth open, the way it smacked its lips and honked, until she lost her breath laughing.

On the third day, when Otta went to the hole, she found it had grown considerably. Now it was so large it could have fit two fishing boats comfortably side by side, and blocks of ice drifted on the water, casting ghostly reflections in the late dawn. At first she thought the seals had returned, for she could see movement beneath the waves, saw the surface swell as some sleek body prepared to breach it, only to fall back in horror as a great fin pierced the sea right in front of her.

It was taller than she was, and it wasn't the only one. Soon the pool was alive with three, four, five black whales rolling and splashing, while Otta sat on the edge, unable to move.

Sea wolves, her father used to call them, and a primal fear beat through her as she saw them arch their backs against the surface. She knew she shouldn't stay. On their crossing from Norway to Canada, she and her husband had watched from the deck of their ship as a pod of orcas tipped a ringed seal off an ice floe directly into the waiting jaws of the bull whale.

They were perfect machines, built for speed and stealth and strength, and Otta did not doubt they could lunge and grab her if they wanted to, yet it was impossible to tear her eyes away. They were immensely elegant in the water. And when one came up for air, she saw that its face was clawed with scars – a hardy old matriarch, she guessed, for she knew most orcas followed their mother all their lives, the mother being both the shield and the sword.

As Otta's father told it, off the coast of Edgeøya, he'd once seen a bull drown an orca calf with repeated smacks of its tail. Her father had suspected that the bull was hoping to mate with the calf's mother and wanted the calf out of the way, but when the grisly act was done, the calf's mother had beaten the bull with her huge skull until the water turned red.

'Canny creatures,' Otta's father had said. 'And a canny creature knows when she's getting the broken end of the stick.'

A canny creature, Otta thought, would not have swum this far under the ice unless it knew it would be able to come up for air. As she scanned the horizon, she almost laughed with relief. Somewhere out there, the sea was opening up. Soon the fishermen would be heading north again, and her long winter would finally be over.

She was still making this noise – this breathless wheezing – when she realized she wasn't laughing at all. Her eyes were hot with tears. The whale with the scarred face was watching her with its all too human eye, and Otta wondered what it saw. Not something worth eating at any rate, just a splinter in the landscape. She could feel the absence of the weight and colour and energy she had lost. She could feel how thin her skin had become, the contours of her skull stark under her fingers when she touched her face, and she thought, if she were to see her own reflection now, would she even recognize herself?

The sea may have been thawing, but the winter wasn't over yet.

Icebergs drifted far out in the bay, with spires and turrets carved by fierce winds further north. Some held holes so tall and wide that a square-rigger of old could have sailed right through to the other side. Arctic turns and eider ducks called overhead. The sun still hid behind the mountains, but now the midday sky was turned out in buttery tones, and Otta and her seal lay on their backs, this new light bursting against their eyelids.

Otta felt she had never seen or heard or breathed as clearly as she did now, though it was a great effort to move, and whenever she checked, she had new bruises, some of them weeping like rotten fruit. There was a little of the dried cod left, but she wouldn't eat it. It wouldn't do any good now. Her body needed sugars, roughage, red meat, fresh fish, and she held out hope that she would get some, if she could just hold on a little longer.

She'd seen her own brother come back from scurvy once, knew that people could and did survive if they were savvy enough, though as she lay there, her husband's voice whipped at her out of the past: 'Otta, if brains were rope, you couldn't snare a spider.'

She sat up, brushing snow from her hair, and looked at her seal, sunning its large, round body with a look of contentment on its blunt, bearded face. By now its wound had scabbed over and did not look so angry. Clearly it could move, and she didn't understand why it wouldn't just go back to the water. The scraps of dried cod she had to offer were poor nourishment compared to the squid, fish and clams a seal like this would normally eat. Perhaps the animal was just being lazy. Or perhaps it didn't know where the water was, its pool hidden by the ridge of snow. One thing Otta knew for certain: her food supply was down to a last measly handful, and if the seal didn't return to the water and start hunting for itself, it would starve, same as her.

She glanced at the cabin squatting on the shore, its boards red from mixing seal blood into the paint. 'Well,' she said to the empty doorway, where she half expected her husband to appear. 'I am standing on the ocean, and you are dead, so what do you think of that?'

With the last flecks of cod, she laid a trail to the water.

It was an arduous journey, both for Otta and the seal, though they barely travelled a few yards. With every movement, she felt her bones bruising her skin from the inside out, heard her own scraping breath whenever she forced herself to take a slightly longer route, flatter ground for the seal, which struggled to heft its great body with its short front flippers. By the time she reached the water, she was almost crawling, saw blood on her trousers where her knees were raw. With the last of her energy, she flung the final shred of dried cod into the water.

She watched it sink, its shape distorting under the ripples, until it was nothing at all.

'Come on, please . . .'

The seal had its head down, busy gobbling up an earlier part of the trail, and Otta feared it wouldn't understand, feared it would just stop where it was now that there was no more food. She groaned at the sky, 'Don't you understand? You're killing yourself if you stay here.' But then the seal looked up. The moment it saw the water, it seemed to summon some hidden reserve of vigour and propelled itself forwards, sliding along the ice, and Otta had to roll out of the way so as not to be tumbled into the sea with it.

At the brink of the pool, it transformed – this lumbering, awkward thing now a streamlined athlete gliding from one world into another, pure grace, a powerful muscle finally able to flex. Otta thought of habitats, how hers was not the dance hall where she had stood on her husband's foot, nor was it the cabin, where she simply collected dust along with the rest of his junk. Where, then, did she belong?

In the water, the seal twisted and rolled with what Otta took to be delight, but it did not resurface to look back at her. She had not expected it to, it was still a wild animal, but she felt the absence of its regard like a bereavement.

She could not say how long she lay there. Hours. Days. She faded in and out of herself. At one point, she saw a pale, hulking shape in the distance and a bolt of panic shot through her, for she feared it was a bear, felt its heavy tread thrumming through the ice. Otta no longer had the strength to claw her way back to the rifle on the other side of the snow ridge, but even if she had, she knew she wouldn't have used it. It was a relic of a world she had somehow stepped out of. Her husband's world, the world of men, and of women too. In the end, the bear did not come any closer, and she watched gratefully as it wandered away, its long snout pressed to the ground, on the trail of some other, healthier prey.

The following morning, as light spilled over the mountains, Otta thought she could feel the world turning beneath her, the slow but certain grind of it inching back towards the sun. Her bare, windburnt face was now completely numb, but slowly she became aware of an iciness creeping up her foot, towards her ankle. Forcing herself up on to a brittle elbow, she saw the water rolling gently over her. The ice beneath her feet had cracked and floated away, leaving only tiny shards that caught and lifted with the tide.

She was surprised how little this troubled her. It bothered her more that her boot was wet. Hauling herself into a sitting position, she tried to untie her laces, but her fingers were too cold, too shaky to be of any use, and in the end, Otta took her husband's skinning knife from her belt and cut the soaking leather from her foot. First one and then the other, revealing toes black with frostbite. For a moment, she simply stared at them, marvelling at her own sense of calm. She felt as if she were outside her body, looking at it from a great distance and not recognizing it at all.

It occurred to her then that if she was going to die, she did not want to do so wearing the coat her husband had bought for her. If she was cold, she would wrap herself in the sealskin; it had kept her warm enough so far. She fumbled with the buttons, but they were quite frozen, and so eventually she cut herself free of this too, head to tail, one clean swipe, removing her carcass from the skin he'd put her in. Now that she looked at the sodden heap of sea-green wool, she didn't think it had ever really suited her.

Kneeling at the edge of the water, she noticed the waves were stronger now, pushing harder at the lip of the ice, or being pushed. It was an effort just to raise her head, it felt so heavy, but as she forced herself to look up, she saw the unmistakeable cross of a boat mast, not far away, travelling down a lead that had split the ice and freed her pool to the open ocean.

The boat was close enough that she could hear voices from the deck, could make out gnarled, bearded faces leaning over the prow, calling out in alarm. She wondered what they saw as they looked down at her. Not a woman, or a man, but a seal slipping into the water, moving quick and clean as a knife.

I'll Be Bound for the Lonesome Woods

For Aude

Grand Lake, Colorado
July 16, 1917

Dear Ale,

Or am I obliged to call you Second Lieutenant Esteves now? So, you see, I have heard the news, even up here, in what you called my 'shabby corner of the world'. Frances rode over yesterday to tell me. She says the snow is still ten feet high up at the pass, and though my lake thawed months ago, I have passed several frozen places on what I like to think of as my reconnaissance treks. Two years, and I am still getting to know my shabby corner.

But I digress – I was meant to be telling you off. It will come as no surprise to you, I'm sure, that I think you are running a fool's errand and allowing yourself to be bought in the process. What good will citizenship do you when you're drowning in the fetid mire of No Man's Land? My cousin Lionel in Penzance was shipped back from Arras in May, and since they do not yet censor Britain's letters to us, he was liberal with his descriptions. Make no mistake, Ale, you are going to get your arms blown off, or half your face, or worse still, your legs, and then how will you come hiking with me in the fall? I think Colorado is worth seeing at all times of year (except, perhaps, in the late spring when the dreaded pollen dust is upon us), but especially in the fall.

Renounce this foolish campaign at once, and I might acquiesce to speak to you again.

Yours most sincerely,
Frederick

Camp Whitman, New York
July 22, 1917

Dear Freddie,

I like the way you wrote 'Frances rode over to tell me', as if your sister were somehow reporting to you, rather than doing what I asked, which was to convince you to come down off your mountain and wish me goodbye. You do realize that I'm going halfway across the world? At least, that is the aim. For now, I am receiving basic training with the 369th Infantry Regiment, and it would mean a great deal to me if you and Frances would come up to New York before I am deployed elsewhere.

I like the men here well enough so far. This is the only regiment in the state that accepts non-white volunteers, and besides Americans, there are a fair number of other Puerto Ricans, as well as Guyanese, Cubans and Liberians, though my CO is a white officer. Captain Ernest Dubois. He relies on me as the Division's unofficial interpreter, since he studied French as his second language at West Point and his Spanish is almost non-existent. I expect his linguistic skills will prove invaluable once we are in France, but for the time being, I am hoping my assistance will stand me in good stead. Perhaps I may be of more use to my fellow soldiers than simply another body for them to scramble over when we go over the top.

You are wrong, you see, my dear Freddie, if you think I underestimate the nature of war. You forget my father fought at San Juan Hill.

As for the matter of citizenship, you are a contradiction, as always. You wish me to stay in America so that we can further explore your wooded exile together, but we are not all as fortunate as you when it comes to possessing aristocratic mothers and immigration papers. 'Free white persons of good character', that's who this government is prepared to naturalize. Who knows how long it would have taken them to make up their minds as to whether that applied to me? Shake your head and tut if you like, but my studies would have come to their natural end, and I would have returned to Puerto Rico. At least this way, by volunteering for this country, my citizenship is secured, and then, God willing, you can show me your mountains.

Sincerely yours,
Alejandro

Frederick Velazquez first met Alejandro Esteves at a beer garden in Dixonville, outside the rapidly increasing sprawl of Manhattan's Academic Acropolis. In the spring of 1915, they were both students at Columbia, Esteves in his first year, while Frederick was trying to scrounge up funding to continue his postgraduate degree, and his limited success was making him reckless.

An Argentinian by birth, Frederick had inherited his Cornish mother's sandy hair and hooded green eyes, though his features were sun-blasted from a recent stint on the Colorado Plateau, digging ancient vertebrae out of ravines. He aspired to be a palaeontologist, but such studies were harder to pursue in Argentina at the time, and so he had come north, much to the dismay of his father, who considered this a superfluous degree and had threatened to cut off Frederick's allowance. Frederick's mother, too, was badgering him to return to Buenos Aires, mostly to appease his father's temper. Frederick might well have folded and traipsed home with his tail between his legs, had it not been for the encounter in Dixonville.

Esteves was seated at a picnic-style table with a mutual friend – one Henry Wallace, who always kept his shirtsleeves rolled up to show off his arms, made thick from years of varsity wrestling. Wallace had recently enlisted Esteves to tutor him in Spanish, and when Frederick finally squeezed his way through the writhing, chattering drinkers, he found Wallace whispering something in Esteves' ear, which made the latter laugh.

'Poor boy,' Frederick said. 'You've acquired some hideous growth on the side of your face.' And he cuffed the back of Wallace's head to detach him.

Even seated, Frederick could tell Esteves was tall, with a narrow, lupine face, dark hair and a prominent nose. It was an unseasonably warm May evening, and the heat of the beer garden, combined with the drink, put great dashes of colour in his high cheeks. Frederick sat on the table with his feet planted on the bench so that Esteves would have to look up at him.

'What are you love birds twittering about?' Frederick said, and Wallace coughed, appalled.

'Watch what you joke about with this one, Velazquez, he's a lawyer. Carry on like that and you might find yourself in need of him one day.'

'Is that so?' Frederick replied. 'Consider me quaking in my boots.'

Esteves gave him a curious look. 'Actually, I'm only pre-law.'

'Oh, well then,' Frederick laughed. 'Consider me pre-quaking.'

'Before you manifested yourself so violently, Velazquez,' Wallace said, 'we were talking about the war.'

'How dull of you, discussing other people's wars.'

'Did you hear Chesterton and Kitteridge went up to Toronto to enlist with the Canadians? They don't think it's someone else's war.'

'More fool them, then.' Frederick took a swig of Wallace's beer. 'What do you think, Esteves? Ought we to race to the rescue of the British empire? They'd snub us on the battlefield while using our corpses to shield them from mortar fire.'

'That's callous, even for you, Velazquez,' Wallace said. 'Men are dying out there.'

'Empires are dying, but such is history. Esteves, do you hike? Some good mountain country in Puerto Rico, I hear.'

'No,' Wallace cut in. 'He blows off steam like a civilized person.'

'I hardly think beating each other senseless in the gymnasium counts as civilized.'

'I don't wrestle,' Esteves answered. Then, cocking his head at Frederick, he added, 'But I don't hike either.'

'Then how on earth do you entertain yourself?'

'Mostly I study. Don't you?'

'Velazquez's studies are merely a means to an end,' Wallace explained, wiping beer foam from his top lip. 'That end being: to be outdoors as much as possible.'

'Tragically, Wallace knows me too well. I intend to hike a trail in the Adirondacks this weekend, if you're interested in seeing a little of the local country.'

'No, thank you, I'm not,' Esteves said.

It was like that, then.

Later, that night, after the three of them had staggered back through Morningside Heights to their separate lodgings, Esteves had turned on the steps of his building to look back at Frederick. It was only for a moment, but though Frederick did not consider himself much of a sportsman, the sound of the door falling shut as Esteves went up to bed seemed very much like a starting pistol.

Camp Wadsworth, South Carolina
October 11, 1917

Dear Freddie,

I apologize for the lateness of this letter. I meant to write you after your visit in August, but we have since decamped from New York to South Carolina, and I have scarcely had an hour to myself in which to organize my thoughts. Some organization was necessary after our last meeting, I think you'll agree. I wish you had come with Frances like I asked. Somehow, she makes you seem more human.

I am getting on all right here, though it is not without its difficulties. The men under my command have a fine sense of humour and we get along well, but we are camped near a town named Spartanburg, and the locals don't seem to know what to do with us. Only yesterday, two of my men and I were refused service while trying to buy cigarettes. The store owner told me they don't serve 'Blacks or Mexicans', and the fact that I am neither didn't seem to hold much sway with him. Captain Dubois spoke up for me, saying that if the store refused to do business with the United States Army, it may as well close down. He meant well, I suppose, but that made it no less embarrassing. I think he is hoping to make major before we're officially deployed. His Spanish is coming along very poorly.

Well, there is no more putting it off.

I can't tell if I'm still mad at you, Freddie. You had no right to come up to New York just to try to bully me out of my commission, and looking like a vagrant, no less. Captain Dubois did not think very highly of that. I refuse to believe things are so bad between you and your father that you can't get the money for a shave and a new suit. You seem like something out of time. Like a frontiersman abandoned in the wilderness and turned half mad. Are you finding many bones in Colorado, or are you just hiding there?

I think what upsets me most, however, is the knowledge that this is, in part, my fault. That you should have ended up this way because of me and what happened at Columbia, and yet you still won't let me apologize. Even now, you punish me.

It's a good thing Argentina has remained neutral in this war, or they would have come and fetched you down from your mountain hut and forced you to be a modern man. God knows I won't do it. I release you, Frederick. I release myself. I go to my duty and pray you find yours.

Respectfully,
Alejandro

PS I heard Lawrence Kitteridge was killed at a place called Passchendaele. I remember he was a friend of yours. My sincere condolences.

'I refuse to believe your studies are the only thing that interests you, Esteves.'

'I never said that. I said hiking with you didn't interest me. Bold of you to infer that it's either you or nothing.'

They reclined side by side on the grass, watching from behind tinted lenses as Wallace attempted to thrash Arthur DeYoung, a ropey fourth-year medical student, at badminton. It was a balmy afternoon, and the Central Park courts were full of women in sunhats and white dresses and men stripped down to their shirtsleeves. Someone's boisterous dog was running back and forth after a shuttlecock.

'Wallace, must you grunt like that every time you serve?' Frederick called. 'It's like watching a hog play.'

Wallace scraped away the gingery hair plastered to his brow. 'Oh, go to hell, Velazquez. I'd like to see you do any better.'

'You don't like him,' Esteves said quietly in Spanish.

'That's funny,' Frederick replied, 'I've never heard anyone accuse me of not liking Wallace. If anything, they say the opposite.'

Nearby, some cross-looking children were riding around on mules, while others were being towed in miniature open-top carriages drawn by goats that kept bleating and defecating on the paths. Esteves took off his sunglasses and fixed Frederick with his black-eyed stare. 'I think you're full of it.'

'Excuse me?'

'I think you're trying to get a rise out of me – implying things about you and Wallace. It won't work.' He rolled on to his front, resting his chin on his lean brown arms. He was as perfect to look at as a river stone. 'I like Wallace, but I don't think I'm obliged to be friends with his friends just because we speak the same language.'

'You think I'm trying to befriend you?' Frederick snorted. 'I'm bloody to my friends, as you've seen. I'm bloody to my tutors too, and my sister, and I like her more than anyone. Learn to take politeness for what it is, Esteves. A way to get through the day with minimal casualties.'

'Goodness, they should call you in for the peace talks. Maybe you could talk Europe politely out of its war.'

Frederick lowered his sunglasses. 'Now, are you being snide because I've offended you, or are you secretly trying to be friends?'

'Nope.' Esteves picked himself up, brushing shreds of freshly cut grass off his slacks. 'When I dislike someone, I don't see a reason to be dishonest about it.'

Frederick watched him stride across the badminton court as Arthur DeYoung threw up his hands in exaggerated relief. 'Here comes the cavalry! Help me take the bastard down, will you?'

Esteves relieved DeYoung of his racket, giving the air a few cursory swipes, before shifting his centre of gravity to his hips and settling low in his stance. Frederick felt hot under his skin. Wallace grinned across the net.

'Come on and finish me off then, kid.'

Frederick thought, Yes, yes, do.

Esteves glanced his way for less than a second, before he let the shuttlecock fly, following through the serve with his whole body, as if he were throwing a left hook, or loosing a slingshot. Even then, fighting in his own private war.

Grand Lake, Colorado
October 16, 1917

Dear Alejandro,

Captain Dubois, Captain Dubois! Did he ever buy you your damn cigarettes? Since you made no mention of it, I have enclosed my last two Camels. (I smoke a pipe myself these days.)

You are wrong if you think my aim in coming to visit you was to bully you, just as you are mistaken if you think I would go begging to my father for a shave. Given all that's occurred, I'm as likely to go to him as I am to go to war. Perhaps you do not know me as I thought.

Yours regretfully,
Frederick

Alejandro's grandfather had been a Basque farmer who settled in Chile, carving out a life for himself, his native wife, and a flock of hardy sheep in the Patagonian Andes. Alejandro came from mountain stock, though he no more wanted to admit this than his mother, who had run away with an affluent wool merchant when she was sixteen, sailed around the Horn, and eventually washed up in Puerto Rico. They were wanderers, his family. Cast adrift with no real home to tether them.

It was a history he kept quiet about at Columbia. His father – no longer a wool merchant, but a factory owner – wanted his son to make something of himself. With so much of his parents' expectation and funding behind him, Alejandro sometimes felt like he was staring down a long corridor with no doors, only windows, through which he might glimpse the lives of others, but not reach them.

In the summer of 1915, he was not invited to Frederick Velazquez's twenty-third 'birthday expedition' in the Blue Ridge Mountains, but was unaware of this fact until he and Wallace departed the passenger train at Roanoke, and Velazquez said, 'I see you brought him along anyway, then. I hope he can keep up.'

They had hiked through knotted mountains, the trail jerking uphill for long stretches, over fossilized tree stumps and jammed streambeds, then down into well-watered valleys. Velazquez set a brutal pace, but every now and then he would stop to inspect an ammonite or a strange claw, which he seemed able to spot from several yards away.

Perhaps what bothered Alejandro the most about Velazquez was that he couldn't actually pin down what bothered him. While Wallace and DeYoung were walking ahead, bickering and swatting at each other as much as at the rampant mosquitoes, Alejandro paused to take a sip of water from his cannister, leaning back with one hand on his tailbone. He watched Velazquez pawing at the ground, turning over ancient seashells with his large hands.

'Did you hike much, back in Argentina?' he asked.

Velazquez glanced up at him, eyebrows raised. 'You know, I believe the perfect wilderness companion is one who can merge into the landscape. When I'm in places like this, the mountains are the only thing I want to hear from, and since the mountains can't speak, I'd rather not hear from anybody.'

'Then why invite anyone at all?' Alejandro said.

'I didn't. Wallace has got it into his head that I need to be socialized, like some kind of foundling pack animal, but I could have done without you and DeYoung this weekend.'

'But you'd have been happy with Wallace's company, is that it?'

'He and I share an affinity for certain pursuits.' Something in Velazquez's smile made Alejandro boil.

'Stop trying to imply things about him. Wallace is my friend, and I know he loathes hiking.'

'What is it that you think I'm implying? More to the point, what are *you* doing with him? All those late nights in his rooms . . .'

'I'm teaching him Spanish. Good God, what would he think if he knew you were talking like this?'

'Perhaps you should ask him,' Velazquez challenged. 'I'm sure he'll get a good laugh out of it.'

But, as it turned out, Wallace did not find it amusing at all. Alejandro wondered, afterwards, if Velazquez had known that from the start and had merely been teasing him, or if he really had miscalculated so drastically. By the time faculty became involved, in what were by that point referred to as 'allegations', it was too late for anybody to laugh it off.

Somewhere in the Atlantic
December 31, 1917

Dear Freddie,

I don't know if I'll get the chance to mail this letter. Currently I am in the middle of the ocean, bound for an unfamiliar country on an unfamiliar continent. We are travelling in convoy with a group of destroyers. They are meant to defend us from U-boat attacks, but we have heard of similar convoys being targeted and sunk, so I apologize if my mood, and thus my letter, is black tonight.

Some thoughts, then, as we close out another sombre year:

This is a good ship. I understand it was once a luxury liner, and as an officer, my quarters are really quite comfortable, or they would be, if it weren't for the storms. Not two days out and we've hit a bad squall flung down from the Arctic. In daylight, the sky and the water are all the same threatening grey, and I only know which parts are the waves when they crash against our portholes. Already one crew member has been swept clean off the deck and sadly lost. I have not been sick yet, though many of the men have, and who can blame them. Perhaps I have inherited my mother's sea legs.

I am now a First Lieutenant. I celebrated my promotion by smoking one of your Camels before we set sail. I can picture you smoking a pipe all too easily, in that quiet little cabin in the woods.

Why won't you come out and say that you blame me for Columbia? It's unlike you to spare my feelings. Aren't you mad, Freddie? If matters were reversed, and you had got me expelled, I would have been incensed. And yet I don't regret it.

Perhaps that ought to have been a separate admission. I am floating in a giant metal tub, being thrashed by freezing water, awaiting any minute to be blasted apart by torpedoes, and if I can't admit this now, then when? I don't regret your being kicked out of Columbia. If you hadn't been, I might never have gone after you.

I can hear the men below, singing 'Auld Lang Syne'. Here's to a better year.

Nauseously yours,
Alejandro

Alejandro spent New Year's Eve, 1915, in a watering hole north of Denver. He could hear the roar of the wind above the timberline, like something long and solid rushing over the clutch of log buildings that formed the mountain town of Lyons. The tailored suits of New York were gone, replaced by thick woollen pants and a scarf tied over his hat, dense socks in sturdy boots. He had come up on horseback from Boulder, battling his mount almost as much as the weather so that he lost a sheepskin mitt outside Loveland. Upon his arrival in Lyons, the bartender had to pour scalding water over his hands to get his finger joints working again.

He did not feel as though any part of him had been working well for some time. Not long into the start of the fall term, Velazquez had been expelled from Columbia, pending a criminal investigation. There were things Alejandro had not fully understood about Henry Wallace – namely that what he had first taken for sensitivity was in fact a blazing, struggling shame, and to have it known that Velazquez went around speaking of him like a lover induced Wallace to show his teeth, as any threatened animal would.

There were accusations of obscenity, of force, of visits made in the dead of night. Alejandro grew to like Wallace less in September. He told him once that he wished he would just shut up, and Wallace said, 'It's you who should have shut up, Esteves. You've been just as bad as him, spreading this around.'

Then one night in October, Velazquez was gone.

'To his sister in Colorado, I should think,' DeYoung said. 'It's not as if he's got anyone else. His father won't have him back in Buenos Aires now.'

Alejandro saw Velazquez's empty rooms. The lack of him was startling.

It was Frances Velazquez who'd lent Alejandro the horse – or Frances Garrett, for she was now married to one William Garrett, who owned the Garrett Silver Mine. The couple had met some years ago when Mr Garrett was prospecting in Argentina, but they now lived in Boulder, which was smaller than Denver and much more rustic, still a mining town at heart. Mrs Garrett looked like her younger brother, which is to say she was hearty and unflinching, and there was a kind of rugged beauty in this. She shared Velazquez's sandy hair and cut-glass eyes, and for the three days that Alejandro stayed with the Garretts, he never saw her wear a dress, only a bulky pair of overalls and a blanket coat.

William Garrett, on the other hand, was a slight, willowy man some ten years older than his wife, with hair so pale it was almost grey. He spoke softly and never disagreed with his wife, or their young daughter, who, at the dinner table, stared into Alejandro's face and declared, with supreme confidence, 'You look like the prince in my book.' She was reading about the gods of South America.

When Alejandro explained that he was looking for her brother, Frances Garrett did not ask why. Only said in Spanish, 'Do you own a pistol, Señor Esteves? You may take mine. My brother isn't always fond of visitors.'

On New Year's Day, 1916, the wind had licked the clouds into ribbons and blown away much of the snow, and Alejandro saddled his horse to set out on a clearer track. The bartender told him a stage ran from Lyons up to Estes Park, which would deliver him faster, but Alejandro was bound for the lakes beyond Shadow Mountain and would not get there without the horse. Besides, he was curious about the countryside and wanted to see it. To understand what had driven Velazquez up here, over and above the proximity to his sister, which, considering the ridges, gulches and rough valleys he had to traverse, was not so proximate after all.

Colorado was all rock and sky. Alejandro watched an eagle, forced from the heights by a lingering snow cloud, swoop vainly at invisible prey below while the wind scythed through stripped aspens and cottonwoods, greying conifers creaking so loudly that sometimes he ducked in his saddle, fearing they were about to topple into his path.

He reached Estes Park around midday, where he washed the cold out of his mouth with a beer and let the horse feed. At the bar, people spoke of a war they did not want but which somehow felt inevitable. There were a number of Mexicans who took Alejandro for one of their countrymen at first and bought him a whiskey, which he did not decline, and on their advice, he bought new mittens and spent the night in an Estes bunkhouse, listening to tales of the Sonoran Desert. Of giant serpents that tried to swallow the world, of cursed wells and demi-god daughters born with animal claws. He left half an hour before dawn. To his relief, the wind had slackened, and the fine air refreshed him.

It was a cold crossing between ruinous peaks. Following Frances Garrett's directions, he made for the Ptarmigan Pass, passing Bear Lake, Dream Lake, Emerald, before he came up alongside the looming wall of Flattop Mountain. The sky was so clear here he felt he could have thrown a stone and shattered it. Beginning the descent, he found a stream flanked by skinny pines. He smashed the surface ice and watered the horse, before continuing down towards Hallett Creek. Mrs Garrett had told him he should follow the creek for two miles until it branched into the North Inlet. From there it was a matter of tracking the inlet to Grand Lake. Anxiety pulsed between his ribs. He had no idea what to expect, and felt for the pistol under his coat.

Mrs Garrett said that Velazquez had leased a small cabin on the east side of the lake, near Adams Falls. By now night was falling, clouds shuddering across the stars as the wind picked up again, and Alejandro had to ask for directions in the town. The locals laughed uneasily and referred to Velazquez as the 'crazy Spaniard'. It wasn't long before Alejandro discovered why.

Having had enough wilderness for one day, he was taking a glass of brandy and some cured elk at Grand Lake's only restaurant when his quarry strode right past him, a clutch of dead rabbits swinging from one fist. Velazquez deposited the rabbits with the cook, who gave him half a bottle of something brown and noxious, which Velazquez proceeded to swallow in front of the clientele. Alejandro was almost repulsed then. A part of him wished he hadn't come, saw the madness of his own errand, but then Velazquez dropped into the seat opposite, reeking of the woods, and grinned.

'Took your time, Esteves. You always did have trouble keeping up.'

Somewhere in Northern France
January 30, 1918

Dear Freddie,

For weeks I have been saying 'I must get back to my letter', but since our arrival in France, I have not had much time to write. The American Expeditionary Force has us doing manual labour. You were wrong, they don't want to use us as human shields – apparently Puerto Ricans aren't fit for the ruthless glory of combat, so we're on ditch-digging duty until enough American boys have been shot.

It makes me think of you, seeing the men in their tents. I'm reminded of your bivouac on Shadow Mountain, and how you taught me to sing that dreadful Argentinian drinking song through the night so that I wouldn't fall asleep and freeze to death. I hum it to myself even now.

It has hardly stopped being some sort of weather or another since we disembarked at Brest. We crossed the country on foot through heavy rain, which became sleet as we progressed north. Last week, my tent blew open during the night, and I woke to find everything covered in as much snow as outside. The worst, however, is when the snow has been marched over so many times that it has turned to slush, and then the mud below it sucks us down and sticks to us like clay. My boots are always wet, and I'm afraid to take them off in case my feet have swollen so much I can't get them back on. They give us cigarette rations, but they are not very good.

I can remember exactly the last time I was this cold, and the circumstances were considerably less dire.

Write to me about something. Anything. This is a lonesome, crowded place.

Yours expectantly,
Alejandro

Grand Lake, Colorado
February 22, 1918

Dear Ale,

Winter has been impenetrable here, and your letter did not get through to me for some time. You must excuse the appalling handwriting. I got caught in a storm coming down from a deer stalk on Shadow Mountain and had to hollow out a shelter in a snowbank for the night. By morning, both my hands were frostbitten. I cut away the worst of the decay myself, but I knew Frances would give me hell when the snow eventually cleared enough for her to come over, so I sought out the doc and had the three offending fingers removed. Now, even if Argentina or the

United States should call on me to fight, I shall be of little use to them. I can barely hold the Beesley, though I have enlisted Frances to help me to learn to shoot again, so at least I won't starve.

I thought of this when I read about your boots. I'd cut them off, if I were you, and let your feet dry thoroughly, or the skin is likely to rot. Would that I could send you a hardier pair. I'd sell my rod, I'd sell my reel to buy my man a sword of steel, or however that old folk song goes. Though I suspect your precious Captain Dubois wouldn't allow that.

In other news, William has been drafted. Frances is furious that I didn't argue with him about it, claims it is proof I've never cared for him. Untrue. I do in fact find William extremely tolerable, but it would go to Frances' head if she knew I approved of her choice of husband.

Write me something happier next time. I don't like to think of you miserable, even if it serves you right for taking my only friend from me and sending him to dig ditches in the rain.

If anything in this letter offends you, pretend you misread it on account of my crippled writing.

Yours somewhat depletedly,
Frederick

PS I remember you being cold. I remember your frozen hands that winter.

'This *is* a shabby corner of the world,' Alejandro said, for the cabin, much like the town, still had a sense of being newly hewn right out of the wild.

Velazquez tossed a log on the stove and set a pot of coffee on the table with two tin cups. He shot Alejandro a taunting smile. 'Well, if I'd known you were coming, I'd have spruced the place up.'

They drank their blackhearted coffee, the horse whickering in the lean-to nearby. Alejandro reported that Mrs Garrett was in good health. He was proud of the journey he'd undertaken, but feared Velazquez would mock him if he thought Alejandro was bragging, so he spoke little and allowed Velazquez to pontificate about trapping coyotes and martens. That was how he made his living now. It was muggy in the cabin, and Alejandro's eyes prickled from the heat coming off the stove. He unlaced his boots and peeled off his socks, planting his feet on the bare boards. Velazquez watched him carefully, while explaining how he kept a whole other change of clothes in a sack under a rock somewhere out in the woods, to wear when he was hunting, so that he wouldn't smell too much like a man. Alejandro nodded, but that was all Velazquez smelled like to him.

There was only the one bed, a straw mattress on a wire frame, so Velazquez said he would sleep on the floor. He had the look of someone who was used to it, which made Alejandro enormously sad and weary, thinking of their comfortable lodgings back in Morningside. This was a place of splinters and gaps.

Alejandro said, 'I'm sorry.'

Velazquez sat there in that cramped, smoky room with his hands half open, as if waiting for someone to take hold of them. 'If all you came here for was absolution, you can head back up the mountain.'

Alejandro wanted to ask what the hell else he should

have come for. But then in the heart of the night, with only the amber glow from the stove embers softening the edges of things, Velazquez came and got into bed with him, and Alejandro, who had come this far, figured he might as well go the whole distance.

Somewhere in Northern France
March 13, 1918

Dear Freddie,

How the hell do you intend to keep trapping when you've cut off three fingers? You are a damn fool. That is all I can think to say, and all I have time to write.

Yours, nonetheless,
Alejandro

Boulder, Colorado
March 28, 1918

Dear Ale,

I am making a brief return to civilization for William's bon voyage party. Frankly, I think they ought to be sending Frances – she'd ride bareback through No Man's Land, smash the Hindenburg Line, and take Berlin in a week – but no one ever listens to my ideas.

Made a killing at the Boulder fur auction, so to speak. Polecat, mink, cherry-red foxes. A lot of the young trappers are gone away now to your side of the world, which leaves more for the rest of us. I can hear you making one of your disdainful little noises at that, but let me tell you, you will not be so disdainful when you see the fine snowy hides I have put aside for you. I know you are a boy who likes nice things. I'm having them made up into a coat and hat set.

Yours affluently (ha ha),
Frederick

Somewhere in Northern France
April 12, 1918

Dear Freddie,

Some good news at last! We have been reassigned to the French Armed Forces. They have provided us with new weapons and helmets (no new boots, sadly), and within the 16th Division, of which we are now a part, there is no segregation. I am stationed with some excellent, hardy gentlemen from Senegal, who no more see this as their war than you do, but at least they do not have to battle Jim Crow along with the Kaiser. The French have been in this conflict longer than we have, and some of these soldiers are worn to shreds. Their officers are a snobbish lot, but I think the regulars are just glad of the additional manpower, no matter where we come from.

We have done a lot of marching, and I have terrible blisters, but I like the French cigarettes better than the American.

There is a sense of things shifting, of change coming to this raw and bloody part of the world. I may be the only one who feels that way, but I feel it nevertheless. Perhaps it is because spring is on the way. I hope it is glorious in Colorado.

Yours,
Alejandro

PS I hope your fingers are doing better.

PPS A coat and hat set? I'll look like a duchess on her way to the opera. Be serious.

Grand Lake, Colorado
April 25, 1918

Her Grace the Duchess of Shadow Mountain,

My fingers are adequate. Top news about the French.

Colorado is indeed glorious in the spring, but you know that already. I was thinking of that afternoon we hiked up to Adams Falls and bathed in the river. The meltwater from the peaks was freezing, but you stuck it out to spite me, I think. It was the first time you called me Freddie. I still have that trilobite you found on the riverbed. The aspens applauded you in colour.

To this day I don't understand how you could return to New York after seeing that part of the world, shabby as it may have seemed to you at times. You told me once that you thought I was getting sick in the head, living so far from other people, and I don't entirely disagree. The mountains fill me with such longing, I am driven by an upwards force, only matched in intensity by the shock I feel when I realize I have to come back down. If there is a wilderness equivalent of homesickness, then I believe I am sick indeed. I think man is unfit to inhabit a world such as this if all he can think to do in it is make war.

But I was being hyperbolic before – I do understand why you left. Unlike me, you are not sick. You like your comforts, and you wanted to graduate. But when eventually you sail back from France with your hard-won citizenship, you will not return to New York, you shall come straight here. I am making this place comfortable, you'll see. At night I wander around howling for you, and the coyotes keep their distance.

Your faithful dog,
Frederick

Somewhere in Northern France
May 6, 1918

Dear Freddie,

We have arrived in our first trench. It was so strange to read your letter about home comforts while drinking watered-down coffee and sweeping rat faeces off the officers' mess table. I fear you wouldn't recognize me out here. My hair is getting long, and I've not had a wash like the kind we took at Adams Falls in many weeks. I'd be ashamed, if the rest of the men didn't stink just as bad.

The captain of the French regiment we relieved said there is not much war going on here any more. Most of the action has moved further north or east, although he did add that, 'Occasionally they will drop bombs on you when the moon is right.' He was so dirty, he looked like he'd been sleeping in the mud.

Yesterday the most unimaginable thing occurred. While making my inspection of the men, I walked past a private with his head bowed. His helmet was spattered with mud, and I made a passing comment about tidying himself up, at which point my sergeant pointed out, rather sheepishly, that this was not a man at all. Everyone grew very quiet then. I had been talking to a skeleton, jammed into the trench wall, still wearing his uniform. War has taught me to stomach some fairly grisly sights, but for some reason this one especially turned my stomach. All night, whenever I tried to sleep, I saw him. I fear I may never stop seeing him, but perhaps that is how it should be. We are inflicting such ends upon our fellow men; what right do we have to avert our eyes?

The war may be moving on in this country, but this country has not yet moved on from the war. There is no birdsong in this place. We have a new Second Lieutenant, a piano player from Harlem, and he is teaching me how to play poker.

Yours wearily,
Alejandro

PS An hour ago we were badly shelled. Captain Dubois took the smallest scrap of shrapnel I've ever seen. It looked like a seed had been blown through one side of his head and out the other. Then he fell forwards on to me and took a great deal worse, sparing me in the process.

Grand Lake, Colorado
May 8, 1918

Dear Lieutenant Esteves,

Am dictating letter to postmistress so must be on best behaviour.

Got a splinter in my eye while chopping firewood. Pinned the lid to the eyeball. Pulled splinter out myself. Blood everywhere but did not puncture eyeball or leak fluid. Yes, Annie, do write that. Doc washed the eye and bandaged my head. Said I was a lucky man. I said that was debatable and would depend on the outcome of certain things (and certain wars).

Blindly yours,
Frederick

Aisne, France
May 31, 1918

Dear Freddie,

I was sorry to hear about your eye, though unsurprised. You are reckless with that axe.

As I write, we are being redeployed to support Senegalese infantry and American gunners in a town called Chateau-Thierry. Apparently there is heavy house-to-house fighting there, and we are needed to halt the German advance at Belleau Wood.

I am glad you cannot see the woods here, Freddie, they are sick and blasted places, with more corpses than trees. Shelling and burning have scoured the earth, and the sight of it makes me desperately sad. In those moments I miss you and your green world like never before. If anything should happen . . .

Paris, France
June 28, 1918

Mrs F. Garrett,

On behalf of the Officers and men of my Company, I wish to offer you my sincere sympathy for the bereavement you have sustained following the death of your husband. Captain William Garrett was mortally wounded on June 26 by mortar shell from an enemy trench. He received immediate medical attention but died almost instantly. Though we had only been stationed together a short time, your husband earned the goodwill and esteem of all his comrades, and his loss was felt with general sorrow by the Company.

Yours sincerely,
Edgar Torrington, Major, 18th Infantry Regiment

Frederick is out back, scraping a bobcat hide in preparation for stretching, when he hears the horse complaining, followed by his sister's curt response. It is summertime, with cloudless skies and simmering air, even though there is still snow on the ground in many places, turned orange from the minerals in the meltwater. Nuthatches walk sideways down the trunks of leafy aspens and larches, and everything is coated with an eye-watering green powder – the seasonal pine dust that forces Frederick to cover his mouth and nose with a bandana while he works. Coming around the side of the cabin, he finds Frances tying her horse to a silver birch, her face turned away, her hat pulled low. When he says hello, she only grunts in response.

'What's the matter with you, old girl?'

'Nothing. I'm alive, aren't I?'

'Indisputably.'

She gives the horse a firm pat on the neck. When she looks at Frederick, he can see that her eyes have been rubbed red. There is something broken in her expression, like a door that has come off its hinges.

'William's dead.'

Frederick suspects it is easier for her to say it in English. To pass it through a filter, to make it another step removed from her. He responds in kind, 'What a goddamn waste.'

'I've telephoned Mamá already. She wants me to come home, bring Isabella to Buenos Aires to meet her grandparents.'

'And what did you tell her?'

'That I can't very well leave you up here to fend for yourself. You'd be dead before the year is out.'

'Well, that's hardly fair. I'm not totally helpless.'

Frances sniffs, wipes her nose with dusty fingers. When Frederick goes to put his arms around her, she wriggles away, like she used to when they were children, racing around the fountain in their father's courtyard trying to push each other in.

'Fran, what is it?'

She stares blankly at a crop of pink campion sprouting from between the rocks behind him, her hands shoved deep in the pockets of her overalls. 'Another letter came, not long after William's. It was my name, you see . . . My name your friend listed, in case anything happened.'

If anything should happen . . .

Alejandro's last letter had been incomplete, but Frederick had thought little of that at the time. Alejandro was in the process of being redeployed; likely he had been forced to move out before he could finish writing.

'Esteves has been killed?' He had not known he would be able to say the words until they came out. 'That's what you're saying? He's been killed?'

'Missing in action, they said.'

'Well, what the hell does that mean?'

'It means he's missing,' Frances snaps. 'And don't raise your voice at me!'

But Frederick knows all too well what it means. *Missing in action* means they couldn't find the body, or enough pieces to tell what belonged to who. He pictures Alejandro's body, softened by sleep, sprawled on the furs they would lay out on the cabin floor so that they could lie comfortably side by side. He sees his hands on Alejandro's waist, and then Alejandro's guts rended from his stomach, legs made ribbons by machine guns, Frederick left holding the pulp of him in the midst of some mortar-scoured wood.

He curses in Spanish, and Frances flinches at that, as if it has somehow made things more real. This time, when he leans against her, she wraps her arms around his back and buries her face in the folds of his flannel shirt. Her hair carries the sweet, almond scent of glaciers. He tells her he is sorry, and she tells him to spare her his apologies, but she doesn't pull away from him. She doesn't move at all, the pair of them motionless in the afternoon shadows, listening to the magpies cackling overhead. Each holding on to the last person either of them has left in this wild country.

Frederick feels himself grow old overnight. He sells his share of rabbit, elk and mule deer to local eating houses and gets drunk in exchange, the rotgut stoking his stunned grief to rage, until his body can no longer keep pace with his gruelling unhappiness. He walks bent close to the ground, feeling for the ridges and bumps of protruding bones, sifting tiny ammonites through his remaining fingers, as though he might come across some ruined part of Alejandro.

Sometimes, on his rare ventures into town to trade meat for liquor, he will cast an eye over the newspapers. Neither the mail nor the news arrives very fast in Grand Lake, and the papers he comes across are often several weeks out of date, but in July there is much ink given over to the Battle of Belleau Wood, and to the US Marines who bayonetted their names into history.

'They were gassed,' Crow Cole says, his voice low as he relieves Frederick of a wrapped elk leg. The cook's moustache hangs like two withered leaves under his nose, which he taps knowingly. 'Hunter Dawlwoody – used to work the mine over in Lulu City – said his son wrote his mama from hospital. Said they were cut down, wave after wave of machine-gun fire, and then they were gassed.'

When Frederick only frowns at him, Cole croaks, 'Mustard gas!' with a kind of riled excitement in his eyes. 'That's what they're using on each other over there. You haven't heard? Burns you and blinds you, pulls your lungs up out of your chest. What do you think of that?'

'I think I wouldn't write about that to my mother.'

There is much that Frederick hasn't heard. Taking his whiskey, he heads down to the lakeside to drink in the sun, and he understands that beyond his communication with Alejandro, he seceded from this war a long time ago. Decided that neither the country nor himself was fit for it, and yet the slaughter kept happening, is still happening, and his avoidance of it has changed nothing. He hadn't asked Frances how William died – had assumed she would speak of it if she wanted to – but now he pictures that quiet, solemn man choking and clawing his throat to shreds for oxygen, and Frances being stuck with that image in her head for the rest of her life.

Alejandro was also at Belleau Wood. His last letter said so.

Frederick drinks until his eyes water and the world is broken into prisms.

Boston, Massachusetts
August 2, 1918

Dear Lionel,

I hope this letter finds you in better health than the last, and that your leg is recovering well. I expect you will have heard from my mother by now of Frances' tragic loss, and that Frances herself intends to return to Buenos Aires before the fall. Unfortunately, the American Expeditionary Forces refuse to ship William's body home for burial. It is customary, as I understand, that men who fall on European soil in this war be buried there, but, as you may imagine, this is troubling for Frances, who wishes to lay her husband to rest in his family plot in Colorado before she departs.

It is essential to her that Isabella start school in Buenos Aires at the same time as the other girls. Don't ask me why, but Frances has become stuck on the matter, and you know how it is when she sticks herself like that. It will be springtime in Argentina when they arrive, and I suspect she likes the idea of a new start. I believe William's death has hit her very hard, although we do not speak of it often, besides this matter of the body, which brings me to the true purpose of my letter.

I am going to France to retrieve what is left of my brother-in-law. Though I understand William is now in the ground, I have been in correspondence with his CO, a Major Torrington, who is still in possession of William's personal effects. Torrington is convalescing in Paris at present, so I have arranged to meet him there. A long way to come for so little, you might think, but how cruel it is when we have nothing to bury of the ones we love. Indeed, I have my own fallen friends in Europe, and I should at least like to know where they lie, so that perhaps I might visit them in more peaceful times, and their ghosts can laugh at my long face.

As it is difficult for a foreign civilian to get in and out of a French port these days, I was hoping you might deliver me. We sailed from Cornwall to Brittany more than once in happier times – could we not do so again, for Frances' sake? From there, I mean to make my way to Paris, and if I am not shot somewhere in between, I shall figure out my own way home.

Upon my arrival in Liverpool, I will travel by train to Penzance, and should reach you Friday, a fortnight from now.

Until then, I remain your affectionate cousin,
Frederick Velazquez

They make port in the French town of Roscoff, nostrils stinging with the reek of seaweed heaped on the shore by last night's tide. The water is the same clear turquoise as the sea that licked the Penzance harbour, the buildings constructed from the same speckled granite and dark slate, and in this mirror of a town he knows, Frederick bids goodbye and bon voyage to his cousin.

It is high summer, but the weather is a turncoat on this stretch of sea, and they were lucky to keep ahead of it in Lionel's little gaff-rigged schooner. In the western corner of the sky, Frederick can see a howler building, and so he does not linger in Roscoff. He buys bread and cheese, an oilskin and a good mare, and sets off galloping through bullets of rain.

It takes him six days to reach Paris. At times he rides along storm-beaten coastal paths, the sea racing away to the horizon on his left, while the land to his right erupts in yellow gorse. One morning, Mont Saint-Michel, the castle in the sea, appears through the early mists like something from a fairy tale, and he thinks of Lionel at home in Penzance, looking out at its twin in Marazion bay. The sameness of these places moves him unexpectedly. He wonders if he might not have felt so unconcerned with this war, had he, like his cousin, stood on a Cornish clifftop and looked out across the sea and thought, They are killing my neighbours over there.

His horse throws a shoe in a quiet, timber-framed town, and the blacksmith who repairs it is a woman. She is startled to see him, even more so the Beesley slung over his shoulder, though he has trimmed his beard since Colorado and only looks half as feral as he used to. By his broken French, she takes him for an Englishman. Assuming she has no use for dollars, he pays her with two pheasants he has shot along the road. He need not ask where all the men have gone.

The weather is fine now, and the sun drinks his sweat as he rides. His thighs are chafed from the saddle, but he cannot bear to stop for too long, as if movement were the only antidote to thinking, and thinking is painful. At night he lays out in the open, watching the moon slide across the sky, and to his eye it seems slighter than the moon over Shadow Mountain, as though everything here in Europe were condensed in scale. His misses the might of Colorado.

His pulse picks up on the outskirts of Paris, where he gallops full tilt past checkpoints, though the soldiers seem uninterested in him, blowing smoke at the sky. He sells the mare at a riverside smithy, takes less than she's worth, and proceeds on foot through the Bois de Boulogne. Arriving in Paris, he learns that the war is in a state of atrophy. A newspaper salesman off the Arc de Triomphe brags it is a Black Day for the Hun – German soldiers are surrendering en masse, he says, and Allied troops are holding firm, throttling the advance towards Paris. The salesman says it'll be over by Christmas. Frederick salutes him and buys a pack of cigarettes.

The city is blazing, and he is exhausted, so he takes a glass of wine on a side street terrace that smells of hot stone. Sitting in the shade, swatting at insects, he recalls his only previous trip to this grand capital, when, as a child, he'd eaten cherries in the Jardin des Tuileries. His mother had chased him around the statues.

Frederick cannot remember the last time he spoke to her. His father's silence has been a wall between them both. What would have happened if she had stayed in Cornwall? She might be a nurse at a field hospital by now, holding men's innards together with her bare hands. In Buenos Aires, she takes tea on the balcony in the afternoons, breathing in the scent of lemon trees from the courtyard below, and she knows nothing of this. Of the bodies that pile up here day by day, most rotting where they fall, men split like firewood, splinters of men, missing in action.

Frederick has carried Alejandro's absence ever since Frances brought him the news, and he tells himself it does not weigh him down, but he can feel his own body moving slower these days. In no hurry to get anywhere Alejandro won't be.

His motivations for coming all the way to Europe were perhaps a little selfish, for he hopes to make enquiries while he's here. To find out where Alejandro's remains most likely lie, and to see if he can't get out there and find some small piece of him to bring home.

Frederick downs the last of his wine and departs. He is angry with himself. Such hermit-like avoidance of the world has only made his re-entry into it more brutal – a fact brought into sharp relief when he arrives at the Grand Palais to meet Major Torrington.

An ambulance is unloaded. Men on crutches, men on stretchers, men carrying other men padded with gauze, burnt men, halves of men, men with mustard-coloured blisters, men stuck together. Nurses in their nun-like garb gesticulate, direct and reprimand one another, while a bespectacled doctor beneath a tree watches it all unfold, smoking silently. Nobody seems to notice Frederick.

Inside, under the immense glass vaulted roof, uniformed boys are undergoing retraining exercises, supervised by white-coated doctors whose shouts lurch from one end of the hall to another. The patients lie prone with their bayonets, slack-faced, not quite ready to be soldiers again. On the wards, the nurses are turning pyjamaed men out of their beds to make way for the new cases. The reek of carbolic soap makes Frederick's eyes sting.

A ward sister barks at him in French, tells him he can't be here. He explains, as best he can, that he is looking for Major Edgar Torrington from the 18th Infantry, that the major was moved here following a gas attack. But he can tell from her face that this is true of many men. She tells him again to get out of the way, and then she is pulled back into the stream of moving bodies.

Frederick has no desire to explore the wards further, to see more of the carnage for himself. He retreats outside, sitting down on the steps of the museum palace to smoke. Even in the sun, he can't seem to stop shivering. Two doctors are conversing behind him, one with a strong French accent, the other Canadian to Frederick's ear. They sound almost bored with their cases, though Frederick cannot find it in himself to judge them. They must wonder what good they're really doing here, saving what they can of a man then sending home his shadow, or sending him back to the front only to be cut down again.

They are the first people whom Frederick has heard speaking English since his arrival at the hospital, however, so he gets to his feet and clears his throat. 'Excuse the interruption, gentlemen, but I was hoping you might be able to help me locate a patient.'

The French doctor, whipcord thin from a diet of mess meals and sleeplessness, looks Frederick up and down, taking in the travel-stained clothes and matted hair with Parisian cynicism. 'And what is your business here, *monsieur*?'

'I'm looking for a Major Torrington. He was my late brother-in-law's CO, he has some things belonging to him. He's expecting me.'

'Ah, Torrington.' The Canadian, with his short neck and hunched shoulders, has something vole-like about him. 'Yes, I know him. American fellow. He's on one of my wards. Lucky he got his gas mask on when he did, or his injuries could have been a lot worse. He's recovering well. I can have one of the nurses show you to him.'

'I appreciate that, thank you.'

'You Americans are taking a beating out there,' the French doctor says, presumably having picked up on the Transatlantic inflections of Frederick's English. When Frederick corrects him, however, the Canadian doctor looks up abruptly.

'Argentinian, you say? Sir, I hope you'll forgive the imposition, but a patient of mine keeps trying to talk to me in Spanish and I don't speak a word.'

Frederick glances at the French doctor, thinking surely they must have someone on their staff who can translate, someone who can stomach the sight of maimed and bloodied bodies better than Frederick. But the Frenchman only shrugs, and his colleague goes on, 'Please, sir, it would be a great help to us. They found him wandering the outskirts of the city in a very bad way. No identification on him. Didn't even seem to remember his own name. If we could only speak to him, we might be able to figure out who he is, notify his family that he's alive.'

Frederick thinks of Frances moving about her house in Boulder, packing up one room after another, making ready to start her life anew. He thinks of his own distant cabin, which had never been built for two, but now feels far too lonely a space for one. He imagines how it would feel for either of them to receive the news that someone they held so dear was not dead after all and might yet come home to them, and in his mind it is as if Frances has drawn back a curtain and daylight has fallen over her face. The world is dark enough at present, he thinks. Who is he to keep the drapes closed in someone else's home? Turning to the Canadian doctor, he nods, and then follows him back into the hospital.

'The young man' is how the Canadian doctor refers to his patient, and indeed he must have been young at some point, but the figure Frederick glimpses as they make their way along the ward to his bedside looks lifeless. The doctor explains that a Gatling gun took off most of the young man's fingers, and Frederick can see that his hands are wrapped in bandages, lying still and shapeless at his sides. Aside from these, the only other parts of him uncovered by blankets are his neck and head, but at the sight of his sleeping face Frederick stops in his tracks, and the doctor says, 'You look faint, sir. Are you well? Sit down and I'll fetch you a glass of water.'

Frederick waits for the doctor to depart, and then takes a step closer to the bed. To his right, a man moans, twitching sporadically under his sheets, while on his left, a burnt boy is reading *The Loom of Youth* in silence. Frederick sits down on the edge of the mattress. When he tries to speak, his throat is so dry all of a sudden, the name is a physical object he has to eject by force: 'Alejandro.'

His hair has grown long, his complexion turned grey, and when he opens his eyes, they seem sunken in their gaunt sockets. For a moment, Frederick fears Alejandro does not recognize him. Alejandro merely blinks up at him, his gaze dark and wavering. Then Alejandro's tongue darts out to wet his chapped lips, and he whispers, 'You were hiking a trail in the Adirondacks.'

Frederick leans forward and grasps his wrist. 'Ale—'

'You asked if I wanted to join you, and I said no. Do you remember?'

'In Dixonville, yes, I remember.'

'I was lying. I was winding you up.' Alejandro's face crumples as he tries to sit up, the movement of his hands making him wince. 'I kept thinking, maybe, if I kept walking . . . I thought I'd find you in the woods. But the woods are no good here, Freddie. They're all burnt and ruined.'

'Hush.' Frederick shakes his head. 'Or speak, tell me everything. I want to hear of every step you've taken, and then, by God, I'll take you out of here, Ale.'

'There's not much left of me to take.'

'Your fingers, you mean?' He holds up his own weathered stumps. 'Don't be defeatist, we've still got enough between us for one hand.'

In his mind, they are already home, coming along the North Inlet, Alejandro on horseback and Frederick leading him. There will be snow heaped on the mountains. The orange lights from cabin windows will seem a part of the autumn, the aspens and birches like streaks of wildfire on the ridges. In the alpine pastures, the bellowing of elk rings down the slopes. In this vision, Alejandro stands at the lakeside, the scent of pine blown in from the forests by a sharp wind that tugs at his long hair, his snowy fur coat, and he looks back at Frederick the way he did that first night in New York, as if to say, *Come and get me, then*.

It is this image Frederick holds in his mind as, ever so briefly, he permits himself to cup Alejandro's jaw in his hand.

'Come home,' he says. 'I mean for you to have nice things again. Venison steak and black coffee. Sheepskin gloves, and a gramophone. I'll build you a little terrace where you can sit and look at the lake. Wine glasses, if you like, and French cigarettes. A proper goose down mattress, boots that will last for miles, and the woods, Ale. I'll give you woods of living trees.'

Coal Country Beauty Queen

Nate takes a right at the intersection, heading away from the suburban sprawl, into the criss-cross of country roads that scar the Cumberland foothills. Perhaps there are other cars, but he doesn't see them. A seam of summer blue still lines the western horizon, and when Nate was a kid, he used to convince himself that if he drove towards it, he was going somewhere and that things were getting better.

He'd be the first to say he was a pretty dumb kid.

Nate keeps driving straight and thinks about Wavey. Jesus, does he think about Wavey. She was frying green tomatoes on the stove, lamplight picking out the sleepless hollows around her eyes. Some of the hair at the back of her neck had fallen out of her ponytail, and it felt vital, somehow, that he'd noticed this. She'd looked up when he called to her. They'd both been surprised to hear him say her name.

*

When Nate was nineteen, he robbed a gas station. Or he tried to. He didn't have a gun, but he held his hand inside his denim jacket like he was preparing to draw. By that point the ache of too many missed meals was catching up with him, making him desperate and stupid.

Back then, in Kentucky, it was an hour's drive to the nearest school that still had the lights on. Nate's truck was old, no heater, one windshield wiper and bald tyres. When the transmission went, there was no money to fix it. He had wanted to be a senior, felt the word carried some kind of merit, but instead the truck broke down and pitched him straight into a world of Oxycontin and bloody knuckles.

The judge gave him the same choice that so many other wrung-out boys had gotten in the short history of their country. Jail or the army. Nate didn't think he was leaving much behind in either case. His father was dead, lungs rotted from coal dust, and his mother sold Xani bars at a two-dollar profit out of her bungalow on the outskirts of Lexington. But a life of running and dodging had given Nate an itch in his muscles, a need to keep moving, and the thought of squatting in a prison cell for the next five years was not compatible.

Looking back on it now, it's almost funny. If a failed hold-up was the best he could do with a fake gun, what did they imagine he'd achieve with a real one?

In basic training, he'd learned how to carry twice his own weight, how to see in the dark, how to clean and reassemble no fewer than twenty different tactical weapons. He'd learned how to eat and how to starve. He'd learned how to crush what was left of Nate, the real Nate, down into the depths of himself like an empty Coke can.

*

He pulls in at a gas station. Not the one he'd tried to rob – that one is long gone, flattened to make way for a shopping mall where kids drink stolen liquor behind the dumpsters. This gas station is brightly lit, busy. A couple of reedy men in camo pants are chatting nearby about the upcoming hunting season, while corn fed boys in basketball shorts stumble out of the store, arms laden with snack food and bottles of Royal Crown. Nate vaguely recognizes some of them, kids of people he went to school with.

He thinks about Wavey again. She was a friend of a friend when he met her, a put-together kind of person, training to be a teacher. Too good for him, really, but she knew how to make Nate laugh. She probably still could, if he let her, but once you've made up your mind to leave someone, there's little they can do to make themselves beloved again. He watches the kids at the gas station, and is astounded that life is just ongoing. His marriage is over, and people are buying candy bars.

He remembers one afternoon, the platoon dug in at some middle of nowhere camp. Away west, a mountain range on the horizon looked like a bite taken out of the bottom of the sky, dark thunderheads piling up behind. The men were lounging in the shadows of their jeeps, the air heavy with the ripe, unwashed reek of them, and Sergeant Ric Marchetti caught Nate by the neck and stuck the stub of his cigarette between Nate's lips.

There was nothing to it. Army boys were all touchers. Maybe it came from working with their hands all day, but for better or worse they were always handshaking, groping, back-handing, embracing.

'Machete Marchetti' the men called him, because none of them were poets but they knew on sight that he deserved an epithet. He came from Brooklyn, said his father was a boxer and his mother was a wild dog, and you could believe it from the way he held himself – spring-loaded, always ready to go off. He had a rich, wry voice that made you want to impress him. He was the best sniper in their unit.

'Corporal,' he said, because this is what Nate was then. 'Corporal, you are one ugly son of a gun. What the hell happened to your face?'

'A fire. When I was a kid.'

'What, your mama's meth lab exploded?'

It was close enough to the truth – his mother's forgotten cigarette setting the bungalow alight – that Nate had to laugh. 'Ruined my shot at being Miss Kentucky '99, that's for sure.'

Sergeant Marchetti snorted, clapping him on the shoulder and declaring to the men, 'Hey, he's all right. The kid's all right.'

Marchetti called him a kid, but he couldn't have been much older than Nate. The desert had taken its toll on him, though, his skin stiff and dark, his forehead corrugated by permanent furrows. A tattoo of Sicily on his right bicep had faded to a murky green smudge. He used to ride in Nate's jeep, told him he was ugly about five times a day and that his own dead nonna could drive better than Nate did, but whenever they stopped to make camp, he'd always offer Nate a cigarette and they'd smoke in comfortable silence.

One evening Marchetti came swaggering back from a briefing with the lieutenant, and Nate pretended not to notice him. Kept his head down, staring intently at the porn magazine their navigator had lent him, huddled into his jacket to ward off the cold of the desert night.

'Well, if it isn't the coal country beauty queen,' Marchetti said, and some of the men laughed. 'You think I don't see you lurking over there?'

'Nothing to see. Can't a guy enjoy some quality literature in peace?'

Marchetti came and leaned against the jeep, close enough that Nate could have bitten the buttons off his jacket. 'You don't look like you're enjoying it.'

'You got some idea how I'm supposed to look when I'm enjoying myself?'

'The mouth on you, kid. Thought you southern boys were famous for your manners.'

The eastern horizon was shot with plumes of fire where the air force was razing a city to its bones. Nate could feel the vibrations of each explosion through the soles of his boots, shooting up his legs to the fork of his body. It made him feel like he was on the brink of something.

They drove by the outskirts of the city the following day. The heat made the air above the tarmac shiver and dance, while displaced children picked through what was left of their lives, tower blocks smouldering behind them.

'What do you want to bet they didn't find no weapons of mass destruction in there either.' Marchetti said it like he said everything, like it was sort of a joke, but his face was grim. He nodded to Nate. 'What're you doing here, Corporal?'

'Dunno. Not going to jail, I guess.'

'That's not good enough. This is why you can't shoot for shit – you've got to be aware of what you're doing, always. All your life. Doesn't matter if you're setting explosives or doing your taxes, you've got to keep both eyes on the goddamn road, understand?'

He was speaking to all the men in the jeep then, but Nate thought of his mother falling asleep with her cigarette still lit, and he touched the burn scars on his cheek. Yes, he did understand.

Nothing ever happened between them. There was no time or space or culture for that sort of thing to happen out there. They carried on as they always did, except sometimes when Nate saw the sergeant, he would get this feeling like an animal had suddenly jumped into his lap.

Nothing happened, but when Nate's tour was over and he was waiting on the tarmac for the chopper to take him to the airfield, he heard a familiar voice. Smelled a familiar brand of dirt cheap cigarettes.

'If you're ever in New York, kid, gimme a call. We'll get a beer. I'll make a proper mess of your pretty face.'

Nate decided he was being threatened, rather than hit on, because that was easier to digest.

But some years later, he did find himself in New York, for a friend's bachelor party. He even tracked down Ricardo Marchetti in the phone book, but he didn't call, and he watched himself not doing this as though it were happening to someone else. He had learnt by then that Nate in the real world wasn't like Nate in the army. He couldn't hold down a job, or strike up conversation, or maintain friendships. It was unfashionable to talk about the war by then. He didn't know what to do with himself, and he was ashamed of this.

*

Lately, he has been thinking again about what Marchetti said. If he'd kept an eye on himself these last few years, perhaps he'd have noticed sooner that he'd already left his wife a long time ago. It's just taken his body a while to catch up to the fact.

At the gas station, now, the night smells like petrol and hot road and the deep fat fryer that's churning out corndogs. Nate waits while his truck fills up, watching the fluorescent lights turning people's faces blue.

He still has that number for Marchetti. Wrote it down on the back of a receipt he keeps in his wallet where another man might have kept a photo of a girl. The payphone is a greasy, ancient thing, scored with graffiti and oily fingerprints, but the weight of the receiver feels good in his hand, and he thinks of the gun he never carried at a gas station just like this one. Gets that same feeling, like he's about to do something stupid.

The dial tone rings on, and then a voice seven hundred miles away says, 'It's so late, Becca, oh my god.'

'I'm not Becca . . .' Nate swallows. 'I'm looking for Ric Marchetti.'

'Oh.' The girl on the other end of the line repeats the name like she's pulling a piece of taffy out from between her teeth. 'Yeah, I think he used to live here. We still get his mail sometimes. Army guy, right?'

Nate hangs up. He leans against the wall, staring up at the light pollution staining the night sky, and lets out a long, slow breath.

Maybe it's better like this.

Like this, he'll never have to know if Marchetti remained a god, or if he unravelled into another loose end, as Nate did.

Like this, in a life of cigarette burns and comatose mothers, scraped skin and Oxy comedowns, broken trucks and broken marriages, he still has this: the fact that, once, he wanted someone and was wanted in return. One bright and beautiful point, like the star he can see above the distant piney ridge. It could just be a satellite, but no one can stop him dreaming otherwise.

Stray Dogs

In 1939, Margaret set out from Liverpool on an ocean liner. Nine days later, after a grievous crossing on February seas, she arrived at Ellis Island, where she was required to complete an immigration form. Margaret was twenty-four, five foot eight inches tall, brown eyes, blonde hair. She had been born in Edinburgh, and her last place of residence was a small hamlet outside of Inverness, where she had, for the past six months, resided with her listed next of kin – the Much Honoured Lady Rosamund Ross, her mother.

At customs, she was quizzed by an official with a few reddish whiskers. The evening light made it look as though his jaw was faintly aflame as he asked Margaret about her final destination in America.

'Right here,' she said, 'New York City.' She understood that he probably needed to ask this, but she thought it rather an impertinent question nevertheless. When the same official asked her how long she intended to stay in the country, Margaret told him briskly, 'As long as it takes.'

She really did not see that the world and his dog needed to know her business in New York. Certainly, if the news made it into the wrong ears, her mother would not forgive her. Margaret felt this was somewhat her mother's fault for sending her when she could have sent Alec or George, even young Julian, but Margaret's brothers were at present all tied up in the ever-so-serious business of warmongering and apparently could not be spared. Never mind that Margaret had been dealing with her own little war of late. Never mind that Richard had stopped telephoning her, and even though he had admitted to fault, it was still Margaret who had fled London society in the wake of his affair, convinced that their friends were looking at her differently now.

Divorce. The word seemed somehow profane, like something she would have heard snickered by her brothers at the back of their Sunday-school classes, whenever they were all home together for the holidays.

She felt completely unprepared for divorce. It was almost as if it were happening to someone else, and Margaret was only passing by a window and catching a glimpse of it. She felt disconnected, is what she meant, and this was how she felt about being in America too.

Before her mother had ordered her to make this secretive ocean crossing, Margaret had never considered travelling to somewhere so far away before. It was so different from what she was used to. She and Richard had been planning to visit Venice together – of course, that was all off now – but at least the Continent had a sense of continuity, familiar traditions being upheld. Here, when she arrived at her hotel, they called her 'Lady Ross', and Margaret thought, My God, these people don't know anything!

Lady Ross was her mother. Margaret was just Margaret.

The place where she was staying was called the Pierre Hotel, a towering cream-coloured building on the corner of Fifth Avenue and Sixty-first Street that couldn't seem to make up its mind as to whether it wanted to be Art Deco or Parisian Baroque. No doubt Americans probably thought this very elegant, but Margaret didn't care for things that were new pretending to be old. Perhaps, in some way, because she felt like the opposite. There were days, especially since her split with Richard, when she felt like a much older person crammed into the body of this gangly girl-child, unsure to whom she could relate, or how she should move through this world, because nobody else her age was going through the same pain.

At reception, while the bellboys were loading her cases into the elevator, Margaret lowered her voice and said, 'I'm looking for my brother, Mr David Ross. I believe he's staying here. Could you let him know I've arrived?'

The concierge glanced at a leather-bound ledger on the desk and told her, no, they'd had no guests going by that name lately. Margaret felt her stomach drop.

'Are you certain?'

'Quite certain, ma'am. Oh, but there was a Mr David Smith. An English gentleman. From London, he said.'

'Scottish,' Margaret corrected. 'A Scottish gentleman?'

'Yes, ma'am,' the concierge replied, but he raised his eyebrows as he said this, as if it was all the same to him.

She should have guessed David would be using a false

name. Wasn't this entire escapade to the States supposed to be some sort of reinvention of himself?

'Where is Mr Smith now?' Margaret asked. 'It's most urgent that I speak with him.'

'I'm terribly sorry, ma'am,' the concierge said, not sounding particularly sorry at all, 'but Mr Smith checked out the day before yesterday.'

Margaret could not really have said why, but she got the sense the concierge was making fun of her a little bit. *I'm terribly sorry.* He had rolled his Rs when he said that, as if attempting some gross exaggeration of her accent, which, admittedly, did sound very English – the result of her teachers' tireless work at her London boarding school to iron the Highlands out of her tongue. This man's imitation of her made Margaret feel suddenly hot under her armpits, and she beat a hasty retreat upstairs.

The suite her mother had arranged for her was probably very nice, but Margaret struggled to take it all in. She kept feeling as if her mind was going to float up out of her skull and escape, like a wisp of smoke blown away in the wind. This was very bad news about David. Their mother had sent Margaret specifically to bring him home, before he could, in the words of her ladyship, 'inflict any further damage on the family name'. But he was not where the private investigator had said he would be, and Margaret had no idea where, in this whole huge country, she ought to start looking.

It was unthinkable that she return empty-handed. Her mother had made that quite clear.

'Your brother will run us into the ground if left to his own devices, and this family simply cannot endure another scandal.' She had looked pointedly at Margaret when she said this. Divorce was as shameful to the ancient institution of Clan Ross as high treason or women driving motor cars.

Margaret went to open the window. A sinewy gust of wind rushed against her as she did so, but she didn't mind the cold. The taste of rain in the air opened up a wordless seam of longing for home, for the high-backed hills that encircled her mother's house, and the furtive mists that rolled in from the firths. From the window, Margaret could see a wide, dark lake down among the bare branches of Central Park, and though this was a far cry from Beauly Firth, the sight of trees and water comforted her somewhat in the midst of this immense grey city.

The truth was – and Margaret could admit this because she was thousands of miles from her mother now – she felt sorry for David.

Of her four brothers, David was the third, and something of the odd one out. Their eldest brother, Alec, had inherited their late father's somewhat obsolete title of laird and his all-too-relevant legacy as a successful Great War general. Alec's future had been written since birth, which, Margaret considered, did have its own kind of sadness, though Alec seemed quite content, all things considered. He was certainly chomping at the bit to test his mettle in this new war that Daddy's old crowd kept insisting was going to happen.

George, the second eldest, had done terribly well at Cambridge and had gone into politics, while the baby of the family, Julian, was still buried under tomes of Homer and Ovid in his dorm at Trinity – all of which he would probably toss aside in order to join up with Alec, if Britain really did go to war. He was very eager to please. This was arguably true of

David, too, except the person he most wanted to please was himself.

At nineteen, he had been sent down from Cambridge for as many offences as he was years old, including arson, quarrelling with the college vice-master, and challenging another student to an honest-to-God duel when the student in question critiqued David's attempt to grow a moustache. He had promptly run off to Paris in hope of becoming a poet, until Alec was sent to fetch him, only to find David living above a flower shop with an artist's model.

'It finished your father,' their mother had said, when David was finally brought home. 'The shame of it! You as good as killed him.'

'*I* killed him?' David had replied. 'And here I was thinking it was all that mustard gas he inhaled at Ypres.'

Her brother was a dreadfully unserious individual, Margaret thought. But, in a sense – though she loved all her brothers – this made David her favourite. She was fond of the others the way one might be fond of one's own arms or legs, which is to say you would notice if they disappeared, but you didn't tend to think about them a great deal otherwise. David, meanwhile, made it impossible not to think of him. Even as a child, he would come tearing into her room to show off the brace of grouse he had shot, oblivious to the bits of gore and gristle he was dripping all over her books and clothes, just wanting her to be pleased with, and for, him. Margaret didn't believe he ever meant to hurt anyone, even that fellow at Cambridge who'd criticized his moustache. David simply didn't think very far beyond the scope of his own desires.

The problem now, however, was that said desires had led her brother halfway across the world, where he was drinking himself unconscious, and it wouldn't be long before *Tatler* or some other tabloid got hold of the news that a British aristocrat was making a fool of himself for all to see.

She would have to find him. If not for their mother's sake, then for David's, and her own along with it, since their mother had clearly decided to lump her two errant offspring in together. It occurred to Margaret that this was possibly why her mother had sent her, rather than insisting that Alec or one of the others pursue their sibling. Thinking, perhaps, that it would take a misfit to find a misfit.

And what a misfit Margaret had become. Divorced at twenty-four. It humbled her, really. She had gone through life convinced that this sort of thing only happened to other women; those who somehow deserved it.

She remembered once, as a young girl, being allowed to stay up late for a birthday party that her mother had thrown for her father. Margaret – she could not have been more than fifteen or sixteen at the time – had gone out on to the terrace and overheard two women talking about another woman whose husband had had an affair. One of them had said, 'But really, my dear, how could she have been so oblivious? How could she not have noticed? It's not as if he tried very hard to cover his tracks.'

And Margaret had thought, Yes, that sounds right. And now it had happened to her. And it humbled her because she understood how a woman *could* fail to notice this about her husband. She understood that these kinds of things were probably being said behind *her* back now.

What would her father have thought, had he been alive, when she came traipsing home to Scotland with her tail between her legs? How would he have borne it if he knew his only daughter was the talk of London society in the very worst way?

Mustard gas would have had nothing on that.

Margaret very badly wanted to see David – not only to be secure in the knowledge that she hadn't failed her mother, but also because she felt David would be the only one who would truly understand her situation. It would not be shameful to him that her husband had been unfaithful to her. He'd probably offer to challenge Richard to a duel too, at dawn with their grandfather's antique pistol set.

After a late supper, which was served in a very large ballroom, under a set of enormous crystal chandeliers that Margaret quite frankly found rather gaudy, she went back to the front desk and asked for the forwarding address of Mr Smith. Her brother, it turned out, had left rather abruptly for Pennsylvania, and the staff at the Pierre had been obliged to send on a pair of his shoes to a hotel in Harrisburg.

Pennsylvania was a state Margaret had heard of only in the vaguest sense. Hadn't some battle occurred there, back when the Americans were fighting one another in the last century? But Harrisburg was completely unknown to her, and it sounded like the name of any other town in this part of the world, like a lazy attempt at commemorating something or someone most people had forgotten about. She could not think what business – or, indeed, mischief – might have drawn David to a place like that.

The following morning, determined not to fall at the first hurdle, Margaret made her way to Grand Central Station, taking with her only one suitcase that she could manage by herself. She still had that feeling of not being entirely connected to her body, and sensed herself moving through the crowds of men in long, beige coats, with their elegant trilby hats, and elderly women dressed in black like gnarled little widows. One man rolled out from beneath a bench, accompanied by the eye-watering scent of urine. Margaret moved through them all, but never felt as though she was one of them.

She thought that this city was not a place someone was supposed to come to by themself. She recalled the trip to Venice that she and Richard had intended, how they had sat together in the evenings and mulled over restaurant recommendations and theatre schedules and tide times, and Margaret suddenly thought now: I am in another country. What she meant was that her loss had made her a stranger in the world.

Harrisburg turned out to be a much larger city than she was expecting. It was the capital of Pennsylvania – Margaret read this on a sign when she disembarked – and she felt slightly foolish for having thought that it wasn't anywhere important. In some ways, it felt a lot like New York, in that there were some large old buildings, some much larger newer ones, and a hotel where, once again, her brother was absent.

This hotel was a good deal less luxurious than the Pierre, however, and less delicate about causing offence as far as the reputation of its clients was concerned. The woman at reception, who had thin greying hair and ate sunflower seeds by the handful as she spoke to Margaret, explained that 'Mr Smith' had got very drunk and broken the mirror in his bedroom, which needed paying for. Margaret wasn't entirely sure if she believed this, but when she took out her book of traveller's cheques, the woman nodded, as if Margaret were fulfilling some unspoken part of an agreement, and said, 'Yup, he's gone to New Mexico.'

'I beg your pardon?'

A wireless was playing in the little office behind the reception desk, Bing Crosby warbling about pennies from heaven. As Margaret started counting out her cheques for the broken mirror, the woman said, 'Your friend. Mr Smith. He told everyone in the card room the other night that he was going to New Mexico to be a cowboy.'

'Good heavens. How do I get to New Mexico from here?'

The woman leaned back slightly, looking Margaret up and down. 'He your husband or something?'

'David?' Margaret could feel her eyes widen. 'Lord, no! Even if he were, I certainly wouldn't chase my husband all the way to New Mexico.'

The woman must have been pleased with this answer, as well as Margaret's cheques, because she told Margaret to get back on the train and keep heading south-west.

'He telephoned to leave an address for his mail. Hotel Farragut in Knoxville, so I guess he's not in New Mexico yet.'

'Knoxville,' Margaret said. 'Is that far?'

'Honey, that's in Tennessee.'

The woman gave her a little guidebook with certain rail routes marked at the back, and she didn't charge Margaret for that.

In Virginia, at a town called Winchester, Margaret had to get off the train and change on to another one, on the Baltimore & Ohio line. By this time, it was so late at night that she felt time had almost stopped happening altogether, and that there was only the darkness that unfurled beyond the platform seemingly without end. Strangely, she was cold in a way she had not been further north, and an idea went through her head that this was because there were fewer people here. There was a loneliness to this part of the country, she felt.

As she sat waiting for her train, Margaret thought about what she had said to the woman in Harrisburg, about how she would not have chased her husband all the way to New Mexico. She had meant it. She wondered if somehow Richard had known that about her. It was an act of love, wasn't it, to follow David like this? It showed that she cared for him. But when Richard left her, Margaret had not gone after him at all, and even when she thought they were very much in love, she could never have imagined herself waiting on a dreary platform on another continent in the middle of the night for him. Had he sensed this lack of commitment to him? Had he looked elsewhere for love because she had pushed him to it?

Then she thought, Stop it, this is ridiculous.

If David were here, he would say, 'Only a very boring man lets himself be pushed, old girl. A man of any worth already has places he wants to go.'

Even her father would have agreed. He would have said, 'Maggenpie', because that was what he called her, 'we can only judge people by what they do, not what we think they might do.'

Action – it has always been about action in their family, from the warrior chieftains reducing each other and their English foes to gore, to her father and uncles in the trenches, all the way down to this young woman shivering on a faraway station platform.

In a great flood of yellow light and metallic sound, her train finally arrived, and Margaret thought, *Action, action.* She climbed aboard and left Virginia behind.

*

On the train there was this: a man in a brown suit who was reading a paperback. He was the only other passenger in Margaret's carriage. She said hello when she boarded, but went and sat at the other end of the carriage, so as not to intrude on his reading.

Almost as soon as she sat down, her exhaustion hit her like a truly physical thing. She felt pinned under it, and her head was so heavy she could feel her pulse in her brain. She was afraid then, and felt very alone. After a little while, she walked sheepishly back up the aisle, holding on to the backs of the green vinyl seats, and said to the man in the brown suit, 'Excuse me. I'm sorry, but would you mind checking to see if I'm awake when we get to Knoxville? I don't want to miss my stop, but I fear I might fall asleep.'

And this man, who was a total stranger to her, looked up from his book, and he had a very everyday face – the sort of face that could easily blend into a crowd – but when he smiled! When he smiled at her, she fell in love with him a little bit, even though he was quite old and the skin around his eyes was drooping.

Of course, he said, he was getting off at Knoxville anyway, so he would be sure to check on her.

There was a faint southern twang to the way he pronounced 'Knoxville'. He asked if she wanted to borrow his book to keep herself awake, but she said no, she didn't want to be any bother. She went back to her seat, but didn't feel quite so exhausted. The exhaustion had been part sadness, she realized, and now she thought this was not entirely a country of strangers after all.

Tennessee surprised her. So far, she had travelled either by night or through domesticated farmland wedged between cities, but as they headed towards Knoxville, they passed through wide green countryside stippled with pines. Here and there, in the milky light of the rising winter sun, Margaret caught sight of wooden houses back among the trees, the occasional ribbon of smoke unwinding from a chimney. These settlements were few and far between, and there was a promise of wilderness here that made some long-smothered part of her sit up like a dog.

She thought of the woods around their parents' estate where she and her brothers used to run wild. During what felt like a very distant childhood, when she was still tutored at home, she would long for the holidays when the boys would come back from their boarding schools, and she could cast off her petticoats and don her wellingtons and become, for a very brief but vital time, one of them. Together they would trek over the braes, learn the oak-throated calls of the red deer, build cairns of pebbles and animal bones by the wayside of paths only they knew. It used to be that the Ross children were infamous for their 'savagery', as one of their father's grouse-shooting friends had termed it. Indeed, Alec and George had once both been hospitalized for taking potshots at each other with a rifle until they hit something that induced a sufficient blood spatter, and Margaret had taught David how to make petrol bombs, which they'd thrown at the Bentley of a visiting bishop.

Then Margaret had grown up and got married, and marriage was a place – even more so than London – where one had to tuck away parts of oneself, trimming them down in order to fit neatly beside one's partner. Only David, it seemed, had retained this savage streak, this spirit of the wild landscape whence they came. Margaret was more like New York farmland now, ordered and tamed.

But she also remembered this: lying on the floor of the nursery with David, when they were both old enough that the room had long since outlived its use, and David tracing his finger across the page of an atlas, saying to her, 'Do you see here, the coal valleys of Wales? That same seam of coal stretches all the way under the ocean to this place, Appalachia. You could put a Welsh miner down a shaft in West Virginia, and he would know exactly what he was about. It would be like going home. I wonder sometimes,' he said, resting his chin on his hands, 'what else is the same but different over there? I wonder if I would make more sense in that kind of place.'

Hotel Farragut was a tall brick building with white stone accents and a motor car parked out front. The nice gentleman from the train had given her directions, but even without his help, Margaret thought she would have been able to find her way. This was not a city like New York or Harrisburg. There were not so many towering buildings that she couldn't see the rise of brown hills beyond, the continuation of the pines. Besides the cars, and a billboard for Pepsi Cola that she had passed in the centre, she thought she could be seeing Knoxville at any given point in the last hundred years. The architecture was mostly Victorian, and some of the smaller shops even had a Frontier look to them. This felt much closer to the sort of place she could picture David inhabiting.

She was disappointed but unsurprised to discover that, despite travelling through the night, she had missed her brother once again. He had checked out that morning, the clerk said, and left a forwarding address in Arkansas.

The clerk was an older man with hefty white whiskers, and

he was sympathetic to a young woman travelling alone, looking for her brother.

'*My* brother ran off to Alaska when he was fifteen, looking for gold. Froze to death, I heard. Served him right for taking the family savings.'

'Oh,' Margaret said. 'I'm sorry to hear that.'

She tried to smile at him, but she felt as if a dark, fat stone were falling through her, all the way down to her gut. Although she had slept a little on the train, she felt totally depleted, and the thought of having to journey on again was overwhelming.

'Say, whereabouts in England are you from?' the clerk asked. 'London? I've got cousins in London.'

'I'm not from England,' Margaret said wearily. 'I'm from Inverness.'

'They live in Hackney,' he said, 'near Victoria Park.' As if she was suddenly going to remember that she knew them after all.

Margaret went across the street to what she supposed would be called a saloon. She had asked the clerk at the hotel for a cup of coffee, but he'd said the kitchen was closed, so now here she was, in this long, dingy room built like a train carriage not going anywhere.

There were no other women in the bar. Margaret felt a small spike of alarm as she sat down with her suitcase, near the window so that she could get a bit of light through the greasy glass, but the bartender brought her a coffee and did not tell her to leave, which is what she had been afraid of.

It was still fairly early in the day, and the only other patrons were a man in a rather tired-looking suit nursing a whiskey, and a group of men at the far end of the room who appeared to be engaged in a game of cards. A thick haze of cigarette smoke hung above them, and Margaret got the impression they had been playing through the night.

Sipping her coffee slowly, she tried to decide what to do. The coffee was strong and earthy and went straight to the core of her body, but it did not help her feel more awake, only perhaps more alert, which was tiring in its own way. She knew she ought to get a few hours' sleep, but she was closing in on David – he had left only this morning – and if she were to set out now, she might make it to Arkansas before he slipped away again.

She was mulling this over when she heard the sound of glass shattering, and looked up in time to see a stocky fellow in a plaid shirt jump up from his chair, grip another man by the hair and slam his head against the table.

'You cheating little bastard . . .!' It was David, blood pouring between his fingers as he clutched his face. Margaret hadn't noticed him because he had been sitting with his back to her, but now he leapt to his feet, shirtsleeves rolled, brandishing his fists like a boxer. The man in the plaid shirt merely slugged him in the face, and Margaret heard the crunch of his nose from across the room.

She was on her feet before she even really understood what she was doing. Marching across the room, she picked up half of the shattered beer bottle that had rolled across the floor and pointed it at the man who was holding her little brother by his hair again, his fist drawn back in preparation for another swing.

David blinked at her through the blood. Margaret didn't say a word, but her body thrummed like a plucked string as she stood her ground and held the other man's gaze.

Then, from behind her, the bartender said, 'Better do as

the lady suggests, Edgar.' His voice was weary, as if he'd had to break up many such fights before. 'Go on, why don't you get home now. All of you. Show's over.'

Afterwards, when she turned around, Margaret would realize that the bartender had a shotgun propped up on the bar, which was probably why the man in the plaid shirt had acquiesced. But this almost didn't matter. In the moment, she had felt a sudden sense of clarity and power that she had not known since before she was married. If only briefly, she had been in command of the room. She had been in command of herself.

'You still haven't told me what on earth you're doing here,' David said.

Margaret had wanted to take him to a doctor, but he had resisted. Then, when she'd suggested taking him to the Farragut to patch him up, he said they needed to find somewhere less reputable. So now they were holed up in a one-storey building that David called a 'motel', in a room containing a single bed and a woven mat on the floor.

'Mother sent me,' Margaret said, as she wiped the blood from his face.

'I know, but—' David winced, flinching away from her as she tried to dab around his bleeding nose.

'Darling, stop squirming, it'll only make it worse. And what do you mean "you know"? How can you know?'

'I telephoned Mother when I was in New York. Needed some help with the old cashflow, you know how it is.' He flashed her a queasy smile then hissed through his teeth. 'You're being a bit heavy-handed there, Mags.'

'Don't be such a baby.'

'Wounded in pride and body.' David clapped a hand to his chest. 'Well, anyway, Mother said she was cutting me off unless I agreed to come home with you, so naturally I said, "Yes, absolutely." I envisioned you and I having a jolly dinner in New York and then skedaddling back home before the moths in my pockets started starving to death. But then a pal of mine told me about this opportunity down in New Mexico. Big cattle branding season coming up, chance to earn a bit of cash.'

'I find it hard to believe one need go all the way to the bottom of this country just to earn some money. You could have got a job in New York if you were so desperate, instead of malingering at your hotel.'

'Malingering!' David grinned. 'I've missed you, Maggie. But you must have seen New York – it's perfectly adequate, but they have *real* landscapes down in New Mexico. That's what I want.'

Margaret frowned, tossing aside the towel she had been using to clean his face. 'It doesn't matter how magnificent the landscapes are down there, you're not going to see them. We're getting on the next train back north and heading home.'

'Mags, be reasonable.'

'I've chased you across half the country. I'm tired and I'm hungry, and now I've got your blood all over my sleeves. You'll forgive me if I'm not feeling very reasonable.'

'I've made up my mind.' David all but pouted at her. 'I'm not a child you can pinch by the ear and cart back home.'

Margaret threw up her hands. 'Why in heaven's name do you want to go there so badly? To brand cattle, of all things! You could help out on the McPhearsons' farm at home if you're so desperate to be with cows. Why does it matter where you do it?'

David looked at her sadly then. He sat back on the bed with his legs drawn up and rested his chin on his knees; and suddenly he didn't look twenty-two any more, but like the awkward, long-limbed brother Margaret remembered from her childhood.

'Because I'm going to go to war,' he said.

'What?' Margaret shook her head. 'We're not at war. Who's been telling you that? Alec?'

'He doesn't need to. Everyone's talking about it. Even in New York, everyone kept saying, "By the end of the year, you Brits will be at war with Germany. You can't help yourselves." That's what they said.'

'Well, stuff them, what do a bunch of Americans know about it? I've seen their newspapers. They only read about things going on in their own country.'

David sighed. 'But they're right. Alec's right. Whenever we were in London, didn't it feel like being in a pot that was about to boil over?'

Yes, Margaret thought, yes, it did. But that was because of Richard and what he had done to her, and had nothing to do with the Germans.

'That's why I had to get away,' David said. 'This might be the last chance I get. I need to be somewhere wilder than I am. Don't you ever feel that?'

She knew that she had felt an intimation of it on the way here, as she'd gazed out of the window of the train. But she was also wary of letting her brother talk to her like this, because beneath David's wide-eyed earnestness, there lurked a scowling, sulking little boy. It had always been there, even as she loved him. A propensity to blame this person or that for whichever circumstances David landed himself in. And she felt, too, that he was blaming her now, projecting into the future and thinking, If I go to war and am killed, it will be because of Maggie. Because she did not permit me to go and shovel cow dung in New Mexico.

'I saw you, back in that bar,' David said. 'You were wild.' Shuffling across the mattress, he took her hands in his. 'Come to New Mexico with me. It'll do you good. You'll be yourself again.'

Margaret remembered the way her body seemed to sing as she'd gripped that piece of broken glass. But she remembered, too, that all the weariness and dread of the past few days had been David's doing, because he could not bear to be dragged home by his sister, and so he had played her. Running across the country in a grand game of hide and seek, as if it were nothing to make a fool of her, when she had thought that he out of everyone would understand her best.

'You are a child,' was all she could say. 'You don't know me at all.'

He knew her well enough, however, to recall that she was a deep sleeper, and that once she was asleep, it would be no trouble for him to slip out of the motel and circle back to the saloon to collect his scant belongings. When Margaret awoke, she felt his duplicity like a physical smack between the eyes. Out of breath, she just managed to catch up with him at the train station, scrambling into the carriage moments before the station master slammed the door.

David looked up and said jovially, 'Oh, good. You got my message then.'

'What message?' Margaret collapsed into the seat beside him. 'You didn't leave any message.'

'Now, Mags, don't get upset. I told the motel clerk to tell you to—'

'Oh, spare me, David.' She sat for a moment with her head in her hands, the neat, intricate braid she had done for herself in New York fraying gently at the edges. 'I suppose this train is going to New Mexico?'

'It's going to Arkansas,' her brother replied. 'But from there we can travel to Texas, and then it's a cinch.'

Margaret did not care for Arkansas. Perhaps she was just wrung out, but as the train rolled on through the Ozarks, there seemed to be a wretchedness to this wintery landscape, with its bogs and bare trees. Everything looked slightly burnt somehow. She saw labourers working in a far field, and she felt terribly lonely. She thought, I am in a place where nobody knows me.

This was why she eventually said to David, 'Will it be warm where we're going?'

It had always been this way when they fought. Whoever became the loneliest first would do the business of approaching the other and making up. But wasn't this the way among all siblings? Sometimes Margaret had to remind herself of this. That the frustrations and sadness she sometimes thought belonged to her alone were in fact entirely commonplace, and to experience them did not mean that she and David did not love one another, but rather that they loved each other the way so many other brothers and sisters did. There was a comforting universality to their quarrels sometimes.

'We'll be in the desert,' David said, evidently delighted that she had finally changed her tune. 'It might be cold at night, I suppose, but you can have my jumper.'

He put his arm around her shoulders, and she leaned

against him. They were both relieved, she thought. He had wanted her approval, and she had wanted her journey to be over, which she now supposed it was. This was David's adventure, and she was simply being carried along by the current of it.

The first green blades of spring were rising throughout the broad open country when they arrived in Copper Flats. This was the name of the township closest to the ranch, to which, on the advice of his friend, David had written and signed up for work, and it was a very quiet place. This is what Margaret thought when the train deposited them at the side of the railroad tracks. There was almost no sound at all, except the faint stirrings of a nearby windmill. Everything was the colour of ochre, and the sky soared overhead, deeper and wider than anything Margaret had ever seen, except perhaps the ocean on her Atlantic crossing. The might of it reminded her a little of that, the constant unfolding towards a far horizon. Indeed, the land was so flat and bare here that she and David watched for almost half an hour before their train finally disappeared from view. Then a dusty black motor car pulled up, driven by a woman in a wide brim hat, who said she had come to collect 'the British guy'.

The woman's name was Teresa Baiz, and she was the ranch owner's widow.

'Does that not make you the ranch owner then?' David asked genially as he opened the rear door for Margaret, and Teresa gave a squawking laugh.

'You'd figure, wouldn't you. But I got a foreman thinks he's running things. Thinks he's going to run me too one of these days. I'd like to see him try.'

Teresa had long, straight dark hair and a slightly hunched posture. She drove with her hat on and one arm lolling out of the window, while all around her hung the unbroken smell of livestock. On the drive to her property, she glanced back at Margaret only once and did not seem bothered by her presence, though she didn't attempt much conversation beyond, 'Hope you ain't getting bumped about too bad back there, miss.' Margaret was, in fact, getting bumped about quite badly, though she didn't see what could be done about it, and had already resolved to take New Mexico on the chin.

Mostly Teresa spoke of the landscape through which they were passing. This, Margaret gathered, was where David would be put to work, heading out on horseback before daylight with the other ranch hands to round up cattle from among long-dead volcanos and rimrock mesas.

'Brandings run bigger, rougher and longer in the desert,' Teresa explained. 'I got thousands of acres, and as many calves need branding before heading to the summer pastures, so most of my boys work out under the stars for several days at a time.'

'How marvellous,' David said, whipping out his silver cigarette case. He leaned back to offer one to Margaret, which she accepted, and the fact of having something to do with her hands seemed to steady her, even as the car bounced along the rutted dirt road.

Teresa, meanwhile, declined David's offer, though her smile seemed to indulge him. 'You ever brand cattle before, Mr Ross?'

'Oh, all the time. Absolutely. Can't get enough of it.'

Teresa laughed at that too. 'Rope-and-drag is our go-to method out here. Heel a calf, drag it to the fire, then the boys on the ground will flank, brand, castrate. Then up that thing jumps and runs right back to its mama.' She squinted at David from under the brim of her hat. 'I'll start you on the ground crew first, I reckon. You'll pick it up quick enough. You'll have to, or you'll be out on your ear. This ain't no hotel.' She said nothing about what Margaret might do to avoid such a fate.

The ranch house was not what Margaret had been expecting. There were tenant farmers on her family estate who kept pleasant, neat cottages, but somehow, perhaps because this was so far removed from the world she was used to, she had imagined an American farmer might live in some sort of barn. Indeed, there was a barn – an enormous structure, far bigger than the village hall back home – but the house itself was made of white wood, and there was a veranda that went all along the front of it, painted blue, with baskets of flowers hanging from the eaves. Between the house and the barn there was a yard with a large pen, which Teresa said was the corral where they trained up horses. Then behind the barn was a squat timber bunkhouse, where Teresa's foreman and ranch hands slept, and she said this was where David could put his belongings.

As David was getting out of the car, Margaret caught a glimpse of the foreman. Or rather, she assumed he was the foreman because it was there in his bearing. Pride, but not arrogance. He was older than Margaret by some twenty years, but there was a liveliness to his movements as he came around the side of the barn, leading a tall white and grey dappled horse. He had a little grey in his hair too, but not unattractively so, and he wore blue jeans tucked into pointed boots, which seemed to Margaret somehow both rustic and elegant, like a soldier of old.

When he gazed at Teresa, it looked as if someone had lit a fire underneath him. He did not wave or say good day, and Teresa did not acknowledge him, but he continued to stare after her, even as the car drove away towards the main house, and Margaret thought, Oh, he is in love with her. And she felt tenderly towards this man, although she knew next to nothing about him, except that he loved a woman who, just now, had not noticed him.

Inside, the house was deep hued and sober. Aside from a tiny statue of the Virgin Mary, tucked away with coloured candles in an alcove in the hallway, the decor was plain and without frivolity, which Margaret found that she liked. Too many flourishes in a home, in her experience, usually meant that a woman lived there who was expected to do womanly things. But this was a practical place, and the woman who lived here was practical too.

'I used to have a girl who helped me with the housework,' Teresa said. She had insisted on carrying Margaret's suitcase, and now set it down on the cool tiles of the kitchen floor. 'But she went and got married, works on her husband's place. He butchers hogs, as I understand it. I never could stand hog farms. Awful stink to them.'

'I'm sorry,' Margaret said, because she felt somehow there was a note of mourning in Teresa's voice. She noticed that the dining table was very long, as if designed for great gatherings, but there was only one chair.

'You can have her room, is what I'm getting at,' Teresa replied, 'if you don't mind making it up yourself. I didn't know to expect you, see. Mr Ross said nothing about bringing a lady with him.'

She didn't say 'lady' the way people at home might have, as

if the word came with a curtsy attached. There was, Margaret felt, some kind of implication here, as if Teresa were sliding it to her face down along the kitchen counter.

Margaret recalled the hotel clerk in Harrisburg – it seemed like a lifetime ago now – and said, 'Goodness, I'm not his mistress! David's my brother, and as for him not letting you know I was coming, I can only apologize. Although I suppose, in his defence, he didn't know it himself until fairly recently. I can make myself useful, though. If you need someone to help with the horses, I've plenty of experience, from my father's stables.'

She thought she saw Teresa's shoulders slacken a bit. 'Your brother . . . heck, I'm sorry. I didn't mean to make assumptions. It's just that, well, a lot of the men we get out this way, often they come here to hide from one thing or another. The law came round last season and took one of my best cowpunchers because they said he was wanted for robbing a man in Santa Fe. I don't need trouble like that.'

'I can promise you I haven't robbed anyone,' Margaret said.

Teresa gave her that same look she had flashed David in the car, indulgent but shrewd. 'But you are running, aren't you? You're light on your feet. Noticed that as you were getting into my car. Noticed you staring off at all that distance too.'

'Oh, no . . . I wouldn't say I was running *from* anything. Avoiding, maybe. My husband, Richard . . .' Margaret felt her whole face stiffen just saying his name. 'Well, I'm glad to have some respite from London, anyway.'

Teresa went to the cupboard and fetched two cups made of a misty blue glass, and then she took a pitcher from the sink, which was covered over with a damp cloth, and poured them both a drink of lemonade. 'I loved my husband,' she said, handing one glass to Margaret and gesturing for her to sit down at the long table. 'He was real steady, dependable. That ain't always a given in a man.'

'No, it's not.' The lemonade was bitter, but fresh, and Margaret drank it down gratefully. The last time she and David had changed trains, they had bought a little food and filled up David's flask with water, but she realized she had not had anything to drink since that morning. 'I'm very sorry for your loss, Mrs Baiz.'

'Ah, don't be. They say the second year of widowhood is harder than the first, because no one gives you the patience they would to someone who's been recently bereaved. Well, I never asked no one to be patient with me. And I don't miss Rustin half as much as everybody told me I would. He was a good husband, like I said, but I didn't even know a person could live as much as I'm living now until he was dead. You understand what I mean?'

Margaret hesitated. She wanted to say yes, she did understand what Teresa was saying, but she wasn't sure why Teresa was saying it to her.

'I had a stray dog once.' Teresa leaned against the counter and drank her lemonade like she was swigging whiskey, wiping her mouth with her knuckle. 'She used to run off sometimes, be gone hours or even days. Then one morning, I came out to the yard and found she'd slipped her rope, and in the very far distance I thought I saw her bounding towards the horizon, and I knew somehow that this time she wasn't coming back. She'd been born wild, and to the wild she returned. All that energy had to go somewhere.'

'I'm not sure I take your meaning.'

Teresa tilted her head towards the window, where Margaret

could see the sun sinking behind a mesa, filling the valley with purple shadows. 'I never said you were running *away* from anything, miss.'

For the rest of the evening, Margaret helped Teresa in the kitchen, making fried potatoes and cornbread, which Teresa cooked up from cornmeal and flour and egg, and Margaret made gravy from the bones of yesterday's chicken. She thought this a rather odd assortment of things to qualify as dinner, but she helped Teresa carry it out to the bunkhouse, where the eight ranch hands fell on it, calling Teresa and Margaret angels.

'Careful now, boys, that's my sister.' David had been engrossed in a poker game when Margaret arrived, but he tucked into his dinner just as ravenously as the rest.

Upon returning to the house, Teresa gave Margaret a big, shapeless wool coat, a blouse embroidered with roses, and wool trousers like the kind she was wearing. 'Spring's coming,' she said, 'but the desert at night is its own mistress, and she can be a cold old bitch.' She grinned and handed Margaret a thick pair of socks, adding, 'You might have to sleep in these.'

Upstairs, in the former housemaid's room, Margaret took off her dress and stockings – she also took off the silk shift she had bought to surprise Richard on his birthday the previous year – and put on the things that Teresa had given her. There was a looking glass propped up against one wall. It had a dark patina around the edge, so Margaret could not see herself very clearly, but as she examined her reflection she thought, I am in a place where nobody knows me, and this time it did not weigh on her as it had on the train.

*

Teresa was right, Margaret did have to sleep in her socks, and the great coat too, which smelled a little of the grease Margaret remembered rubbing on her horse's saddle when she was a girl. The familiarity of the scent comforted her, and despite the chill, she was already drifting off to sleep when there was a knock at her window.

At first she thought it must be a branch tapping against the glass. Then she remembered there were no trees out here for miles, or if there were, they were stunted little things that could not possibly reach this high. She was beginning to think she must have dreamed it, when the noise came again, this time as an insistent tapping.

Pulling the big wool coat around her, Margaret lit her oil lamp and padded over to the window, where she found her brother clinging to the sill outside.

'David!' she hissed, freeing the catch and being careful not to knock him off in the process. With the window pushed open, she could see that he was balanced on the roof of the veranda. 'What on earth are you doing? Did you climb up here?'

'Maggie,' he whispered, beaming at her, 'come and look at the stars!'

'You idiot, get down at once before you fall and break your neck.'

'Oh, don't fuss, Mags, it's really quite secure. Now, I know you must be in a dreadful state out here—'

'The only state I'm in is one of trying to get some sleep, David.'

He snorted and then beckoned emphatically with one arm. 'Come and look at the stars with me, Mags. You'll be glad you did.'

*

The darkness out here was like nothing she had ever known. She had chosen to come down the stairs and let herself out the front door, rather than clamber around on the roof, but as soon as she was outside, David had to guide her across the yard. She could barely see him standing next to her, and when she held her hand up in front of her face, there was nothing. And then she blinked. And suddenly the lights came on.

From horizon to far horizon, stars spilled as if from a toppled sugar pot, and as she craned her head back and stared, Margaret felt the curve of the Earth beneath her, felt the night sky arching its back above. The desert was no longer black and bare, but mauve and indigo and silver. This is how the world looked before people came into it, she thought.

David leaned against the corral fence and lit up a cigarette, which he offered to Margaret.

'Why did you tell them you were English?' she asked quietly, as she leaned beside him. 'In New York, the concierge said you told everyone you were from London.'

'Oh, that.'

She was not looking at her brother, but she heard him sigh, as if he had been expecting the question. She took a drag of the cigarette and passed it back to him.

'I don't know,' he said finally. 'I suppose it's this great unspoken thing in our family, isn't it? The idea that English is the thing we should aspire to be. We were all of us sent away to English schools, and then Cambridge, Cambridge, Cambridge. Alec with his wife in Hertfordshire and his boys at Harrow. You with your husband from bloody Kent.'

In the dark, Margaret held her breath and did not move, but she felt that stone dropping through her again at the mention of Richard.

'You know,' David said, 'there was a fellow in the rooms below me at Trinity who came from Cardiff. He used to rib me a good deal, so one day I told him, "Listen here, old chap, I'm not actually English," and he said no, I was worse than that. I was a Scotsman pretending to be an Englishman, and he thought that was really quite pathetic. I felt so wrong in my own skin afterwards.'

Margaret considered this, listening to her brother sucking the smoke in and out of his lungs. Somewhere, out on the flats, a bird took flight, calling in alarm at some unseen predator. At last, she said, 'Is that why you're doing all this? You're unhappy with yourself because of something someone said to you at Cambridge?'

David laughed weakly, handed her the cigarette again. 'Now that really does sound pathetic, doesn't it? But isn't it strange to think that you're one thing, only to discover people see you as something else? I'm proud of being Scottish, but I'm not very good at it. Our parents put a great deal of money towards making me an English gentleman, but it doesn't fit either. When I got to New York, I think I wanted to try it on for size. I wanted to see what it would feel like to be English in a place where nobody knew that I wasn't. I can't say it made me happy. I suppose,' he said, after a moment, 'I've come to the great melting pot so that I can be anonymous. So I can work out for myself who I am.'

'You're David,' she said. 'You're quite mad, and a wretched brother, but I do like you very much as you are.'

He kissed the side of her head, taking the cigarette from her as he did so. 'If I get very good at this rope-and-drag business, I could flank and brand and castrate Richard for you, if you like?'

But Margaret was only half listening. In her mind, she was on the terrace at her father's birthday party again, overhearing those women gossiping about the other woman whose husband had been unfaithful, and recalling David's words from a moment ago: *Isn't it strange to think that you're one thing, only to discover people see you as something else.*

Yes, she thought, exactly that.

She came to learn that brandings mostly happened out on the range, where cattle were ushered together by mounted riders. Crews moved from one ranch to another throughout the spring, often working hundreds of calves daily with practised ease, and it was a community event, with neighbours expected to show up and assist the cowboys.

Margaret liked the way people dressed here. Equal parts buckaroo and cowpuncher, Teresa called it. Slick-fork saddles, tall post horns, sixty-foot reatas, and riders who could throw a grand loop even in a windstorm. Flat brim hats, wild rags and tapaderos swung over polished stirrups. These were cowboys who rode light-handed bridle horses and, though they weren't showy, they took pride in their horsemanship, which Margaret, who had ridden since her girlhood, could appreciate. Out here, a good horse was one that handled quietly, could hold a rope, and could wait for hours without making a fuss.

'Though I reckon they say the same thing about women too.' Teresa glanced over at the foreman as she said this. When he did not immediately look up from the cart he was hitching, she cleared her throat loudly until he did, and Margaret thought, Oh, I see. And she felt less sad for him then, though slightly embarrassed that she had got caught in the midst of this shy and peculiar courtship.

Because she could sit a horse, Margaret rode out with the rest of them most days, though Teresa wouldn't let her join the ground crew with David. The stench of singed cattle hair made her nose sting. At lunchtimes, while the families and workers sat smoking and licking their plates clean, Margaret would sometimes mount up, putting her horse through figure-of-eights, then setting off on a hard ride across the scrubland, followed by a long walk to allow both beast and woman to cool down. Occasionally, when he wasn't cheating his way through a hand of cards, David would come with her. Then they would race one another, waving their hats with their heads tossed back, howling at all that sky, and though they were far from home, at times like these, Margaret swore the air tasted as it had when they were children, playing havoc in the glens. Something electric in the air.

As the spring wore on, the cowboys expected to move towards the foothills of the Sangre de Cristo mountains. This was tougher work, among draws and timber and tighter ground. You were just as likely to rope in a narrow canyon, the foreman said, or along a pine ridge, as in broad open desert, and David surprised Margaret by proclaiming that he wished to stay on and see the season through to completion. Physically brave though her brother might be, roping had more than once burnt his hands, and he complained frequently of having to camp out on the flats with only a skinny bedroll separating him from the snakes and the scorpions.

'But it makes a change, doesn't it?' he said, that evening, when he and Margaret were trotting back from their ride. 'The men here don't care whether I'm English or Scottish or God knows what, and they certainly don't care for titles. I'm rather getting to like this plain old David fellow.'

'And I'm rather getting to like plain old Margaret.'

David grinned at her. 'You, Mags, are anything but plain.'

They would have to go home eventually, she knew that, just as David must have known, though they did each other a kindness by not speaking of it any further that evening. Instead, they sat around the campfire, well fed and comfortable, with the sprawling night at their backs, and they listened to the foreman's guitar, while Teresa sang softly, almost to herself, about wayfaring strangers.

Three years from now Margaret would be back in Scotland, sat about in similar fashion with the Women's Timber Corps while they took a break for lunch. She would be perched on the length of a felled spruce with fellow pink-faced girls in jerseys and boots, and she would listen to the array of accents, Lowlands and Newcastle and North Wales, and think again of this. Of how people have more in common than they have differences. She learned this in the desert, and she would learn it anew in the Highland forests, where she was once again no Englishman's wife, and no laird and lady's daughter.

Some nights, she would slip away from her digs and follow the coursing tributary that she knew wound its way down to the River Ness and her old home. There, she would tilt her head back and look up at the sky, propped up by giant pines, scattered with stars, and she would think of David. By then he would be fighting far to the south, in a different desert, in quite a different uniform to the plaid and blue jeans he had worn in New Mexico, but the stars above would not have changed. And as long as Margaret could see the stars, she would tell herself that he was looking at them too.

Only once would she write to her mother. The letter that she received from Lady Ross in response spoke ungenerously of David, claiming that he had led Margaret astray. Then Margaret would put her mother's letter aside and would think only this: He brought me home to myself. As much as anyone could do that, her brother had done that for her.

How to Have Your Children and Eat Them

I

There was always a quietness to the land after a big storm. On the drive out to Hope House, Eve and Cyrus been humming along to Madonna, but then the radio hit a dead zone, and now the silence was so thick Cyrus felt he could reach out and touch it. The sun was coming up in the rear-view, clouds tinged orange in a petrol-blue sky. Branches and cacti lay scattered over the hard shoulders, while turkey vultures hovered idly overhead, and a lone tumbleweed hesitated before skittering across the road. Cyrus had to swerve to avoid a stray cow lying flattened on the tarmac.

Eve, riding shotgun, had one bare foot up on the dashboard and was painting her toenails black. Goth girl, Cyrus teased her, and Eve told him to go to hell. It's this thing you do, she explained – you paint your nails one colour, and then you put this special black polish over the top that cracks and separates as it dries, so that you can see traces of the true colour underneath. You wouldn't get it, she said. I'm actually red all the way down.

'I've really got to go all the way past Haring?' Cyrus asked. He did not like driving in the desert. It tickled at some caveman part of his brain, all that empty space. No way to keep watch in every direction. No way to see who or what might be stealing up on you.

'Yup.' Eve sucked on her lower lip as she tried to concentrate on her nails. The skin around the corners of her mouth was flaky from cold sores that reappeared whenever she was stressed, and ever since the phone call last night, from Kathleen Buck, Cyrus had caught glimpses of her slathering anti-viral on the raw, cracked skin when she thought he wasn't looking.

'Kathleen's worried about storm damage,' Eve added, swiping polish over her big toe. 'That house is a piece of crap. I told her it's going to fall down anyway one of these days, but she's still hung up about it, so I said we'd go check on the place. Whatever.'

'Kathleen's your stepmom, right?'

Cyrus had only met her once, a couple of years ago at Eve's graduation. A woman in a baggy flannel shirt, Tony Lama boots and feather earrings, her ginger hair already streaked with grey so that it bore some resemblance to the red clay river in Cyrus's hometown where the locals tossed their scrap metal. Some people give off a feeling of being abandoned – not broken up with, not jilted, but dumped the way that unwanted things are – and Kathleen Buck had given him that feeling.

'Just because she married my dad doesn't make her anything,' Eve said.

'Didn't she pay for all your books and stuff in college?'

'So? I didn't ask her to. She just called me up one day and said she wanted to give me some money, and I thought okay. Not up to me how she spends it.'

Eve had not liked college much. Cyrus knew this because he had met her on a bridge over the snarl and exhaust fumes of I-10 traffic, and although she had not said it in so many words, he'd had a feeling she'd been planning to jump. She had left her wallet and her shoes on the sidewalk.

Cyrus had soon learned that Eve did not like much of anything, besides giving herself impromptu piercings and naming stray cats and melting plastic with her lighter. She took the latter very seriously, said it calmed her down. Cyrus got that. He was two years clean and built card towers to focus his mind whenever he got that bad itch. He had expected her to laugh at him when he asked if she wanted to come to his recovery group. She had this way of laughing with one eye closed, like she was aiming at a target, and he loved it and dreaded it in equal measure. But to his surprise, and maybe hers too, she'd agreed. She'd smiled and said she liked the idea of dating a boy with his own trauma, because then he wouldn't try to fuck her.

The afternoon was nothing but miles and heat. Cyrus's car churned up clouds of yellow dust that would linger in the soupy air long after they'd torn through this stretch of highway. They passed a sagging fence that must have marked the boundary to some far-out ranch, and nailed to one of the wooden posts, Cyrus spotted a coyote pelt with the head still attached. A hand-painted sign said something about a reward. Eve made a sound of disgust in the back of her throat.

'People don't know how to work the land any more,' she said. 'Proper ranchers know that coyotes keep the prairie dogs in check, and you can lose a whole lot of stock from cattle stepping in burrows and getting their legs all twisted and broken.'

'Your dad,' Cyrus said, carefully, because he knew her father was dead. 'He was a "proper rancher"?'

Eve sucked on her lip some more. 'Assholes these days use cyanide. About as good for the rest of the food chain as mercury in the ground from the oil wells. Imagine dying like that, poisoning every other living thing you touch.' She leaned forward to squint at her toenails. She could get kind of weird about death, and Cyrus thought this probably had something to do with her sister, who had died young and very unpleasantly.

'Trap 'em, snare 'em, shoot 'em,' Eve said. 'That's what my dad told us, but he wouldn't do poison. He said there was a difference between hunting and murdering. He would know, I guess.'

Cyrus glanced at her, trying to look her in the eye. He wanted to ask her what she meant, but then she swore loudly, holding up her thumb where she'd reached out to touch her toe. Red polish smeared like blood.

It was late afternoon when they reached Hope House. Various signs around the gate read 'No Hunting', 'No Trespassing', 'Turn Back'. These were professional looking and had not been drawn by hand.

'Kathleen told me the keys are in the eye socket,' Eve said, raking her dark hair back. She had cut it some weeks ago and was still not used to how short it was. Sometimes Cyrus thought she seemed very far away from her own body, and he wondered if, wherever she was, it was closer to him, or even further away still.

Eve's father, Joseph, had bred horses here at one point, but later foals had been afflicted with dwarfism, and her father and stepmother had been forced to sell everything, or so she said. Eve also said she could read palms and that she'd been born with a sixth finger, so Cyrus usually took her stories with a grain of salt, or perhaps a whole spoonful. In this case, however, the small, weathered horse skull sitting on the front porch hinted at a kernel of truth with regards to the dwarfism. Eve slipped her fingers into one of the eye sockets and pulled out a set of keys, shaking off the dust that had collected during last night's storm.

'Don't just stand there,' she said, stepping inside. '*Mi casa es su casa.* Jeez, it's roasting in here.'

The house was utterly quiet. Cyrus hovered in the doorway, watching as Eve dialled up the air con.

'Cy, you're letting the bugs in. At least close the screen door.'

'There's no damage that I can see. Just dust everywhere. Not much we can do about that.'

The storm had been a real howler, and Cyrus had expected to find fences pulled down and broken glass everywhere, but the house was in surprisingly decent shape. If all Kathleen Buck wanted was to know the place was okay, then surely they could tell her that and be on their way. Cyrus did not especially like being here. He thought perhaps it was because the house was so far away from anything he was familiar with.

Still, he bent down to start unlacing his boots. Eve snorted and started scuffing her Converses on the rag rug in the middle of the floor.

'Evie,' he said, and she gave him her one-eyed smile.

'What? Like you said, there's already dust everywhere.'

Cyrus did not generally think of himself as someone who noticed how a room was decorated. Indeed, it had only recently occurred to him that the rec hall where his recovery group, Fresh Start, met every Sunday was painted lilac, and he had surprised himself by deciding that it was a little ugly. His upbringing had not encouraged him to think in terms of what looked nice or what didn't. There were only things that served a purpose and things that did not. Looking around Kathleen Buck's living room, he thought there was a great deal in here that served a purpose, but he did not think it was a nice room at all.

There were rugs and a TV and a couch and a big desk, but there were also rows and rows of guns on the wall. Shotguns, sawed-offs, hunting rifles, a tactical rifle that did not look particularly legal, pistols, revolvers – some relatively modern, others that could have been used in the Civil War for all he knew. Cyrus had lived in Texas all his life and was generally unfazed by firearms. Whenever the pastor worked up a sweat during a sermon, he'd take off his blazer and the whole congregation could see the .33 on his hip. But Cyrus didn't think he had ever been to anyone's home before and seen guns on the wall the way other people might have put up paintings or cross-stitched Bible verses. There was something showy about this. Even the more trigger-happy of his neighbours would have agreed it was tasteless to demand too much attention over such a thing. Same way they thought anyone who said 'amen' louder than everybody else in church was kind of an ass.

But what especially startled Cyrus were the circumstances. Sure, Haring and its far flung properties were out of the way, and maybe some people were a little out of touch, but he'd have thought the Bucks would have been the last people in the world to put guns on display, after what happened to Eve's sister.

Eve had told him about it the first day they'd met, on the bridge. Cyrus was there as part of Fresh Start's outreach programme, trying to save souls from the tyres of so many passing cars below. When he'd asked Eve what was so bad she didn't feel she could live with it any more, she had told him that her little sister Marnie had gotten killed. A shotgun had gone off, right through the middle of her face, when she was only nine years old.

Cyrus had listened, of course, and felt sorry for Eve, because clearly the pain of this loss was immense, but privately he thought she had told him this because she felt obliged to tell him something. To give him some explanation for why she was on the bridge, clearly thinking of jumping. He thought maybe she'd felt embarrassed. He thought she missed her sister a lot, so she'd told him about that, but he didn't really think she blamed herself for Marnie's death. How could she? It had all been a terrible accident.

Eve sat down on the big desk and gave it a considering look, then without warning she picked up a pot of pens and hurled it to the floor, smothering a laugh as they rattled across the tiles.

'Jeez, Evie!' Cyrus had decided a long time ago that he was allowed to say 'jeez'. He always pictured one of the Apostles saying, 'Yo, it's my main man Jeez,' and after that it was impossible to consider it a serious form of blasphemy.

'Jeez, Evie, what the heck are you doing?'

Eve rolled her shoulders back, turning her neck from side to side. She looked like she was gearing up for a race, or perhaps a fight. She said, 'Are you hungry? I could die I'm so hungry,' and she hopped off the desk and disappeared through the living room door. Moments later, he heard the sound of chairs scraping and cupboards slamming in the kitchen. This time, when something fell and shattered, she did not try to stifle her laughter, but she did sound surprised. Almost as if her doing this was completely unexpected.

Cyrus did not know what to say. He felt like a parent trying to ignore a disruptive child's behaviour. His first thought was that somehow the house was making Eve act like this, but then he thought this kind of superstition was beneath him, so he went outside and sat on the concrete slab that served as a porch and stared at the horizon. It seemed impossibly far away to him, and again he was struck by the sense of being cut off, floating on waves of heat in the middle of nowhere. A person could go crazy out here, he thought, a person could easily lose their mind and go full-blown nutso. But he knew this sort of thinking was beneath him also.

After a while, he heard the screen door open and felt the warmth of Eve's body as she came to crouch behind him. When she buried her face against his neck, Cyrus felt relief the way he used to when he found a vein in the soft crease of his elbow. She had not gotten so far away from herself this time that she had forgotten him. She kissed his jugular, and for a second he thought maybe she was going to bite him. Then, more alarmingly, he thought that he would let her, but she only said, 'Let's get going.'

As they left, she slammed the front door so hard that its little diamond window cracked, hairline fissures spreading outwards like rays of light from some Old Testament angel. The air felt thicker than before, as though someone had left an oven open nearby, and Cyrus could swear he smelled the sickly, chemical reek of melting plastic.

'Evie,' he said, as they climbed into the car. 'Did Kathleen do something to you? Is that why you're so mad at her?'

Eve raised her eyebrows. 'Nope. Kathleen did absolutely nothing.'

When he glanced in the rear-view, Cyrus could see the first tendrils of smoke uncurling from the windows. He watched the house burn behind them for fifty flat miles until it looked no bigger than a cigarette stub discarded in the vastness of the landscape.

They stopped at a Braum's on the way home. Eve's dark hair shone pink as she sat on the hood under the neon sign, dipping curly fries into her chocolate milkshake, and together they listened to the grackles poking at junk food wrappers, the stop and start of trucks in the drive-thru. Cyrus was glad to be in the vicinity of people again. Eve, too, seemed more relaxed, and when she slid down on to the asphalt, saying she was just going to run to the bathroom and then they could get moving again, this made Cyrus glad too. Everything felt very normal. Here he was, just this guy having a milkshake with his girlfriend, and then they would drive home together.

Sometimes, like when he caught up with old friends who had moved away and come back to find the Cyrus they used to know full of gaps, people would ask him what are you doing with a girl like her? And Cyrus would laugh and say hey, Eve's all right. She's pretty great. Because the truth was, he had grown up watching his parents go about love as if it were the greatest chore on their to-do list. They'd worked at marriage the way they had worked at their jobs, building callouses and getting a sweat on, even though both had been on the outs since before Cyrus was born. Picking himself up and trying again was in his genes. He had seen, that day on the bridge above the hurtling traffic, that it was in Eve's genes as well, and this mattered to him.

She had not come back from the bathroom yet. Cyrus got down off the hood and went to start the car, to get the AC flowing. The dashboard clock said it was almost 9 p.m. He hadn't realized until then quite how exhausted he was – too many hours crammed behind the wheel, too much tension back at Hope House. He didn't want to be driving too late into the night, didn't want it for Eve either. Clearly today hadn't been easy for her, even if she wouldn't say why.

He went back into the diner, thinking he'd order a coffee or a Red Bull, anything with caffeine. Glancing towards the bathroom, he saw that there was no line, and that the bathroom door itself was ajar with no one inside. Eve must have gone back to the car. Well, good, he thought, they would be on their way again. But as he headed back out into the parking lot, he heard someone say, 'Oh, Kathleen!'

Eve was at the payphone, clutching the receiver in both hands. She didn't seem to have noticed him, though he was close enough to hear her speak.

'Kathleen, I'm so sorry – the fire! That storm must have been really wild. Yeah, it's all ruined . . .' There was a tremor in her voice that Cyrus hadn't heard since meeting her on the bridge, except this time, as he watched her wipe her eyes, he saw her smile at the sun that was setting the horizon ablaze, and that smile was all teeth.

'I wish there was something more I could do, Kathleen,' she said. 'The storm's totally wrecked the place. I just feel *so bad*!'

II

It had been rough weather the day Kathleen first came to Hope House. This would have been back in the seventies. Thunderheads were swarming above, and the wind, following the path of an old streambed, sharpened itself on the rocks before trying to knock the Stetson off her head. Further out, though, the sun picked out the mesas in shades of gold against the black sky. It was a big sky here, Kathleen thought, climbing down from Joseph's truck. There was no getting out from under it.

Hope House was a low-slung adobe building with a corrugated roof and wooden shutters that banged in the wind. It lay on a stony plot on the far flung edge of Texas, a hundred scorched acres with the streambed running down the middle like the crease in the centre of a Bible. When the monsoons came, they reminded the desert that it had once been under water, the heavy rains disgorging fish fossils and the jawbones of extinct aquatic predators for children to find. In the summer, there were the sandstorms. Winds that could blow the jelly right out of your eyes, Joseph said.

In reply, Kathleen had crushed her Stetson firmly on to her red curls and smiled. 'Good thing I wear such big sunglasses then.'

Kathleen had grown up in the nearby town of Haring. Her father had been what you might call a gentleman farmer, in that he dressed like he worked the land and complained about the government-induced price ceilings of the fifties without getting too much mud on his boots. Even during the monsoons, when the rains turned the ground to butter, he still managed to look clean-pressed and Sunday-starched and expected the same of his daughter. The actual farm work wasn't too onerous, since they only grew one crop of alfalfa and owned just eighteen head of Holsteins, but Kathleen could remember sitting on the porch with her mother, watching the two cowpokes her father had hired digging out an irrigation ditch, sweat glistening on the back of their necks, and she'd thought: That's what I want to be.

She'd wanted those boots with the pointed toes and thick block heel that made you swagger. She'd wanted to ride off into the sunset and out of the smallness of her life. With her fingers like pistols, she would mime shooting in the yard, and the great sadness of her early years was having grown breasts before she turned thirteen, which brought the attention of older boys and, perplexingly, her parents.

Her mother had urged her to accept a ride home from school with the doctor's son, who was sixteen and had his own convertible. Such a nice boy! There were no such things as backroads in Haring then, there was only the town and 'beyond', where the desert stretched for scorching miles to the seam of the world, and it was there, *beyond* the gaze of any adult, that the doctor's son had stopped the car and tried very hard to push Kathleen's head between his legs. The air was close and heavy, and she fought him hard enough that she broke one of his fingers, though not before he'd unzipped his fly. She was so shocked at the sight of his penis, she'd laughed. Then she'd spent the remainder of the journey telling him she was sorry, because he had cried.

When she got home, she'd almost told her mother what had happened, but she knew that her mother was friends with the doctor and his wife, the boy's parents, and thought very highly of them. Kathleen did not want to make trouble. She would keep on living like this – not wanting trouble – until a few years later, when Joseph Buck cut through the stage dressing of her life.

She was deeply in love with Joseph. Everybody was, in those days, but it was she who won him. He had his mother's Germanic complexion and his father's bare-knuckle boxer way of standing, which were about the only things either parent ever gave him. Something about his face brought to mind a headshot of some vintage movie star, but only if you'd buried it in the yard and then dug it up again years later. These few things were known about Joseph: that he had two daughters from his first wife; that he made his money rearing horses way out in the scrubland; that his parents had left him at a Panhandle gas station as a child and had never come back. His mix of tragedy and apathy drew women to him in a way that no man could explain and no woman tried to.

His life was hard and bound to be short. Kathleen, along with everyone else in Haring, pictured him being riddled with bullets in a bar fight, or being mauled by a coyote while he defended his livestock. But that sort of expectation is hard to live up to, and in the end, when he collapsed from an aneurysm in the frozen foods aisle, aged sixty-six, there was a collective feeling that he had let everyone down, just a little.

'In the end.' Kathleen does not much like that turn of phrase. What end? Did things come to an end as soon as Joseph died? Is she supposed to just shrivel up and go, because she has put her husband in the family plot?

It's been five years now, and she will be fifty-five next week. When she turns on the radio, she thinks everyone these days sings about being unhappy. What's up with that? Last night, she'd thought, 'I'll ask Joseph about it,' because he had always been very in tune with young people. But then, as she was waking up, she had the clearest sense of Joseph's body beside her. She could perfectly picture his smooth broad shoulders, his fair hair against the pillow, and she realized the version of him she was thinking of was some twenty years younger, and she remembered once more that he was dead.

Lying there, with all that empty space beside her, she felt adrift. She was a tiny speck floating in the vast, lonesome darkness of 3 a.m. The feeling only got worse when she understood that what she had really wanted to ask him had nothing to do with music and young people. She had wanted to ask about Hope House.

What on earth is she going to do with it now?

The recent sandstorms have been brutal out that way. Other properties – though they are few and far between in desert country – have reported similar damage: shutters torn off, windows smashed, yucca ripped out at the roots by the screaming gale. But these things can be swept away, patched up. Not so at Hope House, where the insurance company says the fire was likely caused by old wiring.

'I mean, that place was basically medieval,' the insurance rep had told Kathleen over the phone. 'In weather like this, all it takes is a stray spark and the wind to whip it up.'

The fire had gutted everything. Three generations of Buck history reduced to ash. She cannot clear that kind of damage by herself, but, in a way that she can't really explain, she doesn't want to.

Ever since Joseph passed, Kathleen has spent most of her time at her sister's place further east in Amarillo, where she can look out of the window at night and see the lights of other people's homes and the brilliant neon of bars and chapels and car dealerships, holding out against the desert darkness. Perhaps it is a relief, then, that the storms have rendered Hope House uninhabitable. What she really wants – she understands, as she lies in bed alone– is Joseph's permission not to inhabit that place any more.

Joseph was sixteen years older than her. He has been dead five years, but still Kathleen cannot imagine herself ever closing the gap. Somehow, she can't imagine he will let her. She was always the perpetual child to him, even when she became a partner in his horse-rearing, even when he allowed her to start giving riding lessons to local kids on weekends, or to organize the renting of horses for movies and weddings and quinceañeras. He liked that she had never finished high school, because then she could always be left wondering: Is this something I don't understand because I did not complete my education, or am I just plain dumb? He liked to let her wonder.

It used to make Kathleen think, if she ever had a daughter of her own, that she would force her to stay in school, just so a man could never put her down like that. But she never did. She never had any children of her own. It would have been cruel to ask that of Joseph after what happened to his girls.

Five years ago, the night before the aneurysm, Joseph had told her he was going to die. Kathleen was lying on her side, staring at his back in the gloom. She was watching the slow rise and fall of his shoulders when he said, with a quietness that was unusual for him, 'Kitty-kat, I think my number's up.'

'What are you talking about?'

Joseph grunted something. Then he sounded more like himself again: 'Did you turn off the stove earlier, after dinner?'

'Yes, of course.'

'I don't remember you doing it.'

'I did. I did do it.'

'Go and check, would you?'

'I know I turned it off.'

'Go and check.'

Kathleen put it down to nerves about a studio director who was coming the next day to look at one of the thoroughbreds. The guy was making a Western, but Joseph didn't have high hopes for it, since by that time the bottom had fallen out of cowboy movies. Seemed like the bottom was always falling out of something round here.

Kathleen knew there would be no arguing with him, so she had got out of bed, shivering as she padded across the stone tiles in her bare feet, for it was winter then, and winter in Texas is a raw, skinning thing. She went to the kitchen and saw that the stove was off. Then she poured herself a glass of water and leaned against the sink and thought, I am so tired, and she knew exactly what she really meant, so she stopped thinking it.

When she got back to bed, she found that Joseph had fallen asleep, and she supposed that was for the best. He needed to rest before tomorrow. She didn't get the chance to ask him why he'd thought he was going to die, but at the time she decided this was unimportant. Probably he'd just had a bad dream. So instead of waking him, Kathleen had burrowed back into bed and had a dream of her own.

She was in the yard with Eve and Marnie. It was high

summer, the desert flush with shades of brown and ochre, and both of Joseph's daughters had sunburn peeling on their necks and chests. The girls were young. Eve eleven, maybe; Marnie nine. About as young as they had been when the accident happened.

Kathleen could remember thinking, in the dream, that she did not want to see it. She did not want to watch the accident happen again. She kept her distance from the girls, tried running in different directions, but her legs moved as if on a lag, and she could never seem to get very far. After a while, she realized she wasn't moving at all, but simply standing there, watching Eve and Marnie. They each had a black bag, like a trash bag, and they were picking things up off the ground and putting them inside.

Kathleen thought maybe it was bones. Sometimes the girls would pick up animal bones in the yard. She wanted to tell them to be careful, to make sure they washed their hands, but then suddenly Marnie was coming towards her, her little arms outstretched, holding one of the black trash bags for Kathleen to take.

Marnie's expression gave nothing away. It did not seem to hint at the awfulness of her fate. Marnie simply wanted Kathleen to take this bag from her, and when Kathleen looked down, she saw that the bag was full of shoes. Children's shoes, tiny pink plimsols and miniature riding boots like the ones the girls sometimes wore, except that they were all caked in grime and the leather was half rotted, and Kathleen found she was inexplicably embarrassed by this. What if a big movie producer came driving up to the ranch to borrow a horse, and instead he found her just standing there with a bag of dirty shoes? What would people think? Joseph would be so mad.

Kathleen pushed the bag back into Marnie's hands. 'I don't want this,' she said, and that was when she woke up.

Joseph lay snoring beside her, but he felt a hundred miles away.

III

The smell of raw meat came wafting from the shed behind the house, and Eve could see a body strung up by its hind legs over a low beam. A skunk, by the size of it. Sometimes they got in the coop and stole the chicken eggs, and then Eve's father would have to shoot them, though he explained that he did not like doing this. It was simply what had to be done. Her father already had the skin pulled down halfway, so that the skunk almost looked like a thin, naked child taking off their sweater. Marnie was looking at it too, nose wrinkling, and when their father caught her staring, he gave her a crooked grin, digging his fingers into the seam of hide and flesh. This had to be done too, he said. They could sell the pelt and cook up the meat. A living thing was the sum of its parts, and all those parts were worth dollars.

Her father had always seemed to Eve like some character from a tall tale, like Pecos Bill lassoing twisters. Most folks would probably have believed it if Joseph Buck told them he'd been raised by coyotes. He had yellow teeth, stained from years of nicotine, but with his slanted smile and cowboy swagger, Eve was old enough to understand that there was a roguishness about him that caught women's attention. It had certainly caught the attention of Kathleen, this woman who had arrived at their house a month ago, whose long red hair hung in spirals like a child's drawing, and who slept in their father's bed.

Eve loved her. Or she wanted to love her.

She saw Kathleen crossing the yard on her way to feed the chickens, and Eve stared until she thought her eyes were going to bug out of her head, desperate for Kathleen to notice her. It was something she had been trying out lately – seeing if she could communicate with her new stepmother by thought alone.

Her father must have seen her looking. He said, 'Watch carefully now, Evie,' and he gave the skunk skin a good tug, peeling it down further. Then he reached for his dull knife and began picking at the tendons to work the hide free. You wanted to use a dull knife, he said, or you risked cutting too deep and spilling blood all over the fur. Eve had seen her father skin a skunk before, but she did as she was told and watched carefully, because you always had to be careful with him.

You had to be quiet when he told you. You had to be still when he ordered it. You had to laugh when he laughed, and he could be very funny – he did puppet shows for Eve and Marnie sometimes with the skulls of raccoons and desert foxes, did silly accents and everything – but you had to laugh, even if you didn't want to, because the terribleness would be lurking right there, on the other side.

Her father was down to the skunk's head now. He ran his hands over it, and Eve felt her stomach roll. She watched him tie a rag around the peeled neck to keep from ruining the fur, then take a scalpel and make a swift incision over one ear, a spurt of fresh red landing on his cheek. He was absorbed in his work, so Eve shuffled over the sun-baked boards and sat next to her sister, who was gazing at Kathleen across the yard.

'Does she hate us?' Marnie asked. She was only nine and to her way of thinking, if a person did not love you, then they must hate you. She also thought the opposite was true, which made Eve unspeakably sad.

Eve shook her head. 'No, Kathleen's nice.'

Marnie picked at the frizzy Velcro on her sneakers and made a small hum of agreement. 'I guess she'd like it more if it was just her and Daddy here. Maybe she'll go away.'

'Nuh uh, don't worry, Marn. I bet she stays for ever and ever.'

'You girls sure aren't afraid to get your hands dirty,' Kathleen said. She stood in the entrance of the tanning shed and tried to look polite about the smell, focusing her attention on Marnie, who was now salting the hairless side of the skunk pelt. 'Looks like you know a lot about living out here.'

Their father put a big hand on Marnie's shoulder and said, 'Yup.'

Eve would not say all she knew.

She was often afraid at Hope House, but not only of her father. Sometimes Eve was afraid *for* him. When he panted, it was as though something inside him was about to give out. The faces he made, right before he collapsed on top of her, were not his face. They were almost clownish in their desperation, almost made Eve laugh, except that she had learned early on that these were the moments when she must be the quietest.

She would keep her eyes on the rafters of the barn, on the rods of daylight spearing the roof, where pigeon feathers collected and spiders were born and died and shrivelled away into nothing. It felt disobedient even to look at his arm or his bare shoulder. Such moments were private for him. Then, at last, he would dredge his voice out of the depths of himself. Tell her she was good. Pick the straw out of her hair.

She met others, later on. At college she met girls, and even a boy, who, when lured over the precipice of their past with cheap sangria and home-made cocktails, would giggle and say my uncle used to . . . my dad's friend once . . . They laughed, and Eve laughed with them because none of them knew what else to do. It wasn't real, or it was, but it had happened to some other self, some far away version of themself that they had left behind in their childhood.

Eve met these others and then hated them when she sobered up. She hated the images they put in her head, the memories they pushed to the surface, the way that was all she could see when she passed them in the hall or glimpsed them across the room at a party. If this is what she thought of them, then surely they thought it of her also.

She and Marnie had not possessed the language with which to talk about the things that happened at Hope House. Eve would not have told anyone, even if someone had asked, because she simply hadn't known how to say it. And her father was her father. She bore him the kind of loyalty an isolated person bears to the few facts they have been told about the world: that he was a grown-up, and grown-ups knew what was best for children.

Eve didn't want to have to tell anyone. She wanted someone to stumble upon their lives and notice that something was wrong. Kathleen could have been that person, should have been that person, but she brought so little of herself to Hope House. There were only tiny outposts of her shirts, dishes and books dotted about among Eve's father's guns, knives and liquor bottles. Kathleen encroached no further into his territory than the hungry creatures that came through the wire fence and got a bullet in the head for their troubles. She didn't come in far enough to notice a thing.

Eve didn't want to tell, and so, when the nice boy on the bridge with the sensible haircut and the Jesus Loves You pin on his shirt asked about her sister, Eve said it had been an accident. What good would it do, so many years later, to explain how they were both raised on the sweet end of a shotgun. How Marnie could take apart a firearm, clean it and put it back together with no mistakes by the time she was seven. How no gun would have gone off in Marnie's little freckled hands, unless Marnie had wanted it to. What good could come from saying any of that now?

Driving home from Hope House that evening in the tail-light glow of the highway, Cyrus said nothing, but Eve didn't need him to talk. She liked the steady presence of him beside her, just as she liked the rumble of the trucks in the slow lane, the vibrations of the road beneath the car, grounding her in the moment.

When those men went up and walked on the moon in '69, she remembered how her sister had come home from school buzzing. A whole week of classes on outer space! Marnie had loved every second.

'Did you know . . .' she'd told Eve, so small her feet didn't touch the floor when she sat at the kitchen table. 'Did you know the stars are already dead? But it takes so long for the light to travel across the universe, we only see it now?'

'I did not know that, smartass.'

Over the years, Eve had often wondered why the stars bothered shining at all, if nobody would see them for millennia.

She'd asked herself what good was all that blazing energy if it burned itself out before anyone understood what it was for. What was the point of doing something that mattered only to you?

But now, when she shut her eyes, Eve could still see the trembling glow of Hope House on fire, and she thought it did matter. God, did it matter. What had happened in that house had come and gone, but that was no reason why it shouldn't burn. No reason why, a million years from now, people shouldn't see it burning still and understand what she and Marnie had never been able to put into words. When Eve rolled her window down, she thought she could still feel the warmth of that fire, even from all those miles away.

Jack the Devil

I

Jack Howl is 186 years old, not that anyone would know this to look at him. If you pickled a black-backed jackal in Old Number Seven, then prettied it up with a pair of Tony Lamas and a leather jacket, you'd be somewhere in the vicinity. Jack's face is sharp, often hysterical, framed by black hair. Though he is scarce about the waist, he thickens at the shoulders and arms, his legs long and lean, a body made for running after things. One of his eyes is dark, the other the translucent blue of a corpse. The story, as he likes to tell it, after a few fingers of bourbon, is that the latter belonged to the Devil, who lost a bet to Jack over who could fill his coal cart the fastest and had to pluck out one of his own eyes in recompense.

'But that was a long time ago,' Jack will say, wiping a drop of liquor from the corner of his mouth, lip curling just enough to show a hint of one sharp canine. 'Things like that don't happen any more. Hell, if you believe that, you'll believe anything.'

The day Ellis learned about Jack, he was making his way through the deepening afternoon down the Spine. An elongated thicket of firs, oaks and hickories that climbed the Blue Ridge Mountains, the Spine had outlived the worst of Appalachia's logging frenzy, its mountaintop blasting, its toxic slurry running down from the mines. Survivor country, Ellis's grief counsellor called it in their fortnightly Zoom calls, presumably with the implication that Ellis was a survivor too. He could not say that he felt like one. When he went to the woods, it was to press on the bruise of Beth's absence.

Six months back, driving home through blue dawn from a night shift at her hospital in Roanoke, Ellis's wife had pulled out of an intersection too early. Easy to miss things on these winding hill roads. She probably hadn't seen the truck coming up perpendicular in the gloom, not until it was already ploughing into her hatchback.

EMTs said she died on impact. Said it like that was supposed to be a comfort. But the thought of Beth – the ferocity of her, the warmth, the unapologetic loudness – being snuffed out just like that made Ellis want to claw his face off.

He didn't go to the Spine to hunt, but Ellis did take a gun. He'd been living in Virginia barely a year then, and he used to tell Beth that the Colt .45 was to scare off bears and mountain lions, a lie that made her laugh. The truth was, he was still a Bostonian at heart, and he had reservations about the people down here. Back Creek was the kind of town where the annual Founders' Day celebration included a parade in historically accurate Civil War uniforms, and they didn't skimp on the Confederate side.

Ellis Sherborne was tall, broad in the shoulders, curly haired, and although he was only thirty-five, his face had the wood-like quality of a man with only one expression. His arrival in Back Creek was still something of an anomaly, both to the townspeople and to himself, in fact, but Beth had cut her teeth on this country, had been born in the next valley over. Because of her, people had acknowledged Ellis's presence here, even if they hadn't entirely understood it. He couldn't see how he fitted in Virginia now that she was gone.

The greys of winter were just beginning to give way to living green, the trail spotted with mountain sorrel and bleeding hearts, though the warmth of spring had yet to sweep all the way up into the Spine, and the air had a frosty weight to it. Ellis's cheeks were scuffed red with cold. Through the trees, he could see the Blue Ridge hills, edged with gold in the gradually waning light, and Ellis thought again how Beth had loved this place. This boundless forest country in which she had lived and loved and perished. For Beth's sake, he thought he must do his best to stay on here. To remain in Back Creek was a way to remain with her, though he felt strongly that he did not belong. Even, perhaps, that he was unwelcome.

It was a shade of that feeling that came to him now, as he paused in a clearing still littered with last autumn's leaves. He could not have said why, but he had the strongest sensation that he was no longer alone.

Nothing moved. Not even a breeze stirring the rain pools that had formed in the tangles of tree roots. There was no sign of man or animal that Ellis could see, yet some primal part of his brain was convinced that if he were to turn around now, he would catch someone watching him. He was also aware that, here in the clearing, he was utterly exposed.

Hesitant, he drew the Colt. Then he turned.

He meant to move back into the trees, to conceal himself somehow, but with that motion, he caught a flash of metal, and something in his mind supplied the word: *gun*.

In a panic he did not know himself capable of before that moment, Ellis fired, and then he heard a man's voice curse loudly, and the thump of something heavy hitting the ground. For a few seconds, Ellis could only stand there, stunned, before he realized what he had done, and rushed forward into the trees where he had heard the man collapse.

He expected to find blood. He expected to find someone writhing on the forest floor in agony, and already Ellis was pulling out his phone to dial 9-1-1, but instead he was met with the sight of Jack Howl, sitting up and probing a hole in his leather jacket with one finger. The metal Ellis thought he'd seen had merely been the rivets.

In those days, Ellis knew Jack only tangentially. Whatever the folks of Back Creek thought about Ellis's presence in town, there was nothing as holy to them as gossip, and at McClusky's bar on Friday nights, they could talk Ellis's ear off about how sometimes Jack went down to Roanoke to raise a little hell in the city. Then there were those who swore he'd inherited a fortune from some distant relative. No, others reckoned, the Howls had always had money, squirrelled away from their moonshiner days.

Moonshine? My ass. They had a stash of Confederate gold.

Wherever the money came from, Jack had put a great deal of it into an environmental charity to help combat the damage caused by the mines, and a methadone clinic, which was sorely needed in these parts. For this reason, people were generally reluctant to speak ill of him, though there were still girls who called him 'strutty'.

'Sure likes the sound of his own jawing.'

One thing everyone seemed to agree on, however, was that the Howl family – generations of quick, lean men, of whom Jack was apparently the last – had always been elusive, 'quare' folk. In fact, nobody even knew that Jack's father had passed, until Jack showed up in Back Creek five years ago and announced that he had come to clean out his old man's house. Before then, no one could remember having seen any of the Howls in a long time.

One old-timer said she could recall Jack as a little boy, but others dismissed her. No, they said, as a child he'd been sent away to school up in Richmond, or was it down in Raleigh? Only his father had lived here, and his father before him, on and on, one of those families with deep mountain roots. Arnallt. Meurig. Simwnt. Names that sounded like they'd been dredged up from the bottom of a well.

At any rate, Jack and Ellis had never shared more than a passing glance on the street. Jack revving his engine at the one stoplight in town, top down on his Mustang. Ellis stuffing groceries into his truck outside the mini-mart, leaning over to Beth to mutter, 'Compensating much?'

In the aftermath of the gunshot, however, Ellis held out a hand to Jack and said, 'Jesus, man, you okay? I'm sorry, I thought it was . . .' He wasn't sure he knew what he'd thought. He could still hear his ears ringing, and his blood felt like shook-up soda in his veins. 'Did I hit you? You need an ambulance?'

'Nah, I'm good.' Jack ignored the hand, still frowning at the hole in his jacket, where, presumably, the bullet had passed right through into his shoulder.

Ellis guessed he was in shock. To be simply sitting there made no sense. Jack should have been in pain, but instead he looked up, those mismatched eyes narrowed, and said, 'You owe me a new jacket, Sherborne.'

Ellis couldn't figure it. 'Can you raise your arm? No? Let me take a look.'

Jack was very pale. It was possible that he was bleeding heavily and Ellis simply couldn't see because of the jacket, so he demanded Jack take it off, which he did with a clipped laugh. 'Not like I'm going to wear that again.'

But Ellis, crouched on the ground beside him now, could only stare in mute disbelief. On the grey Henley that Jack was wearing underneath, there was not a speck of blood. Even stranger, though the bullet had clearly torn through the fabric, there was no sign of injury at all beneath it, except a faint discoloration of the skin, like the aftermath of a bruise.

'That's not possible.'

Jack's smile drove the corner of his mouth up high on one side, like someone had caught him with a fish hook, and his eyes took on a slightly manic glint, which made Ellis stand and take a step back.

'Relax, would you?' Jack said. 'I'm not going to eat you.'

'The hell are you talking about?' That primal throb in Ellis's brain was back, telling him to go for his gun again, and it was all he could do not to listen. 'What's going on? Who *are* you?'

Jack merely cocked his head, calm as anything. 'Well, that's the million-dollar question, isn't it?' Then he got to his feet, rubbed his hands on his jeans and slung his ruined jacket over one shoulder. 'Probably best we keep this between ourselves. You were shooting your piece off without a hunting licence, after all. And besides, Yankee, no one would believe you anyhow.'

Barely half an hour later, Ellis was making his way back down to his car when he came upon a break in the woodland. Here, a rocky crag overlooked a steep drop into the pasture below. There were deep wheel ruts where other vehicles had come and gone, probably hunters at this time of year, out looking for bearded turkeys, and Ellis had a good view of the houses that had once stood here, their stones scattered throughout the pasture by the bitter reckonings of the past. Beyond that, the mountains repeated themselves in shades of blue all the way to the horizon until they became haze.

What drew his eye now, however, was a deer going hell for leather through the grass, its hind legs pumping up almost level with its front. A moment later, he saw what was chasing it.

Jack sprang free from the trees and ran through the pasture, faster than any human had any right to move, a single black streak across the landscape. Ellis felt his scalp shrink with horror, but he couldn't tear his eyes away. From his vantage point on the crag, he watched Jack close the impossible distance between himself and the deer, sling one arm around it and sink his teeth into its neck.

II

Of the ship that took him and his father away, Jack has only pieces of memory, as if he is looking back at it in a broken mirror. It was crowded in the hold, and loud. They were slotted in between the merchants' cargo and there was always somebody snoring, even in the daytime. After a week or so at sea, a woman from Liverpool began to teach him and a handful of the other children to read in English. He told her his name was Ioan Hywel, but she could never quite fit her mouth around it, so she called him John to start with, and then just Jack.

They could have been down there for a month or a year – all long times are the same length to a little boy, no matter what the clock says – before they were deposited on a Boston quay, and from there they were funnelled into the migrant's life. Jack's father, Morcant, was a wiry man with the bearing of an undertaker and sharp shoulder blades that protruded through his undershirt like wings snapped off at the base. He wore his curly black hair down to his jaw, which slanted a little to one side, on account of him having taken a fist to the face from the rent collector.

Jack did not blame his father for taking them away. The lords and ladies of Wales spoke like Englishmen now, and they wanted their people to be English too. They made it so that a man could not afford to live in his own country or speak his own tongue. In the end, Jack and his father had been going barefoot, sleeping in ditches along the Afon Wysg, and so Jack did not blame Morcant for taking him across the ocean. All the same, he was not glad to be with him. He was too young back then to be able to put it into words, but he knew there was a badness in his father. He absorbed this knowledge the way his clothes and hair absorbed Morcant's pipe smoke in the evenings, and sometimes in those evenings, when Morcant was cosy with a bottle of rum, he'd tell Jack about his own childhood. A brother who used to tie him to a chair in the kitchen. A brother with a cruel smile. More than once, Morcant said, 'You've got a smile just like him,' and then he'd chase Jack around the campfire.

Jack was skinnier in those days and light on his feet. He imagined himself like a wisp of smoke, but if Morcant caught him, which he usually did, he'd remind Jack that he was just meat.

They did not stay long in Boston. There were many people already starting their lives anew there, and Morcant said he wanted elbow room, so they headed south, working every job in the book along the way. Throughout the 1840s, they picked fruit, shucked corn, dug ditches, mended saddles, painted signs and built parts for a stagecoach, but the little bag of coins Morcant stuffed into his boot was always light, the coins themselves filthy from changing hands so many times. It seemed to Jack that there wasn't enough money to go around in this country, so you had to pass it on quick, just like people got passed around too.

Skimming from one town to the next in the back of rattling wagons, father and son were honed down to the bone, ankles blistering, their hair often stiff with dirt. Jack watched whole states pass by in a parade of chokecherry trees and skeletal larches, long stretches of woodland through which phosphorescent eyes peered at him from between the trunks. He saw rusted farm tools standing in empty fields, the remains of wooden houses kneeling in the weeds, miles of country with no signs, or signs pointing to places that were so many miles away. On the ship, it had seemed like every person in Europe was coming to the New World, but now that he'd arrived, Jack got the sense that it had already been abandoned.

It was warm the day they arrived in Back Creek, Virginia.

Summer had finally made its way into the mountains, and every surface was thick with ferns and moss, the air smelling of sunbaked bark. It was beautiful land, but squinting through the twist of trees, Jack could see that the hills on the other side of the valley were scraped bare. This was where the mining company had cleared the timber away. Squatting in the cleft of the valley, the town seemed hastily constructed – cabins hammered together so recently that the planks still had sharp edges, and chimneystacks battled for space among the fierce mass of pines. It did not feel like civilization; it felt like a faraway land where anything could happen.

Even as a child, the irony of having left the pits and spoil tips of South Wales to come out west and dig coal was not lost on Jack. But it could be that way with newcomers in America, people resorting to the familiar in a country that was determined to make strangers of them. At the age of twelve, he began work at the mine, a job his father had got for him, crawling on his hands and knees for long black hours. He would come up from the mine soaked through, and his shirt and pants would freeze stiff in the winter air, sounding like rocks scraping together as he walked home. There was coal dust in the whorls of his fingers that he couldn't wash out, never mind that he scrubbed the skin until it split.

When Jack was thirteen, he was down in a tunnel with another miner. John Fog was a white-haired man with narrow features sharpened by years of working the coal yard, but he wasn't just a worker, he was a *knower*, with an understanding of the mines that bordered on spiritual. Seams of coal had a way of speaking to him, luring him deeper underground, where only he, with his wizened body – and those like Jack who were not yet fully grown – could pass. So it was that they were down there together, hacking at the underside of the mountain, when they felt the floor heave, and the tunnel swallowed itself, sealing them under a thousand tons of rock.

Jack had no way of knowing how long he had lain there, his whole body frozen. At least, he hoped it was the cold that was making him immobile. 'Mr Fog,' he said, though his throat was cracked and parched as a gulch. 'How do you know if your back's broken?'

'You can't always know. When your spine goes, you don't hardly feel it.'

Jack heard a splash as John Fog moved towards him, and he realized the cold he'd been feeling was not a broken spine, but water rising around him.

'They'll be up there now, trying to get to us.' John Fog's voice was tense but controlled. 'Just do what you can to stay dry, or you'll freeze to death. And don't use your lamp neither. Save the matches. Like as not we'll need them in the coming days.'

'Days?'

'Plenty of men have survived worse than this,' John Fog said, but when Jack asked, 'Who? Which men?' he did not answer.

Holding on to one another's shoulders, they waded through the icy water until they found a ledge of dry stone barely two feet wide, where they curled themselves up until their muscles pinched. The rock sucked the heat out of their bodies.

'We got any food?' John Fog asked, and Jack had to confess that he had dropped his biscuits in the water. 'Ah, well. Guess we won't eat each other, at least.'

'Sir?'

'You ain't never heard of that? It can get that way sometimes, when things is bad enough. But don't fret, boy, there's not enough meat on either of us to make a decent meal.'

The water came up over their boots. Jack pictured his feet swelling, growing pale and bloated like wet bread, though he had lost sensation in them hours ago. There was a rattling as fragments of rock dropped into the water, and he imagined their fellow miners somewhere overhead, tunnelling towards them. Any minute now, they would be saved.

The water had now reached their groins, and Jack's eyes strained, unseeing in the blackness. Somewhere beside him, John Fog retched.

Hours. Days. Without light there was no way to measure the passing of time, except for this water, rising, rising slowly, lapping at his mouth now like an eager lover. Or how he imagined one might feel. He was just thirteen. He had never danced or gotten drunk or been kissed. He was going to die down here.

Sometime after this thought, though only God knows how long, Jack realized that John Fog was no longer by his side.

'Mr Fog, sir,' he called into the darkness, 'are you still there?'

Somewhere he could hear the calls of men, or ghosts, answering him, and Jack wondered how many bodies this mountain had swallowed. The Appalachians were older than bones. Years from now he would hear such a statement from one of his more educated officers – that the Appalachian Mountains pre-dated any findings of remains, human or animal – and Jack would think that sounded true enough, because those mountains could eat up bodies so they would never be found.

But Jack was found, in the end. The mining company said that he had done damage to company property, and they compensated him for the accident by sacking him and his father. Morcant, in turn, exacted payment from Jack with his belt buckle, but in those first tentative moments after his discovery, the men were gentle with him. Gentler than Jack thought anyone had ever been, carrying him up to the light, their arms encircling him as he shuddered and blinked.

They had to cut his boots off. His feet had bloated inside the slimy leather, but the men were careful, so careful he could have wept. Perhaps he did. He doesn't remember now. The last thing he had any clear recollection of was the sound of his own voice, calling out again for John Fog. One of the rescuers' headlamps swung around the collapsed tunnel, and in the arc of that light, Jack saw the body floating back against the rock wall, his eyes wide open.

'You have to take him,' Jack mumbled to the men who were carrying him. 'You have to take that man too.'

'Company says to leave him be,' someone said. 'He's already gone, son.'

Jack protested all the way up to the daylight, but as far as he knows, no one ever went back down. They just left John Fog bobbing in the water, staring all around in the dark.

III

'Hey, Sherborne,' Jack says, leaning in the doorway. 'Aren't you going to invite me in?'

It's hog killing weather, late autumn mists sweeping down from the peaks, the valley full of cold light. Even in town, the resounding clack of battling antlers can be heard coming from the pastures, and on any other Saturday afternoon Ellis might have hiked out in search of the stags, just to watch them. Just to feel a little of that wildness reverberating through the landscape. This weekend, however, he is supposed to play host to the Back Creek council, to oversee preparations for the town's bicentennial celebration.

Ellis himself isn't on the council. That's the kind of position a person only achieves in Back Creek when they have a few generations' worth of bones buried in the hillsides. But he teaches history at the community college on the other side of the State Park, and he's got plenty of material when it comes to nineteenth century Virginia. For the sake of Beth's memory, he has offered to help out. However, by right of bloodline, the town council also includes Jack Howl, who has taken it upon himself to arrive a whole hour before anyone else.

'What happens if I don't?' Ellis asks. 'Invite you in, I mean. Will you just have to stand out there on the stairs? Is that part of your whole deal?'

'My deal?' Jack says. 'Sherborne, it's just good manners to invite your guests indoors.'

It's been two years since that afternoon Ellis shot Jack in the woods. These days they aren't exactly friends, but now and then they will both find themselves at McClusky's, propped up by a bottle of bourbon. And once, on the anniversary of Beth's accident, when Ellis was so smashed he passed out at the bar, Jack had picked up his tab.

Ellis wouldn't say that he is any closer to understanding what Jack is, exactly, but he is arguably a little closer to believing it. He has come to understand that things drift out of human memory in Appalachia. One need only drive down Main Street to see the windows knocked out of old offices and shopfronts, the insides rain-rotted, timbers splintering.

Rusted railroad tracks run through the weeds, parallel to the road where the Prince Panda takeout, the Fine Ladies' Wear, and even the Guns n' Ammo are all in the process of shutting down. Final sale, everything must go, thank you for your business. This is a place where the rest of the country leaves things it wants to forget about, and Ellis can believe, if nothing else, that Jack is no different.

With a sigh, he stands aside and gestures into the apartment. 'Come on in, then.'

Not like he can just leave him lurking in the hallway, although Ellis can't smother the faint prickle on the back of his neck as he watches Jack wander into the living room. He is suddenly aware that this space hasn't had another person in it since the realtor handed Ellis the keys.

This isn't the apartment where he and Beth lived together. Their old bungalow on the edge of town had become 'a place', as in, it's a place that Ellis doesn't like to think about, because it was the last place he had seen his wife alive. He'd been intending to use this last hour to tidy up a little. Now he aims for surreptitious as he clears some room on the dining table. No need for anyone to total up just how many beers he'd finished alone last night, or that his lesson plan for next week has pizza grease in the margins.

'I like it,' Jack says, leaning against the plastic counter in the kitchenette. 'The exposed brick, and the not-one-but-two unopened *Die Hard* DVDs, the single-serve Chef Boyardee cans in the trash. It's very divorced dad.'

'Don't go through my trash.' Ellis frowns. 'What are you, a raccoon?'

'Can't blame a guy for being curious. You're something of an enigma round here, you know.'

'Sorry, *I'm* the enigma?'

'What? Everyone likes me, I'm a people person.' Jack flashes that strange sideways smile. 'You know that's why the council wanted to meet here, right? Instead of having you bring all your historical junk to the church hall. They're trying to figure you out, Sherborne.'

'Good luck to them.'

Ellis hefts a cardboard box up on to the table and begins unpacking stacks of yellowed local deeds and photocopies of woodcuts and tintypes. Labourers, miners, families with children in bonnets. There is a freed Black couple standing proudly on their new land, right before the government revoked the grants and reissued all those hard-won acres to the white man. There are the original Back Creek founders, faces reduced to smears by sepia, all in a line outside what had once been the Grand Hotel but was later flattened and replaced with a gas station.

A lot of this stuff had belonged to Beth. She wasn't interested in history in a general sense, but she loved where she came from, and collected pieces of it the same way she collected horse chestnuts and hagstones. Among all these centuries old faces, there is even a photo of her as a child with her grandfather, both of them holding up squirrels they appear to have shot. She looks so delighted, Ellis can't even bring himself to be weirded out by the thought of a kid toting her grandad's vintage Browning, although he does slip the photo into his back pocket. Doesn't see that he should have to share that one with anybody else.

The rest of this, at least, should be useful to the council. They are putting together a little exhibit, two hundred years of Back Creek history, and that's the kind of thing Ellis would be genuinely happy to help with. He only wishes he'd had time to sort through all his research first, preferably without Jack snooping around in the background. Turns out he's the kind of dog you can't leave cooped up for too long.

'Hey, Sherborne, did you know you're out of whiskey?'

'Sherborne, who owns CDs and no CD player? Scratch that, who owns CDs any more, period? And seriously, what's with all the Chris Isaak? The guy sings like he's waiting in line for the bathroom.'

'Sherborne, I hate to break it to you, but some of your students are supremely bad at this.'

Ellis drops a textbook with a pointed thump and looks over at Jack, now lying on the couch with a sheaf of unmarked essays in one hand, and a glass of whatever he'd been able to find at the back of Ellis's cupboard in the other. It looks faintly purplish, and Ellis fears it may be the blackcurrant liqueur his mother had sent him after Beth's funeral. Because that's what every grieving widower needs, obviously.

'*Echoes of Valour: examining the human stories of the Civil War*,' Jack reads. '*In the serene embrace of the Rappahannock River, where cannonballs once danced through the air, a tapestry of individual bravery unfolds at the crossroads of history* . . . Is this supposed to be Fredericksburg? Are you kidding me?'

Ellis rubs the back of his neck. 'It's a little flowery, perhaps. But I happen to think the Civil War is a vital part of our national story, and it matters that we remember it.'

'Did you read that off a keychain at a giftshop? Please. Fredericksburg wasn't a serene tapestry of dancing cannonballs, or whatever. It was bloody and loud, and once you've slipped in the guts of another man strewn all over the place, it's not something you forget, believe me.'

'Wow,' Ellis says flatly, 'you say that like you were there.'

'On the banks of the Rappahannock. Sharpshooting boys from Massachusetts.'

'You're screwing with me. You fought at the Battle of Fredericksburg?'

There's an unfamiliar slackness to Jack's face then. The same look in his eye that Ellis's great-uncle would get sometimes, talking about Korea and Pork Chop Hill.

'It was cold enough that the river had started to freeze, but not so cold that a man could stand on it. We could see the engineers on the other bank building this pontoon to try and get across to us. I expect they wished they hadn't in the end, though.' Jack stares into his glass, teeth bared in a hollow grin. 'You know there's a feeling you get when you're waiting for soldiers to come at you? A weird sort of longing for your enemy, like you can't wait to go meet them. I was a sharpshooter, and I kind of loved every man I shot, and mourned him, and reloaded. There were bodies everywhere, and parts of bodies, some without arms, without legs, some with all those things but without the meat to hold any of it together. We were routed eventually, hand-to-hand fighting in the streets, real butcher work, yadda yadda ya. You can read your history books for that. But mostly what I remember is that the guy next to me got a hole right through his wrist, and some of it went in my mouth.

'Took me another year, but I did desert. Ran off in the night at Gettysburg. I took my sergeant with me, but he had malaria or something. Died after a few days on the road, and so I . . .' Jack's expression slides away again into something else. 'Well, that's another story.'

Ellis stares at him blankly for a moment. Sometimes

holding a conversation with Jack feels like he's being swung around the room by his ankles and hitting every item of furniture in the process. The skin between his shoulders twitches. Clearing his throat, he says, 'You were a Confederate soldier.'

'And whiskey is wet, Sherborne, this is Virginia. But believe me when I say there's nothing about those guys worth remembering. Don't put them in your essays, or re-enactments, or town parades. They're dead, so leave them in the past.'

'You're not in the past,' Ellis points out, 'you're in my living room.'

They are quiet for a moment. Outside, grackles are croaking in the mini-mart parking lot, and somebody's souped-up engine peels out on to Main Street with an apocalyptic roar. Ellis considers throwing Jack out. Considers this whole situation to be surreally fucked up, but there is, nevertheless, a part of him, a guilty sliver, that can't help feeling curious. You spend your whole life studying history, and then all of a sudden, here is history, lounging on your couch, drinking your mother's home-made liqueur.

'Could I interview you?' Ellis says, before he can stop himself. 'It's just, you've lived all this stuff, it's insane. Were you at Appomattox? Do you think the Confederacy really funded Lincoln's assassination? What made you fight in the first place? You can't pretend you didn't know what the war was about.'

'Never said I didn't.' Jack drains the last of the liqueur and wipes his mouth with the back of his hand. 'I can hear your gears turning from here, professor. You want to ask me if I supported slavery? If I was a piece of shit? Well, see, I think I was worse, because I was just plain selfish. I'd been down a coal mine so long that when the army sold me daylight, I bought it. This country's always been good at that. Makes your life hell, and then sells you the fix.'

'I don't think that justifies it,' Ellis says.

'Sherborne, I'm not sitting here trying to justify the Confederacy to you. I'm just telling you why I did it. But selfishness explains away a lot of history, don't you think?'

'Then why tell me any of this at all?'

Jack is silent, squinting his mismatched eyes like he's aiming at a target, and Ellis wonders if that's what he'd looked like – Howl the sharpshooter on the banks of the Rappahannock, world narrowed to the barrel of a gun.

'Same reason you invited me in,' he says at last. 'Time comes around, a man gets tired of having only himself to talk to.'

IV

McClusky's bar occupies a shabby brick building, which used to be a barbershop, which used to be a taxidermist. Jack remembers taking a fox there to be mounted, a long time ago, and the spindly man who ran the place had looked at the little body, wrapped so carefully in sacking, and said, 'This thing's mangled to hell. Can't do nothing with it. What killed it, do you know?'

'Something hungry, I expect.'

This wasn't long after the end of the war. Jack had been young then. Or rather, he had still been twenty-five, but he felt brand new. Just born. He did not yet have a handle on what he had become, and as such his kills were often sloppy and savage. Back then, the town council blamed the bloody deaths of local livestock on a bear they believed had migrated to the area, but it was only a matter of time, Jack thought. If he didn't clean himself up, one day someone would catch him in the act. They would put him down for what he was – this aberration of the natural order of things – but he couldn't help it. He had come home from the front so very hungry.

It's generally quiet at the bar during lunch. Just Jack nursing a glass of something cheap and fiery, and a few old-timers with crinkled faces, talking about so-and-so's grandson who went away to college, somebody claiming she made her own cornbread for potluck when there were clearly Martha White boxes in the trash, Merle Haggard on the overhead speakers claiming Mama tried. From the window, Jack can see preparations for the bicentennial parade are well under way, volunteers hanging bunting between the rusted streetlamps. Mayor Bainbridge, with her lonesome eyes and her mother's best wool suit, is directing Girl Scouts and school band members, and Jack has a quiet kind of love for all these people, for their doggedness.

Appalachia has been abandoned by one government after another, left adrift in a sea of opioids, smokestacks and empty coal yards, but still the region clings on. He knows, because he has looked this up online, that it isn't so different back in the old country. Drop him in the valleys of South Wales, and it'd probably be like stumbling through a funhouse mirror, everything familiar, yet not quite right either.

He hasn't been a Welshman in nearly two hundred years. In a natural lifespan, a man gets to reinvent himself a few times over, but for Jack, it's been endless. The only constant he's had in all this time has been Back Creek. The soil and the rivers and the woods here didn't fight any civil war, the azaleas never turned traitor, and these blue hills, repeating away into the mist every morning, never kept anybody in chains. Jack can't help loving this place. It's because he loves her that he's glad she lost the war.

He has tried, down the years, to alter the town's fortunes where he could, hoping, perhaps, that he might change his own in the process. In the fifties, he held firm on the picket line with the miners. A decade later, men came stealing up on Back Creek one night dressed all in white, and Jack lured them into the backwoods and ate everything but their faces, which they had been so keen to hide. As recent as yesterday, he'd argued with the town council against those damn Founders' Day uniforms, but every generation of council members says the same thing. That they dress up as Union troops too. That it's harmless, that it's history, that people have a right to recognize their past, as if that isn't the very essence of the problem. People won't stop clinging to one side of the war or the other, and so the way Jack sees it, he'll never know peace. This morning, he still woke up with that same hunger. The Devil in his belly, gnawing at him from the inside out.

Maybe that's why he tried talking to Ellis. Poor hollowed-out Ellis with his dead wife and his sad eyes and his empty liquor bottles. He is a historian. He's supposed to be objective. Could be Jack's just getting old, but maybe it wouldn't hurt to lay it all out to someone. He doesn't expect absolution, but living like this is a lonely business. These days the clock seems to tick down faster and faster. Soon it'll be time to make tracks again, pretend to put his house on the market, pretend to buy it from himself. He needs to disappear for another few decades, until he can come back as his own son or nephew, until there's no chance of anyone looking at him over a beer one night and realizing that Jack Howl has looked twenty-five for an awful long time. It's a well-honed plan. But maybe there's still time to tell someone his story all the way to its grisly end.

To stay out of sight of Mayor Bainbridge and the parade crew, Jack walks around the back of Ellis's building and climbs up and in through the bedroom window. He finds him with a duffel bag open on the bed, in the process of cramming yet another flannel shirt inside, but when Ellis spots Jack's reflection in the mirror, he throws his fists up like he's expecting a fight.

'Whoa, easy there, Sherborne, it's only me.'

'Yeah, I can see that. What the hell, man? Is the front door a foreign concept to you?'

'This way I saved us both time.' Jack sits down on the bed and peers inside the duffel. 'Word is, you skipped school today. Please tell me it was so you could go get high behind the gym, or whatever it is young people do these days when they're playing hooky. I wouldn't know, I was home-schooled.'

'That explains so much.'

'Do you really own this many plaid shirts? This is uncanny.'

Ellis snatches the duffel away. 'What do you want?'

'Just checking in, making sure you're not passed out in a slick of your own bourbon-scented vomit. You know, as friends do.'

He's doing that thing, Jack thinks. That Ellis thing where he's got to tense his whole body in case he accidentally expresses one meagre hint of feeling anything at all.

'Not that it's any of your business,' Ellis mutters, returning to his packing, 'but I've got to go to Boston. Personal thing. Don't raid my liquor cabinet while I'm gone.'

'Like "job interview" personal, or "dead relative" personal?'

'Your condolences are duly noted.'

'Dead relative, then. Bummer.'

Ellis glares at him, but there's something in his posture now that looks a little relieved. Like maybe he was worried Jack was going to say, *sorry for your loss*, and he was going to have to respond with something beyond his usual lumberjack stoicism. After a beat, he lets his hands fall heavily to his sides, and concedes, 'My great-aunt. I didn't know her all that well, but her daughter's in Sydney and can't get a flight out until Monday. I'm the only family in the country, so it's kind of on me to arrange everything.' He rubs his jaw, glancing at Jack. 'You ever plan a funeral?'

'Not as many as you might think. Which I'm now realizing is a missed opportunity, since black is absolutely my colour.'

'You do dress like you're perpetually on your way to a wake at the world's lousiest dive bar.'

'Oh, stop. Flattery will get you anywhere.'

Ellis has a way of smiling like it's his first time giving the expression a try and he's not sure if he's doing it right. Women probably find that very compelling, though frankly it makes Jack want to shake him by the shoulders and demand, *What's it going to take for you to enjoy yourself for once?* Last year, half joking, he'd offered to score Ellis some coke. Said he could do a bump from the crook of Jack's thumb and forefinger if he wanted, and Ellis had only laughed Johnnie Walker-drunk, and replied, 'Pretty sure there's some kind of folklore warning about that. Accepting gifts from the Devil.'

Then he'd passed out at the bar, and Jack had driven him to the trailer of this nail technician Ellis was screwing at the time. He had dumped Ellis on this girl's lawn, practically comatose, which had no doubt left her wondering – as much as Jack had wondered himself – why a man with a beautiful girl waiting on him kept drinking like he didn't want to see tomorrow.

'I could drive you.'

Ellis looks up from his bag. 'It's like a two-day drive to Boston.'

Jack shrugs. 'I'm a hoot on road trips. And I could do with getting out of town for a while.'

'Sure, nothing says "relaxing weekend break" like a stranger's funeral.' Ellis looks suspicious. 'You seriously want to come all the way to Boston with me?'

'Why not? Come on, show this country boy a good time.' Affecting a little of his old southern drawl, Jack adds, 'Why, in them big cities, I hear they got buildings as tall as the sky.'

That night, Ellis wakes from a dream in which he is in the car with Beth. In which he is trying to warn her about the intersection. In which nothing changes.

He comes to violently, jolted as if the impact of the crash has somehow reached him through time and distance, and he feels betrayed by the supposed comfort of his bed, heads into the kitchenette to gulp down warmed-over coffee.

Even two years on from the accident, sorrow is a forceful thing that leans on him hard, and he can't seem to get out from under it. Sometimes it lays him low for days. In those moments, he can't imagine it will ever let up, but of course eventually it does, and then he feels like a traitor to his grief, for feeling that little bit better for a while.

Lying on the couch with the lights off, Ellis wonders when this acute sense of missing Beth – the cluster of moles on the back of her neck, the scent of her coffee brewing in the mornings, the precise way she turned her socks down over the tops of her hiking boots – will eventually dispel into something more nebulous. A more general sense of loss. He wants to miss her like an old man looking back sagely on the long unfurling of his life, not like a junkie twitching for the needle. But still he finds himself waiting for her to enter a room.

Maybe getting out of town will be good for him. For the longest time, Ellis has been telling himself he needs to stay in Back Creek to stay close to his wife, to be in the place where she was, but talking to Jack puts matters into a strange, strained perspective. Evidently, some things do linger on after death. But why Jack and not her? Ellis just wants to understand. Why this uncanny leftover from the ugliest chapter of their country's history, and not a good woman who did nothing but love, and was loved in turn.

V

They start early, heading north on the highway through autumnal country, Blue Ridge in the rear-view coming alive with the rising sun. Ellis swigs black coffee from his Thermos, wrapped up in his scarf and a thick rollneck sweater because the heating in his truck hasn't worked for years now. One of those things he kept telling himself he was going to sort out, after Beth, like renewing his gym membership, or getting back to his PhD.

'Let me guess, your stereo doesn't work either.' Jack lowers his Aviators, frowning in the passenger seat. 'No offence, Sherborne, but your ride kind of blows.'

'I thought you said you were fun on road trips.'

'I suppose I could sing. You want me to do Chris Isaak?'

'I'll throw you out at the next gas station.'

The landscape turns steep as they near Shenandoah, but the interstate steers them away towards quiet towns and flattened pastures, hay bales stacked high for the winter, and the inescapable Virginia car dealerships. Leaning against the window, Jack says, 'All this used to be forest.'

'Yeah? Must have been a while back. When was the last time you came up this way?'

'Came down, more like. Straight shot through the mountains from Gettysburg.'

'You did all that on foot? What's that, a week's trek?'

'Two weeks for me, at least.'

Well, shit, Ellis thinks, no wonder his sergeant didn't make it.

'I was a deserter,' Jack says. 'Not like I could take the train. Couldn't even go by the main roads, in case I was spotted.'

'You ever thought about writing some of this down?' Ellis asks, and then scolds himself. What exactly would he be able to do with that information? Unverifiable accounts of the Civil War from an undead soldier do not a PhD thesis make.

'I'm not really big on journalling,' Jack replies. 'Doubt there's enough washi tape in the world to make that look like a cute story. Me wandering through the mountains, half starved, half crazy, until eventually I showed up at my dad's place, and he took one look at me, knew I'd gone wrong somewhere in the wilderness. He wanted to put me out of my misery, but by then it was too late.'

Ellis adjusts his grip on the wheel. After a moment he says, 'Do you know how it happened, then? How you ended up . . . like you are?'

Jack just settles back against the headrest, gazing out of the window again as they roll on through acres of rust-coloured farmland. 'Ugly things happened here, when this land was all forest,' he says. 'But I still liked it better with the trees.'

They stop at a roadside café in an idling little town in the shadow of Shenandoah, thick with the dust of so many passing cars. The welcome sign lists the population as 435, and every one of them seems to be getting breakfast at the same time. This is sports jersey and overalls country, loose pieces of straw traipsed across the floor, everyone's hair and clothes ripe with the scent of outdoors. People watch Jack take a seat by the window like they're staring at the ghost of Elvis.

'Next time we stop,' Ellis thinks, 'I'm giving him my jean jacket. Maybe a hat too.' Folks have probably been running their eyes over Jack since long before he wound up whatever manner of creature he is. He's six foot tall with cheekbones you could skin your fingers on, but that doesn't mean Ellis enjoys being stared at right along with him. The waitress who takes their order calls them both *darlin'*. Some of the truckers at the next table look like they want to call Jack something else.

The food is decent, though. The coffee could bring a man back from the dead, and the view from the window of misty fields and logging trucks makes Ellis feel strangely relieved.

'Part of me kind of thought we wouldn't actually be allowed to leave, you know?' he says. 'Like Back Creek would find a way to stop us at the town limit. There's something about the country round here . . . You don't feel it?'

Jack raises his eyebrows. 'Don't tell me you go in for all that Appalachian backwoods magic crap.'

'How can you say that, man? I mean, look at you. You said so yourself, you walked into that forest a soldier, you came out a . . . Jesus, I don't know. Whatever you are.'

'A relic.' Jack spears one of his hash browns with his fork. 'A reminder. Figure I'm still kicking around because some people don't want to take down the Dixie flag bunting. If that day ever comes, maybe I'll vanish in a puff of smoke.'

Ellis shakes his head. 'Sounds like magic to me. The fact that I'm even sitting here talking to you is like one big, screwy dream.'

'How do you know it's not, hm? Maybe you're God knows how many whiskies deep, passed out and drooling on your lesson plan.'

'No, I know I'm awake.' Ellis takes a sip of his coffee, looks out of the window at the faraway skyline. 'I don't dream about you.'

After breakfast they trade places, Jack behind the wheel and Ellis hissing through his teeth every time Jack swerves between lanes.

'Are you insane? The speed limit is ninety!'

'Sherborne, speed limits are a suggestion, everyone knows that. It's like . . . ninety minimum. See? This guy's doing at least one-twenty.' Jack squints as he closes the gap between them and the Chevy in front. 'Bet I can pass him, even in your geriatric truck.'

'Come on, man, don't— Use your signal, Jesus!'

'Oh, so now the guy from Boston is going to preach to me about signalling.'

They're in northern Virginia now, the roads pine-heavy and full of potholes, which at least has the benefit of forcing Jack to slow down. They drive in relative silence for a little while, watching the country slip by in a vista of disused railroads and fire towers, until Jack says, 'You've been holding out on me.'

'For the last time, I promise you the stereo doesn't work.'

'I mean I've been doing all the talking. What about you? You have any secret tragic war stories I don't know about?'

'No war stories, no.' Ellis doesn't like riding shotgun. He never knows what to do with his hands when he's not the one driving, so he just stuffs them up under his armpits to keep warm. 'Grew up in Boston, went to college there, grad school too. Travelled a little for research. That's how I met Beth. I was in the Sonoran Desert for my master's, she was hiking with friends. Then . . . you know the rest.'

'Thanks, that was suitably minimalist.'

'I don't know what else you expected. That's all there is.'

'See, Sherborne, I refuse to believe that. What was your favourite movie growing up? Did you have a dog? A shitty dad? A bad tattoo?'

'What's that got to do with anything?'

'"That's all there is."' Jack scoffs. 'Is that really how you see yourself?'

Ellis gazes out of the window at the charcoal scratches of trees and distant grey hills, the sun a faint smudge, low among the clouds. He tries not to think about Beth, how she had said something similar once, the first night they'd stayed up drinking together at the desert motel where they were both staying. She wanted to talk about his master's thesis. She loved the idea of coming to the great outdoors to study, but he kept turning the conversation around, saying no, he wanted to hear about her. He couldn't beat down this private fear that if he showed her too much of himself, she would realize she didn't want him. He's just not sure why he's doing the same thing with Jack.

They come up behind a big red SUV, the rear window

plastered with stickers for the upcoming election. Among these is an enormous Confederate flag decal, and Ellis glances at Jack.

'You want to say something so bad, I can feel it,' Jack says. 'Would you feel better if I rear-ended him? It'd fuck up your grille, but I'd do it, for the sake of your Yankee honour.'

'You really don't see a connection between this guy and people like you?' Ellis says.

'People like me? What, coalminers? Capricorns?'

'Is this a joke to you?'

Jack's laugh is grim. 'He's a monster of your making too, Sherborne. This guy could google what a bunch of losers we were any time he likes, but he won't, because everyone still makes Appalachians feel like losers. He's got to cling on to his oh-so-proud rebel ancestors, or admit that they did something wrong, and let me tell you, if there's one thing human beings hate doing, it's admitting to a fuck-up.'

With one hand, he gestures broadly at the road. 'You know what Appalachia's like? One of those Third World nations where America comes in and strips all the wealth from it. Lumber, coal, copper, steel, and what did they give us in return? Minimum wage and the opioid crisis. Plenty of people here grow up believing their country's forgotten about them, that your lot think they're stupid—'

'My lot . . .' Ellis snorts, reaching for the Thermos, but the coffee is cold. 'Excuse me if I do think that's a pretty stupid reason to tear the country apart. Same as it ever was.'

'Oh, same indeed, Sherborne. You're so normal about people in Virginia that you literally took a shot at me once. Would you have done that in Boston?'

'Boston has less of a racist asshole problem.'

'Probably seems that way when your dad lives in Cambridgeport, sure.' Jack shakes his head, drumming his fingers on the wheel. 'Long as I can remember, people have been coming to Appalachia, picking it clean, and then saying, "Nah, it's someone else's fault that you've got nothing." In my day, the "someone else" was rich Yankees and free Black folk. Now I guess it's immigrants. Something to distract us from whichever politician's turn it is to gnaw on our bones. The lucky ones . . .' He is staring hard out of the windshield, eyes on the flag decal ahead. 'The lucky people are the ones who find something beautiful out here instead. Some other banner to march under. Something else to be proud of.'

VI

He left Gettysburg in the night, under a horned moon. Later, Jack would not be able to say why then, why that night, of all nights that he had slept on the ground in his stinking uniform, the great, wide darkness of unfamiliar country unspooling at his back. He felt only in that hour that the strength had gone out of the earth. The strength seemed to him to have gone out of the whole damn war, and he didn't care to die for it. He had never known a man who'd owned another. He'd owned little enough of anything himself, and did not like the feeling that he was being used by those who had a good deal more than he ever would.

His sergeant was a man by the name of Linklater. He was about Jack's age, and he had a fair, fine face, like a president on a coin, though by then the coin had lost some of its shine. It made Jack think about those early days when he and his father had come to America, how the money they earned was always filthy from being passed around. Linklater was like that. He had been passed from one platoon to another. Had come up from Texas originally, and he was crazy to get back to desert country, said he didn't like the way the trees blocked the view up here. Said he could never see what was coming.

At first they had started out on horseback. Sitting a horse for days at a time was hard on a man in all manner of places, seemed to grind an inch off Jack's spine with every mile, but he missed it after one horse got lame and then the other snapped a leg, and in the end both horses had to be shot. They left the sun-stiffened carcasses in Maryland and continued on foot. Jack insisted there wasn't much of Maryland to cross before they would be back in his neck of the woods, and he got some kind of feeling that Virginia would know him once he set foot within her borders again and would somehow guide him home.

But it did not happen that way. It did not happen like that at all.

About a week into their journey, Jack and Linklater felt like spoiled meat. It was July, the sky preaching blue so bright it was almost white, and the sun beat on Jack's body as bad as his father ever did. They were doing all right for food, at least. Linklater had taken his pistol with him, though he was near out of bullets, and Jack still had his Enfield rifle, so they could make good eating from conies and the odd bird here and there.

But their span of good fortune was short-lived. That night, bedded down in the soft loam under a towering spruce, Jack awoke to find Linklater groaning and spasming, and when he got the fire going again, he could see that the sergeant's handsome face had gone the colour of an old candle. Come morning, Linklater seemed a little less delirious, but his mood was uncharacteristically sour. He reckoned they had eaten something bad, and he scowled at Jack as he said this, because it was Jack who had been doing the cooking.

Jack had grown up as good as a wife to his father, had been required to put a meal on the table every day or no one else would, and so he knew there was nothing wrong with the way he cooked. Knew Linklater was sick, but he didn't like to tell him. They had watched plenty of soldiers perish from typhoid, dysentery and malaria these last couple of years, and it seemed especially cruel for a man to have lived through so much warfare, only to have the sickness come over him like he was no better than a barely weaned babe. So Jack hefted Linklater's haversack up on his shoulders along with his own, and got his arm around Linklater's middle, and they walked on together like that.

Jack figured it didn't matter that the going was slow. He wasn't in any rush to get home, didn't know how he would explain his desertion to his father, but he told himself he would cross that bridge when he arrived at it. He was, after all, a soldier now, and one who owned his own rifle at that. Morcant could threaten him with the belt buckle all he wanted, but by that point, Jack had seen men with their jaws hanging off, blasted apart by artillery. Wickedness had been done in this land that would take many years to undo, but at least he could say he was factual about it, not like some of those men who carried on waving their flags and talking like this war was something grand. Jack had not averted his eyes. He would not avert any part of himself from his father either. Fear had gone out of him entirely, or so he thought.

*

On the fourth day, they were walking through craggy, ridged country peppered with coyote scat. The stunted trees did little to shade them from the sun, and Jack was trying to keep the sergeant from falling into some kind of stupor.

'What's the first thing you're going to do when you get home?'

'Not go back into the army,' Linklater said, his voice hoarse. 'My sister said they got militia rounding up men for the draft, but I'll be dead before that's me again. The sole of my foot's come clean off, we been marching so long now. Why should I skin my feet for generals who do nothing but draw their pay and wear gold braid?'

'It's a rich man's war,' Jack agreed. 'They're just getting poor men to fight it.'

'My sister lost her harvest last year because I was away fighting. And no offence to you and yours, Howl, but I don't give a damn about Virginia. You know how many miles away Texas is from here? Y'all can sort out your own mess. My old man used to say—'

But whatever wisdom Linklater's father had imparted was swallowed up as the dirt under their boots loosened and Jack felt his foot go clean through into nothing.

He still had his arm around Linklater's waist, and the weight of both their haversacks was dragging him down. Jack's split-second thought, as the earth gave way beneath them, was that they had tripped on a prairie dog burrow, or perhaps a whole warren. But the ground just kept on opening up, and whatever they fell into may as well have been a mine for how dark and deep it was.

The next thing Jack knew, he was blinking awake, black spots dancing in front of his eyes, the taste of soil in his mouth.

Above him, there was a glimpse of night sky, a scattering of stars. Beneath him, the broken body of Linklater, who had cushioned Jack's fall.

Trying to stand sent bolts of pain shooting up his left leg, and after cautious probing, Jack realized that one of his bones wasn't sitting where it ought to be. There would be no climbing out, then. Even if he'd had two working legs, he doubted that would have been possible anyway. He could see that the walls of this hole were packed tight with earth, and it was a long way up. One wrong move, too much weight placed in an unstable spot, and he could bring all that dirt piling down on top of him, smothering the life out of his lungs.

Horror washed over him then. For a moment, he was thirteen again, trapped in the flooded tunnel under the mountain with John Fog, only this time it was the body of Linklater keeping him company. Jack did what he could to shuffle over so that he was no longer sitting on the sergeant. Kept saying he was sorry, like a wagon with only one wheel, just going round and round. Then he curled up beside the corpse and tried to sleep, clinging to the hope that, when he woke, daylight would reveal a way out.

It was like this: he had their haversacks, but nothing inside them was edible. He had their canteens, but no water. He had the Enfield, but nothing to shoot at, unless he wanted to shoot himself. If suffocation or gangrene didn't kill him, starvation surely would.

Jack could not say how many days he spent down there in the earth, for he drifted in and out of wakefulness, but it was long enough that the sweet scent of early decay started filling the hole.

Linklater was on the turn. Jack reckoned this was why nobody butchered hogs in the summertime. He tried not to think like that. Tried to think of Linklater as the man he had been, good-humoured and fine to look at, but he was neither of those things now. Just ripe.

Jack pushed the thought down as long as he could, but his insides were clenched up from wanting. The idea had come to him that this might not be a collapsed warren, but some hunter's trap he had fallen into, and that sooner or later, the hunter would come to check it. If he could just hold on another day or two, he might be saved. But in order to do that, he would have to eat.

One thing a man learns in battle is that the only true reason a soldier kills another soldier is so that he can go on living. Honour, glory, love of country, all those things fall away when armies collide, and there is only the blasting and the fire and the need to survive. As he cut into Linklater's body, Jack told himself it was like that. Just a helpless need to go on living.

Some nights, when the wind is blowing a certain way, bringing all the summer smells up out of the forest, Jack is flung back in his mind to that July evening in 1863 when at last he staggered home to Back Creek. What a sight he must have been, if there had been anyone besides the bats and the snakes to see him. His uniform had been torn to ribbons in the wild, and what was left still dangling from his body was stiff with dried blood. His mouth hung open, his jaw smeared red, teeth glinting in the moonlight, far sharper than any man's teeth.

After he'd eaten, Jack could tell that something had changed. He'd crawled up into the daylight as if the height and the depth of the hole were nothing, like a spider moving up a wall, and when he emerged on to solid ground, he found that his leg had healed, the bone set just right. But he was still hungry. As he made his way through the mountains, stalking through the woods and ridges of Shenandoah, he tore into any animal he came upon with a savagery that both alarmed and delighted him, until at last he arrived on his father's doorstep, and found that he could not enter the house.

'Let me in.'

The door was open, but Jack's feet stopped at the threshold as if they had a will of their own.

'Pa, let me in, I'm in a bad way.'

But Morcant leaned over the windowsill above and cursed him in their mother tongue. 'You are not Ioan,' he said. 'Whatever you are, you are not my son!'

Jack did not know what he was. Only knew that he needed to eat, his guts twisted into knots of agony. And when he looked up at Morcant – this man who had dragged him to America, who had made him go down into the dark of the mine, who had beaten him with belts and kindling and his bare fists, who even now was turning Jack out of his own home – he thought his father was leaning a little too far out of the window. Jack thought he was leaning just far enough.

VII

There are certain places Jack can step into as seamlessly as a good pair of boots. Alleyways behind nightclubs where people go to smoke, the bedrooms of wealthy women he has no intention of speaking to again, and dive bars, the seedier the better. The kind where the jukebox still rules and the bartender keeps a sawed-off taped beneath the cash register. The bar adjoining the motel, a stone's throw from the New Jersey state line, is one such dive, and Jack falls into it gladly.

'WL Weller, neat,' he tells the bartender. 'Hell, make it a double.' As they'd driven through Pennsylvania that evening, they'd passed more than one sign for Gettysburg National Military Park, and now the evening has an edge to it that Jack is eager to shake off. 'Make it the same for my friend here too.'

One thing he appreciates about Ellis is that he has never told Jack to slow down when it comes to racking up the bar tab. Birds of a bourbon-soaked feather flock together, it seems. Even when tongues started wagging around town that Mr Sherborne was a drunk, that it sure was a tragedy what had happened to his wife, but passing out in a bar full of onlookers was a bad look for anyone, especially a teacher – even then, Jack couldn't bring himself to raise the matter with Ellis. He knows full well that the liquor goes a long way to softening Ellis towards him. Take it away and maybe he'll decide he thinks Jack is a son of a bitch after all, and somehow Jack finds that idea unacceptable.

Nodding to the bartender for what's either their third or fourth round, Jack rests his chin on his fist and asks, 'How come you don't dream about me?'

'What?' Ellis's expression is bemused, unsteady. Functioning alcoholic or not, he gets drunk fast, which is kind of endearing. Like watching a dog run headlong into a glass door.

'Back at that diner this morning, you said you don't dream about me.'

'Did I damage your ego or something?'

'A little. I'm not even there in the background, like . . . having a beer?'

'You don't drink beer,' Ellis points out. His finger traces the curve of the whiskey glass, and he addresses its contents rather than Jack. 'Self-preservation, I guess.'

'What is? Not thinking about me after hours?'

Ellis shoots him a strained smile, but the silence sits there, and they let it.

The jukebox is playing 'Angel of the Morning'. A couple of tipsy girls with wispy bleached hair are singing along off key, occasionally interrupted by the rumble of pool balls rolling across the balding table in the back. Jack swirls his whiskey in his glass, thinking that subtlety is probably what's required now, but unfortunately he's aware he has always been about as subtle as a knife in the gut.

'You want me to blow you in the bathroom?'

Ellis blinks, brow creasing momentarily before his whole body seems to loosen, and he laughs quietly. 'Jesus, man. You almost had me there for a second.'

'Well, I'm a regular comedian.' Jack raises his glass in something like a toast. No doubt it's for the best, he thinks. The bathroom in this place probably sucks.

'Self-preservation'? Jesus, what a line. And of course Jack had to go and run with it; Ellis walked right into that one. Now he's got another full day's drive ahead of him tomorrow, which he'll have to endure with a murderous hangover and whatever running gag Jack inevitably makes of this evening.

After staggering around his motel room, it becomes apparent this isn't the kind of establishment where the staff helpfully leave out little paper cups for you, so Ellis is forced to stick his head under the faucet to drink as much water as possible. He decides he's too inebriated to risk a shower, and instead crawls into bed with his socks still on, because the heating in this place is about as evident as the paper cups. In attempting to check his phone, he only succeeds in dropping it on his face, at which point he resigns himself to lying there in the dark, trying to focus solely on funeral arrangements.

How come you don't dream about me? Seriously, who asks that?

Scratch that, Ellis tells himself, that is exactly the kind of thing a guy would ask when he thinks he's the personification of a smooth shot of rye.

Rubbing a hand over his face, Ellis breathes out deeply. Lilies are traditional for funerals, right?

It's not as if he never thinks about Jack. Actually, it's difficult not to – he just gets in, like cold weather under the door. This afternoon, in fact, as they drove by signs for Gettysburg, Ellis was thinking how impossible it seemed that Jack should have walked all the way from there to Back Creek, but then Jack is kind of impossible. He can catch a deer with his bare hands. He can take a bullet and not even bruise. He isn't human, not even close, and yet Ellis can remember being twenty-five himself, volunteering at a museum in Nantucket for the season. He'd had a crush on a research assistant, even though she kept calling him Elijah. He'd gotten high for the first time. He'd finally gotten contact lenses and decided maybe he didn't totally hate the way he looked, all of which makes him feel a weird kind of ache when he considers Jack now. That's what your twenties are supposed to be like.

Do people still do hymns at funeral services? he wonders. Great-Aunt Esther was a Lutheran. She'd probably want a hymn or two.

Jack's not a bad-looking guy, Ellis has to give him that.

Maybe he smirks too much, and Ellis knows for a fact that he straightens his hair, but sometimes, when the days are growing shorter and the cold wind puts a little colour in Jack's cheeks, you could almost believe he was human. That's a heartening thought, but it's not as if Ellis is jerking off about it, so what the hell was that 'self-preservation' crap about?

Poems?

Do people actually read poems at funerals, or is that just something that happens in movies? Ellis knows a few verses of *Beowulf*, but that's about it. Nothing says 'goodbye elderly relative' like troll children devouring your thanes.

Alone in the dark, he draws the sheet up over his head and mutters aloud, 'Jesus, what are you even talking about any more?'

On the pillow beside him, his phone lights up suddenly, and Ellis re-emerges to read: *kinda thought you were going to come over.*

Why? he types back. *Need someone to invite you into your own room?*

if i said yes would that work?

Ellis stares at the screen. He's not used to people hitting on him – even Beth kind of crept up on him slowly – so maybe that's not what this is. Jack would flirt with the furniture if given the chance. And he's drunk. They're both drunk. And now Ellis is just making excuses.

I'm in bed, he replies, not entirely sure what he's hoping to achieve with that, but then a knock on the door makes his whole body go rigid, and a voice on the other side says,

'Hey, Sherborne. Let me in?'

Ellis feels his pulse going like machine-gun fire. You're wasted, man, he tells himself, you open that door and you are in for a world of hurt tomorrow morning. But the thing about whiskey is it tends to separate Ellis's mind from his body, and he's already up and stumbling across the motel room before he can muster the discipline to stop himself.

He opens the door in his T-shirt and boxers, feels the rush of frigid night air against him. There is only a brief pause in which they look one another up and down, before Ellis grabs hold of Jack by the front of his shirt and pulls him inside, Jack kicking the door shut as he goes.

They stumble backwards through the dark until Ellis hits the wall, cursing, hands either side of Jack's face, and he can't see for shit with the lights off, though he reckons Jack can see him just fine. He feels like someone's cut his legs out from under him. Feels like a bastard because he's not even thinking about Beth, except for noting how much he's not thinking about her, but his brain is marinated in top-shelf liquor, and the only thing he can focus on at all is the way Jack kisses him like he's trying to knock Ellis's teeth out. Then Jack draws back, looking at Ellis with his head cocked to one side like he's waiting on something. A round of applause, probably.

He drops into a crouch, and Ellis clutches his shoulders and then his hair, like he can't make up his mind whether he's trying to stop this happening or not. Jack digs his nails into the skin around Ellis's hipbones until it hurts, and even when the room seems to narrow to the point of a tongue and the heat of Jack's mouth, even then, Ellis isn't sure he's actually enjoying this. It's just a relief, more than anything else. Like waiting for a blaze during fire season – the way not knowing how or when it's going to start sometimes drives you crazier than the burning forest itself.

His hips jerk without him meaning them to, and Jack makes

a sound in the back of his throat that Ellis feels all through the fork of his body. No, if he's enjoying anything, it's the ragged edge of Jack's breathing and the way he's clinging to him. It's feeling like this isn't only something Jack is doing to him, but something that Ellis is doing to Jack in turn.

He shoves his knuckles in his mouth as he finishes. Never liked the sound of himself during sex anyway, but somehow the context makes it feel twice as awkward, especially when Jack presses his mouth to the juncture of Ellis's thigh and bites down on the tender skin there.

Ellis flinches. Has to take hold of Jack by the jaw and shake him off. 'Hey,' he warns, 'none of that,' but he doesn't stop touching him, stroking Jack's hair back from his face. He's a weird kind of animal, Ellis thinks. You'd think no one had been feeding him.

VIII

Ellis wakes with the kind of headache that's not so much a hangover as the tail end of still being drunk. The motel room lurches viciously as he sits up, and he has to swallow down the nausea rising at the back of his throat. A twinge in his left hip alerts him to the teeth marks just above his thigh, and Ellis's mind supplies: *crime scene evidence*. There goes any plausible deniability on the drunken hook-up front. He manages to stretch some of the stiffness out of his leg, but his skull throbs as the door opens, and the motel's vacancy sign thrusts a spear of neon into the room.

'What time is it?' he croaks, squinting as Jack sets a cardboard cup on the nightstand.

'Time for caffeine and Lucky Strikes.'

'I don't smoke.'

'It's Pennsylvania, they came free with the coffee.' Jack looks much the same as he always does when the two of them have been out drinking, which is to say, a damn sight better than Ellis. Kicking off his boots, he sits down on the bed and says, 'Don't sweat it, Sherborne. It's barely daybreak. If we leave in the next half-hour, we should make Boston before your ridiculous New England 4 p.m. sunset.'

Half an hour does not feel like enough time for Ellis to shake himself into anything remotely resembling a human being. He clutches his coffee cup like it's a lifeline, while Jack appears to be studying his face intently.

'You're making it weird, man,' Ellis says.

'I brought you coffee. That's not weird, that's . . . heartfelt.'

'You're staring at me.'

'Well, it's a small room, Sherborne, and you happen to be right in front of me. Look, it's no big deal. I go to bed with my friends all the time.'

'Oh, great, thanks.'

'What, are you jealous now? Are you going to do the Ellis thing and get all silent and mopey? See, I'm adaptable, I can give a damn or not, but considering I'm going to be stuck in a car with you for the next five hours, I'd appreciate it if you'd stop looking like you want to take a swing at me.'

'I would never take a swing at you,' Ellis says, and means it. 'I just think maybe we shouldn't . . . make a thing out of this.'

'Fine by me. But for the record, it's a little late to walk it back. The horse hasn't just bolted, it's left the racetrack altogether.'

Ellis takes another sip of coffee, half hoping he can disappear behind his cup and the conversation can vanish along with him. Somehow they've ended up at each other's throats again, and he's not even sure how they got there. At one point last night, he'd had that dream again. The car spinning across the median, Beth's face blanching, staring at him in the headlights, only for Ellis to wake and find Jack still stretched out beside him, one arm flung carelessly across Ellis's chest. It had felt strange and unfamiliar, but not unsafe.

He hadn't meant for them to argue, but Jack is already sliding off the bed and reaching for his boots again. 'How about you get dressed and have your crisis in the car? I'm about done with Pennsylvania anyway. Don't want to stick around any longer than I have to.'

It's dawn, but cars are already rushing up the highway, commuters on their way to Newark or New York, punctuated by solitary truckers driving endlessly through the hours. Jack is at the wheel because Ellis can't look at taillights for too long without his eyes watering, and he figures that'll teach him for falling asleep with his contacts in. Wiping his glasses on his sleeve, he says, 'I need you to do something for me.'

It's the first real thing either of them has said since they got back in the truck. Swerving violently into the passing lane, Jack balances one wrist on top of the steering wheel and answers, 'How can I be of service, Sherborne? Need me to google "sex with guys WikiHow" so you can stop running up your data bill?'

'That's not . . .' Ellis frowns at him. 'I'm not doing that.'

'My bad. You've just been staring at your phone very intently for the last ten minutes.'

Ellis rolls his shoulders, stuffing his phone back in his

jacket pocket. 'I need you to be, you know, normal. In front of my relatives. No crawling up the walls, no doing that thing where you make your teeth really long, no talking about stuff that happened a hundred years ago. I mean, I'm being hyperbolic, but this is a funeral. Things are already tense enough.'

Jack hums as he narrowly avoids clipping the wing mirror of a pickup he's trying to overtake. 'For argument's sake, why might I be tempted to show your relatives my teeth? Hyperbolically or otherwise.'

The road ahead wavers in the bleary autumn light. Ellis knuckles his eyes. 'My father's going to be there. He managed to get a last-minute flight out of Vancouver; he was lecturing at the university up there. The American Revolution and popular loyalism, if you were wondering.'

'I was not, and even you saying that was enough to almost put me to sleep. I take it you and Daddy don't get along?'

'No, we get along fine.' Ellis puts his glasses back on. New Jersey still looks bleak. 'Mostly we talk about work, when we talk at all, but he finds my career choices a little . . . Well, the guy has three PhDs and lectures internationally. I teach at a community college in smalltown Virginia. All I'm saying is, at some point, he's going to try and wind me up, and the last thing I need is you cutting in to say "Uh, actually, I was there and that ain't how it went down."'

'Oh my god, was that supposed to be a southern accent?'

'I'm serious—'

'Also, this is what you're worried about? Me telling your old man I'm actually 186 just so I can beat him in a historical debate? I thought you were worried I was going to tell him I blew you.'

'Jesus. Well, obviously don't tell him that either. Just . . . behave.' Ellis can see the muscle twitching in Jack's jaw. 'Please?'

'Don't worry,' Jack says, slipping back into that drawl, and Ellis can never tell if it's real or an exaggeration. 'I wouldn't dream of backchatting a big city professor with all his booksmarts. Why, I'm just a boy from smalltown Virginia.'

Traffic slows to a crawl just before they cross the Hudson. Jack's got junkie jitters in his hands. Even at the rate this traffic's going, it won't be long before they're on the bridge, and then he'll have to wait out the whole crossing with his intestines constricting. He can hear the heartbeat of the diabetic trucker in the semi ahead of them, and it makes him grind his teeth.

He should have gotten something to eat when they stopped for gas back at Pine Lakes. There had been a guy waiting near the men's bathroom who looked like he had as much life left in him as a blown tyre at the edge of a highway, and Jack had considered luring him into the trees and finishing him off. Poor son of a bitch probably wouldn't have argued about it either. But from the glazed look in his eyes and the disconnected sway of his body, Jack figured him for an addict, guessed he was waiting for the bathroom to shoot up, and that's a far cry from Jack's cocktail of choice, at least not in this century.

He had learned that in San Francisco, in the summer of '67. Back then, he could scoop Flower Children right off the street, and he didn't have to kill them, he could just take a drink. Nice and slow over the course of a timeless evening in some smoky squat in Haight-Ashbury, rooms thick with incense, guitar reverbs warbling from the record player.

Jack used to get his highs second-hand, mainlining coke from open veins. Always uppers. He was never a weed guy, the aftertaste of which used to linger like he'd swallowed mildew, but he did once lap blood laced with LSD out of a girl's wrist, and then went into the Santa Cruz mountains to try and pull down the moon. He got picked up a week later by an artist who was on his way to Palo Alto. Some poor kid who blanched at the sight of Jack's crawling, desiccated body and wanted to take him to a hospital, and Jack chewed his hand clean off for his troubles. Not something he feels especially proud of these days, but at the time the colours were still bleeding and bending at the edges of his vision, and the old, impenetrable hunger had overtaken him for the first time in a century. You are what you eat, Jack figures, and what he'd eaten too much of in San Fran was total junk.

Ellis glances up from the roadmap spread out on his lap. 'You don't look so good.'

'Thanks, Sherborne, that's what every girl wants to hear.'

'I'm serious. Your hands are shaking. Are you okay to drive?'

Jack can hear Ellis's pulse too, quick like picking on a banjo.

'Do you need to pull over?' Ellis asks, his voice grave. Then, after a moment, he holds out his arm with his sleeve rolled up, wrist exposed. 'Would it help?'

Jack chews on his thumbnail and looks away from him.

'I mean, don't do anything permanent, but if you need a drink to tide you over, if you're unwell—'

'Sherborne, put that away. We'll stop at a picnic spot on the other side. I'll chow down on a few chipmunks or something. Jesus, that sounds bleak. But I'm fine, I'm just cranky. Can you please roll your sleeve down.'

That silence again, the same kind as at the bar last night,

sitting between them like a third person along for the ride. The truck crawls across the bridge, but Ellis's heartbeat still hasn't let up. Eventually Jack tilts his head towards him, says softly but firmly, 'Relax, please. I don't want to do that to you. It would hurt like a son of a bitch, and it would make a mess of your lousy truck. But I do appreciate the gentlemanly offer.'

Ellis shoots him a grim smile. 'Well, you did get me that coffee earlier. And those cigarettes.'

'Which you didn't smoke, by the way. Where I come from, that's a pretty serious transgression.'

Ellis looks like what he is – wrung out and hungover – but his pulse finally begins to slow. 'Sorry about this morning,' he says. 'I know I've been a dick to you since I woke up. This is all just supremely surreal to me. I've been thinking about Beth, wondering what she'd say if she knew about last night.'

'Well, no offence, but she wouldn't say anything,' Jack replies, 'on account of her not being alive. Take it from me, you can't go through life worrying about what the dead may or may not think of you. Either someone was a dick and good riddance to them, or someone died wanting you to be happy, so just get on with it. It's not like you've got for ever.'

'You do,' Ellis points out. 'Man, what are you? Seriously, after all this, can't you at least tell me that?'

'You've read the history books, Sherborne, you know what I am. I'm just hanging around to reflect it back at the rest of you, until y'all learn your lesson.'

They look out at the vast span of the Hudson swirling fast beneath them.

Ellis says, 'Is that really how you see yourself?' His voice is tired, but not unkind.

*

The sky is growing dark around the peaks of the skyscrapers by the time the Boston skyline finally surges into view. Ellis doesn't know what he'd expected to feel. Like he was coming home, perhaps, but instead there is only the fatigue of the long journey and the relief that soon he'll be able to get out of the truck and stretch his legs.

Initially he'd planned to get a hotel in the city, but since it turns out his father is going to be in town after all, they've been invited to stay in Cambridge. Or rather, Ellis has been invited. He hasn't mentioned Jack, largely because he didn't know how to go about explaining his presence in a text.

A friend drove me up here. Why? Oh, it's purely academic.

And he insisted and it's hard to say no to him.

And by all logic I should find him abominable, but it's starting to bother me less what he was; what interests me is what he's become, and how I reconcile that.

'Get a load of this,' Jack says, as they roll through streets of colourful triple-storey houses, all sash windows and tidy wooden porches flying American flags, maples lining the kerbsides strung with fairy lights. 'I swear, every time I come up to New England it gets more twee. Like if a ball of yarn were a place.'

Beyond the truck windows, night is falling fast, the towering lights of Boston coming to life on the far bank of the Charles River as they follow the signs towards MIT and Cambridgeport. Give it a month or two, Ellis thinks, and the river will freeze. The snow will come in sudden and thick, and the wind will whet itself on the bare trees and all these old houses that have probably been here as long as Jack has, because he is wrong about this place. New England has a fierceness to it too, and it has built fierce people. One might even say – considering its long history of revolutionaries, abolitionists, suffragists and scientists – that Boston has always been the nation's real rebel capital. Ellis almost misses it. It is not a city that likes to be told what to do or how to do it, which is perhaps why he and his father have always struggled with one another here.

In no time at all, he finds himself saying, 'Second-last house on the left.' And here it is, a whole life he hasn't looked in the eye for years.

'Jeez, your dad's loaded.' Jack peers up from the driver's side at the stacked wooden balconies and hand-carved woodwork.

'So are you,' Ellis replies.

'Yeah, but I spend it on cool things, like my car.' Jack gives him a searching look, before adding, 'You know, in the end, I bit my father's head off.'

'Sorry, what?'

'Just something to think about,' Jack says, flashing Ellis that bright Devil's eye. 'If this guy really pisses you off this weekend.'

IX

Alistair Sherborne opens the door still wearing his coat and scarf, his suitcase visible behind him in the hall.

'Well timed,' he says, shaking Ellis's hand firmly. 'Just got back from the airport myself.'

He's a giant of a man, with a thick moustache and a full head of white hair combed back from his face. He has always had this way of greeting people, Ellis thinks, like he's a politician visiting soldiers on the front line for a press op.

'Your flight go okay?' Ellis asks, as Jack clears his throat loudly behind him, and Ellis realizes he's still standing on the porch. 'Right. Dad, this is a friend of mine from Virginia. Jack Howl. He drove up here with me.'

'I gathered that from his presence in my doorway.' Alistair looks Jack up and down for one long moment, before concluding, 'Well, don't just stand there, Mr Howl, you'll catch your death. Come on in.' Then, barely lowering his voice, he adds, 'He's very young, Ellis – not one of your students, I hope,' before marching down the hallway into the unlit depths of the house.

'So, where did you go to college, John?'

Ellis should have known his father would get around to asking that eventually, although preferably with the good grace to actually remember Jack's name. The three of them are sitting at the table in what Alistair calls 'the small living room', despite it being about half the size of Ellis's entire apartment, and Alistair has opened a bottle of red that he was given by the faculty at UBC as a thank-you for his time. Not a thank-you he thinks highly of, Ellis notes. In his experience, the only wines his father has ever offered to share with him were ones he didn't particularly care about wasting.

It's always been a difficult house to heat, and with Alistair having been away all week, the central heating is only just coming back to life. Ancient radiators creak as the warmth sneaks back into the high-ceilinged rooms, sash windows shivering in their frames as the wind picks up outside. Ellis's hands are stiff with cold when he reaches for his glass, but beside him, Jack looks oddly serene, wearing the cable knit sweater that Ellis had offered to lend him when they took their bags upstairs.

'I don't actually feel the cold, you know,' Jack had said, and Ellis had felt foolish, thinking that was probably something he ought to have guessed. But then, when he'd tried to take the sweater back, Jack had swiped it out of his hands anyway.

Now, in response to Alistair's question, Jack folds his arms on the table and smiles near-beatifically. 'You know, it's funny you should ask, Mr Sherborne, sir. I actually went straight from school into the military.'

'Oh, yes? Whereabouts did you serve?'

'Afghanistan,' Jack says, without missing a beat. 'US Army Rangers, sniper with the 75th.'

He must have googled that, Ellis thinks, taking a very long gulp of wine.

'Tell me,' Alistair asks, 'what's the feeling among the forces these days? Do you feel like you're making a difference out there, or just turning the gears of the imperial war machine?'

'Hey, ours not to reason why, ours but to do and die, am I right?'

'Ah, Tennyson.' Alistair sounds faintly surprised. He gives Jack a thin smile, and Jack glances at Ellis, evidently pleased with himself.

He probably googled that too.

'We're very grateful for your service to our nation, I'm sure,' Alistair continues, but Ellis knows that tone of voice, knows all too well when his father is planning to pull the rug out from under someone. 'In your opinion, do a lot of young people in the south feel their only option for career stability is the armed forces?'

'Oh, well, you know how it is down there.' Jack beams at him. 'A lot of us just like shooting guns.'

That gets a laugh out of Alistair, at least. 'But in all

seriousness,' he says, 'and I keep explaining this to Ellis, there's only so much good a state education can do if even the kids who graduate feel they're being funnelled into the military. We need change at a federal level, wouldn't you agree? The rural south needs rejuvenating, but in the meantime, educators like Ellis are simply wasting their time in places like . . . what's that town called again? Backside something?'

'I like my job just fine, Dad,' Ellis says.

'It takes all sorts, I suppose. But I would never have been satisfied with "just fine". Nor would your mother.'

That's probably why she lives in Tampa now, Ellis does not say, but he stares pointedly at his father across the table, and hopes Alistair knows he's thinking it.

'You know what's weird?' Jack says, putting one of the Lucky Strikes to his lips. The two of them are up on the third floor balcony that adjoins what used to be Ellis's childhood bedroom, although nowadays his father uses it as a space to store old skis and tents and snowboots. Relics of family outings that Alistair always had to cut short because he was needed suddenly back at Harvard.

Over wine and a hastily cobbled together dinner of whatever his father had in the fridge, Ellis had tried to maintain civilized conversation, but Alistair wouldn't let up needling him. To walk out entirely would have looked petty, but Ellis had needed somewhere to cool off and preferably finish the rest of the wine. He doubted his father would follow him up to the top of the house and out on to the balcony, especially on a freezing night in late October, but Jack was another matter, and the thing about Jack was he seemed clinically averse to sitting in silence.

'I said, do you know what's weird, Sherborne?'

Ellis sighs, leaning against the side of the house, wrapped in a scarf he had grabbed on the way out and is fairly certain had once belonged to his mother. It doesn't smell like her any more, but never mind. She has, for much of his life, been characterized by her absence.

'I don't know,' he says. 'What counts as weird – you being an Afghanistan war vet who quotes Tennyson?'

'Hey, you said I couldn't climb your father's walls; you never said I couldn't lie.'

'You're right, that is one of your favourite hobbies. Up there with day drinking and defending the great state of Virginia.'

'It's actually the Commonwealth of Virginia,' Jack says, hopping up on to the balcony rail with preternatural balance. 'And your dad was being a patronizing dick.'

'Yeah, well . . .' Ellis isn't smoking, but his breath still comes out in clouds. 'No disagreement there.'

'But that's what's weird, Sherborne. I've seen you threaten to beat down redneck drunks at last call because they looked at the waitress the wrong way. And I know you went up against your board of trustees with nothing but that pissed-off look in your eye, all because they wanted you to put some Bible crap on the wall—'

'That was the Ten Commandments, and it doesn't belong in my classroom.'

'See what I mean?' Jack brandishes his cigarette at him. 'I've never known you to back down, but your dad tells you your job's worthless and you kind of suck at it, and you just sit there? Come on, man, that's not you.'

'Families are complicated.'

'What a lame answer. Did you get that out of a child-of-divorce self-help book?'

Ellis removes one hand from the pocket of his fleece and flips Jack off. 'I've got a question for you.'

Jack grins, stretching his long legs out so that he's seated on the rail. 'Will I be your date to the Back Creek Bicentennial Bonanza, or whatever it's called? Yes, but only if you buy me a corsage.'

'You're relentless.'

'Ah, you're getting to like it.'

Ellis shakes his head. 'You were bullshitting about fighting in Afghanistan, right?'

'Things I've seen, they'd cure anyone of fighting.' Jack raises one hand, mimes like he's firing a pistol. 'But every good lie has a kernel of truth to it, I suppose. I *was* a sniper with the US Army Rangers. Hell, I even made captain, but not in Afghanistan, no. North African campaign, 1943.'

'You fought in World War Two?'

'Figured I couldn't afford not to. Hoped maybe it would balance my chequebook, so to speak. A few dead Nazis in return for my eternal rest, but it turns out the afterlife doesn't work that way.' Jack inspects his cigarette. 'Cairo's one hell of a city, by the way. Lots of history there. You'd love it.'

'No, go back,' Ellis says. 'What do you mean, your "eternal rest"? You don't want to die, do you, not for good?'

Settling against the carved balustrade, Jack takes a long drag, the tip of his Lucky Strike glowing bright against a night sky heavy with clouds, the wind ripping the smoke away before it's barely out of his mouth. 'On our way out there, we stopped over in the UK. I thought about driving to Wales, would have only taken me a couple of hours, but it didn't seem right somehow. I hadn't been back there in a hundred years. There wouldn't have been any family to welcome me. I'd have just been another of those Americans going to someone else's country and pretending it means something.'

'Jack—'

'No,' he says, a little irritably, 'I don't want to die, Sherborne. But it isn't getting better – this country's only getting hungrier, and so am I.' Firmly, like he has to take the sentence by the reins and steer it, he adds, 'If you really want to know, I can tell you about Shenandoah. How I ended up . . . like this. You spend enough time in the wild, enough time without food, eventually you'll eat—'

'No, it's okay.' Ellis comes to hunker down beside him, and unsure what to do next, he wraps a hand around Jack's ankle. There's a pulse under there, Ellis can feel it. Thready but real. Somewhere inside, there's still a person. 'You don't need to talk about that.'

Jack grimaces. 'That bad, huh?'

'No, I think good and bad are kind of redundant terms when it comes to history. There's only what happened. The choices people made and the outcomes those choices led to. It's what you learn from it that matters, and what you do with what you've learned. You – well, I guess I'm still figuring that out. But you did desert the Confederacy. You fought against fascism. You try to fix things back home . . .'

He's never called it that before, never referred to Back Creek as home. But being here now, hearing the sound of cars and sirens and backyard dogs barking instead of coyotes howling from the crags, Ellis can't deny it feels like he has left something vital behind.

'You drove me to Boston,' he says, leaning against the rail, looking at Jack, who is looking out at the city skyline. 'That's something you did.'

X

They catch the tail end of the lunch rush at a bougie little restaurant in Downtown.

'Do you think I can get like, a burger here?' Jack asks. 'Or does it all have to be smashed avocado?'

Ellis eyes the drinks menu with some suspicion. 'I hope these are just the brunch options.'

'I can't believe you just used that word.'

'Brunch?'

'It's like watching a porcelain teacup come out of a woodchipper. I don't like it. Isn't your dad supposed to be here? This place was his lousy recommendation.'

'He's probably still arguing with the florist.'

Jack watches Ellis run a hand through his unwashed hair, looking around like he thinks someone's about to come and tell him he doesn't belong here.

'Honestly, I don't hate him taking point on this whole funeral thing,' Ellis says. 'Aunt Esther was actually his aunt, I never really knew her that well, so I guess he's better placed to say whether she'd prefer carnations or roses at the church.'

'I doubt she has any preferences,' Jack replies, 'considering she's dead.'

'You're dead, and I happen to know you prefer whiskey aged in sherry casks rather than bourbon barrels.'

'That's just good sense.' Jack kicks him lightly under the table. 'God, you're obsessed with me.'

'And you're out of luck here.' Ellis brandishes the drinks menu at him. 'It's all kombucha.'

Lunch with Ellis's father is about as much fun as Jack had been expecting. In terms of funeral arrangements, Ellis had got as far as a phone call with Esther Sherborne's minister on the drive up here, so the whole thing is being thrown together at the eleventh hour. Even Jack can appreciate that must be taking a toll, but when Alistair isn't lamenting the supposed uselessness of his son's profession, he's complaining that caskets these days are all poor quality because people don't value their work any more. Even northerners, it seems, buy into the notion of the 'good old days'. Jack could tell him how, after Fredericksburg, he'd seen coffins built from wood cut so thin they'd sagged in the middle from the weight of the bodies. But Alistair would probably ignore the sentiment and merely congratulate him on being able to fit his slack jaw around the battlefield's three whole syllables.

Ellis's father is, at present, explaining to them both the economic motivations of southern nationalism. How Ellis's students can't realistically hope to improve their lot under this current administration, who mostly consider the rural south to be a place to wipe their feet. Jack doesn't even disagree, but it's heartening all the same to hear Ellis say, 'I'm sorry you feel that way, Dad. I like working there.'

Jack feels his phone buzzing in his pocket. Glancing at it under the table, he recognizes the number of the realtor in Virginia he's been talking to about putting his house back up for sale, and he receives this with some surprise. He had forgotten that he'd called her. Outside, amid the clamour of Downtown, he phones her back and tells her he's not going ahead with the sale, at least not yet.

'It's not you, it's me,' he says, trying to talk over the roar of power tools from a construction crew working on a skyscraper overhead. The weather is still bitter, and although Jack can't really feel it, he hunches into Ellis's sweater all the same. It's a hideous thing, frankly, probably weighs as much as a whole sheep and makes Jack look like he got lost on some Arctic expedition, but it does smell a little like Ellis. Jack can see him through the restaurant window, talking to his father with all the enthusiasm of one about to stab himself in the hand with his fork, and Jack tells the realtor, 'I'm just thinking of sticking around a little while longer, that's all.'

One thing Jack has noticed about New England, on the rare occasions he has ventured up this far north for a party or two, is that the cities here tend to skip dusk. Autumn afternoons in Boston adopt a raw kind of light, and then suddenly night comes on like the whole city has been tossed into the back of a trunk. Only been here a couple of days, but already he misses the mountains, the way Blue Ridge knows how to tease out a sunset. How the valleys hold the day a little longer and give you time to make your peace with it.

In a cemetery near Boston Common, he stands beside Ellis and Alistair as the handful of mourners begin to disperse, old friends and neighbours of Esther Sherborne who shake Alistair's hand and tell Ellis they remember him as a child. Judging by Ellis's expression, he's getting weary of hearing this, but Jack wouldn't mind too much if there was someone who could say the same to him. It's something, to be remembered. It's when a man drifts out of human recollection altogether that he feels truly dead.

A twice-removed cousin from Back Bay invites the Sherbornes for a drink following the burial, which Ellis politely declines. Says he could do with stretching his legs, which is exactly what he'd said after he'd buried his wife too, Jack remembers that. Remembers slipping into a back pew during Beth Sherborne's service, attended primarily by her kin from neighbouring valleys, and he had spotted this man all but folded in on himself sitting up at the front.

Ellis had not given a eulogy during Beth's funeral. He'd simply sat there and stared at the casket like it was only him and her body in the whole church, and he seemed to Jack, then, like a figure from a Tarot card. Circled by omens, and not all of them bad. At any rate, Jack had felt drawn to follow him, until the day when Ellis had put a bullet in him for his troubles. Of all the Massachusetts boys who'd ever taken aim, Ellis was the only one to wing him. Jack had found himself oddly charmed by that.

Outside the cemetery gates, he and Ellis watch Alistair and the cousin get into a cab. As soon as the door shuts, Jack notes that, even through the darkened window, there is a sort of falling away of Alistair's face. He comes undone, sinks against the car seat and shuts his eyes. Jack sees this happen, and his dislike of Alistair ebbs a little.

It could be that the man really cared a whole lot about his aunt. Maybe it's the weight of her passing that is pressing on him now, forcing him to turn from the window as the cab pulls away. Or maybe it's being here with his son to whom he can't seem to communicate, no matter how many conversations he begins. It is strange, Jack thinks, the things we can endure and the things we can't.

They wander through loud, bustling streets toward Longfellow Bridge, which will take them across the river back to Cambridge. The Charles has an icy smell to it tonight, and a yellowish tint in the sky overhead hints at snow. Jack smokes the last of the Lucky Strikes as they walk, and glancing at him now and then, Ellis has a sense of being split in half.

Part of him is here, watching the shadows catch and shift in the hollows of Jack's face as they pass under streetlamps, and the other half is back in the Spine, where he scattered Beth's ashes. He knows that by now the wind will have carried what was left of her far and wide. Carried her all through the Blue Ridge Mountains if she's lucky, and so Ellis knows he cannot go back to that spot where he left her. The half of him that's still waiting there will be waiting on nothing if it doesn't move forward.

'Tell me something,' he says, because he doesn't want to think about death any more tonight. 'A memory you have, something good that happened once.'

They're on the bridge now, the water flowing opaque and fast beneath them, the occasional car passing by, but mostly they're alone. Even the sound of the city traffic feels distant here. Jack doesn't answer right away, but he leans against the iron rail, takes a deep drag on his cigarette, then points it at Ellis.

'I know you prefer my war stories, so you might not like this one so much, but I remember when electricity finally came to Back Creek.'

Ellis knows about this too. In 1936, President Roosevelt announced the Rural Electrification Act, but much of rural Virginia would remain in the dark for a few years more. It's something he covers every year in his module on local history at the community college, but he listens nonetheless as Jack explains how, before electrification, they had to do everything by lantern light. There's a different texture to things, the way Jack tells them, because it isn't like listening to an elderly relative half remembering a faraway past. It's sharp, it's present. When Jack talks, history doesn't feel like a sepia photograph. It's more like how Ellis imagines the oral story-tellers of old must have told it, and how many historians ever get that lucky?

'I mean, obviously I didn't need lanterns to see anything,' Jack says, winking his glassy blue eye. 'I don't have trouble seeing in the dark. But there was other stuff . . . no radio, for one – the signals didn't reach our town. No telephones. We couldn't hear from the rest of the country, and it was starting to feel like we'd been totally cut off.'

But then a cooperative came in, he said. They were from the Piedmont, and they asked for a contribution of $5 per household so that they could petition the bank for a loan, and then they set about suturing one town to another with wires and cables and setting up stronger transmitters. There was something almost heroic about it, Jack explains, this simple putting up of poles for the wires to travel along.

'History doesn't usually feel like history when you're living it,' he says. 'But I had a sense of living in history right then.'

It was by no means an overnight process, but at last, one day, the switch was thrown. Then suddenly, like the Commonwealth of Virginia had come to some great epiphany all together, people had telephones and refrigerators, and lights by which they could feed their livestock in the deep black mornings. And they had the radio.

'First thing I ever heard on the radio was Glenn Miller, and I danced in the living room, in my bare feet. When I looked out the window, there was light all over the valley. Few years later, when I was at the Empire Club in Cairo, they played "When the Lights Go On Again", and I felt that. I got what they were talking about.'

'That's a good memory,' Ellis says.

And Jack says, 'It's how I think about you.'

He looks uncertain then, and unlike himself in his uncertainty. He inhales deeply from his Lucky Strike, and Ellis recalls what Jack had said about how the lucky people in this country were the ones who found something beautiful in it.

He thinks again about why Jack is still living and Beth isn't. Beth who was so loved, and Jack who was not. But Ellis figures maybe it's not because Jack is supposed to stick around as some awful reminder of the past. Maybe he is like any other restless spirit with unfinished business. 186 years waiting for this: Ellis putting an arm around his shoulders and holding on to him as they walk across the bridge towards the lights on the other side.

Author's Note

I turned twenty-one sitting on a motel bed playing cards, somewhere on the border between Texas and New Mexico. I remember a pool with no water in it, and there were motorcyclists swarming outside. I had spent what little money I had on a bottle of sangria, which I drank all at once, because it was my most reliable companion out there, where packs of Baptists stalked the vulnerable and men lived by their fists. It took me another two years to work up the courage (and the funds) to finally come home, but I don't think I ever truly got the desert dust off me.

In 2022, my editor suggested I submit something for the BBC National Short Story Award. As someone who had never really written a short story before, I found the prospect daunting, but I was in a writing slump and keen to try something new. I wrote a piece about a man driving the breadth of Texas – a drive I had made several times myself – which became 'Long Way to Come for a Sip of Water' and ended up on the award shortlist. I couldn't believe it. I'd gone from lying hungover in a cheap motel room to discussing my writing on BBC Radio 4.

As complicated as my feelings remain about the US, I'm grateful for my time in that vast, wild place for teaching me how to write about landscapes and for giving me the fuel to start writing short stories. The short story is a medium I have long admired, and to be a contributor to that means so much to me – though not, I think, as much as it would have meant to that lonely twenty-one-year-old sobering up in the desert.

I'm indebted to everyone who has made this collection possible:

First and foremost, to my wife Aude Bailey-Claret for her love and patience, as well as for lending this manuscript her insightful eye. I'm particularly grateful to her for sharing her recollections of interning with the US National Parks service, and for inspiring many of these stories but especially 'I'll Be Bound for the Lonesome Woods', which would not exist without her.

To my brilliant team at Doubleday and Penguin for bringing this collection into being, particularly my editor Kirsty Dunseath for encouraging me to write my first real short story, and my publicist Alison Barrow for continuing to champion my work.

To my agent Alice Lutyens at Curtis Brown for floating the idea of a collection to me in the first place.

To Tamari Fourré and Matthew Willis for listening to me ramble about Civil War manoeuvres and providing the friendship necessary for such a project.

To all the booksellers, reviewers and readers who have supported my work so far, and to the authors who generously took the time to endorse this book.

To everyone at the NSSA for shortlisting me, and to Joseph Balderrama for his flawless narration of 'Long Way to Come for a Sip of Water' on BBC's *Front Row*. Huge thank you also to Nicola Holloway for dramatizing 'Wasteland Girls' and 'Coal Country Beauty Queen' for Radio 4, and to Sarah Twomey and Matthew Needham respectively for narrating and bringing those stories to life.

I'm immensely grateful to Daniela Taitl for sending me so much material about the First World War, particularly Vera Brittain's published letters. And to Barbara Kochman, who provided the initial inspiration and historical material for 'Stray Dogs', in addition to being a steadfast friend.

Further research for this collection includes James S. Griffith's *Beliefs and Holy Places: A Spiritual Geography of the Pimeria Alta*, and James M. McPherson's excellent books *Battle Cry of Freedom: The American Civil War* and *For Cause and Comrades: Why Men Fought in the Civil War*. The videos of Peter Santenello, specifically his interviews from rural Appalachia, were also hugely helpful, as was Swan Land Company's 2025 article 'Spring Cattle Branding on American Ranches: Tradition, Etiquette and Regional Flavor'. Paul McDonough's *Headed West*, Bruce Haley's *Home Fires* and Francesco Jodice's *After the West* continue to be sources of inspiration for me visually, as well as fond reminders of the liminal places one encounters while driving across the country. The town of Haring, which appears in a number of these stories, is a composite of various small towns along the Texas–New Mexico border and is entirely fictional.

Honorary mention is due to my great-great-grandfather Jack Jones, the real-life Jack the Devil, whose epithet I borrowed for the final story in this collection. His devilry was related to his temper and the trouble he caused at the coal mine, rather than anything otherworldly, but he is something of a grim and legendary figure in my family history, and I've long been meaning to put his name in a story.

Perhaps more than anything else I've written, this collection has forced me to confront and re-evaluate my experience of living in the US and what that means to me now. The best parts of those years were always the majesty of the landscapes. The ugly parts crop up in some of this writing. I'm forever thankful to my sister, Lucy Bailey, for being there for me when I returned from this strange chapter of my life, for listening without judgement, and for opening up her home to me when I needed it most.

Anna Bailey is a *Sunday Times* bestselling author from Gloucestershire. Their debut novel, *Tall Bones*, was nominated for the Theakstons Crime Novel of the Year and Goldsboro Glass Bell awards, as well as the Prix Nouvelles Voix du Polar. Their second novel, *Our Last Wild Days*, was also published to great acclaim. Their short stories have been dramatized for BBC Radio 4, including 'Long Way to Come for a Sip of Water', which was shortlisted for the BBC National Short Story Award. They live in Bordeaux with their wife.